CHRONICA

Paul Levinson

Connected Editions

An earlier, very different version of Chapter 2 was published as "Advantage, Bellarmine" in Analog Magazine, January 1998

Chronica was first published as a Kindle book by JoSara Media in 2014. This current paperback is the same as the Kindle edition, with an updated About the Author and other Back Matter text.

Chronica is the third novel in the Sierra Waters time-travel trilogy which consists of The Plot to Save Socrates, Unburning Alexandria, and Chronica.

ISBN-13: 978-1-56178-059-4

hardcover: 978-1-56178-060-0
Kindle: 978-1-56178-031-0

Cover design by: Joel Iskowitz

Printed in the United States of America

Connected Editions, 260 Underpass Road, #161, Brewster, MA 02631

https://connectededitions.com/

To the original four

CONTENTS

PREVIOUSLY IN THE PLOT TO SAVE SOCRATES

Sierra Waters, a graduate student in 2042 New York City, is given an unusual manuscript by her mentor Thomas O'Leary, who soon after disappears. The manuscript is a previously unknown dialogue in which Socrates receives a visitor after Crito on the eve of Socrates's death - a man who claims to be from the future and offers Socrates a chance to escape the hemlock that won't change history: a clone of Socrates will be given the hemlock, so Socrates can escape to the future. Sierra is not sure what to think of this manuscript, but she and her boyfriend Max go off to London in search of Thomas. There they discover a room with chairs which can travel through time, as explained to them by William Henry Appleton, the great 19th-century American publisher, who has used such a chair to travel to the future. Sierra and Max travel to Londinium 150 AD, where Sierra to her horror sees Max attacked and killed by Roman legionaries. She goes to Alexandria, where she meets Heron, the enigmatic ancient inventor, and his student Jonah. Sierra is now attempting to save Socrates - in the way indicated in the manuscript - as much as she is looking for Thomas, and her travels take her to Phrygia (later Asia Minor) in 404 BC, and the bed of Alcibiades, Socrates's beloved student. Alcibiades, who in our history is killed by Spartan mercenaries when in bed with a concubine, is saved from this fate when Heron arrives with legionaries minutes before the mercenaries arrive, and awakens Alcibiades and Sierra.   In the ensuing escape and aftermath, Sierra and Alcibiades fall in love, and Heron enlists them in the plot to save Socrates which he is now traveling through time to set in motion.   But Sierra and Alcibiades gradually come to realize that Heron - or some future version of himself - is trying to kill them. In the end, Sierra not Heron rescues Socrates and takes him to 2042, where Socrates meets with Thomas, who has reappeared and is thrilled to see the philosopher. But Alcibiades is injured in the rescue and he and Sierra are separated. Desperate to find him, Sierra goes to Alexandria, 410 AD, where she has reason to think Alcibiades may have gone, and where she takes on the identity of Hypatia, who in our history was killed by fanatics in 415 AD.

PREVIOUSLY
IN UNBURNING
ALEXANDRIA

Sierra Waters is in the ancient city of Alexandria, hoping that Alcibiades her lover will know to look for her there. But as the months go by, Sierra's personal motive is replaced by a reason much grander and more profound: do what she can to save the ancient Library of Alexandria from burning. History discloses that the Library was burned at least three times, with the flames taking as many as 750,000 scrolls, many of them one-of-a-kind works.

To implement her plans in Alexandria, Sierra has traveled to the far future, and had her face remade to look like Hypatia, who died from a mysterious illness. Sierra as Hypatia increases her power in the ancient Library, and attracts a variety of fictional and historical characters to her cause. But there's danger in having that world think Sierra is Hypatia: in our history, Hypatia will soon die a horrible death, ripped apart by a mob of early Christian fanatics.

Sierra soon realizes that, even with all of her friends and her prowess, stopping the burnings of the Library will be beyond her power. She decides, instead, to save whatever few scrolls she and her friends can rescue from the Library. Her intent is to bring them to the future, where they could be digitally copied and put beyond the reach of any flames.

Heron, indeed, is desirous of seeing the Library burn, first because he is concerned about how the saving of any texts could alter history, but also for a deeper, more personal reason. In his youth, Heron wrote *Chronica*, a detailed explanation of how to construct a time travel device, and how to use it to manipulate history. He does not want *Chronica* to fall into anyone's hands – least of all, Sierra's – and he deploys all of his power to making sure the Library burns, and with it, his *Chronica*.

Sierra and her colleagues begin to get help from an unexpected source: androids from the future, who were likely constructed by an older version of Sierra herself, but who also seem to be doing Heron's bidding at times. These androids have a way of instituting "re-sets," in which pinpoint events in history, such as deaths, can be reversed. One of Sierra's friends benefits from a re-set, and it seems that Max, whom Sierra saw killed on the shore of the Thames in *The Plot to Save Socrates*, may have had his death re-set to life, too.

Indeed, Max proves to be Sierra's most reliable ally, and she needs all the help she can get, since Heron also has a spy deep in Sierra's cadre of supporters. Sierra and her group are almost completely foiled in their attempt to rescue scrolls from the Library, but she and Max manage to save a few books – including *Chronica*. They deliver the scrolls to William Henry Appleton, who promises to do what he can to get them published.

But Sierra, still looking like Hypatia, yearns to return to Alexandria, still hoping that Alcibiades might somehow still show up, after all. On the day in history that
Hypatia is to be murdered, she is attacked by the Christian mob, who hack her to pieces.

Heron, who directed the mob to Hypatia, thinks he has at last disposed of his enemy, Sierra. But all he has killed is an android, who has taken on Sierra's appearance as Hypatia. In New York City in the 1890s, Sierra – now looking like herself – walks down Fifth Avenue with Max, and they consider their next move.

CHAPTER 1

[New York City, 2062 AD]

S ierra and Max didn't have to wait too long to learn the change in the future their time in the past had wrought. They arrived in New York City on November 20, 2062 – the 120th anniversary of Joe Biden's birth. It was not yet quite a national holiday, but it was noted in the press on every screen, where it was predicted that Joe Biden's birthday would indeed soon be a national holiday. He had been the 44th President of the United States, serving two consecutive terms, from 2008 through 2016. The nation loved him for many reasons, most importantly because he had revolutionized life in the U.S. with the 200 mile-per-hour fast-rail system he had begun to install across America in his second term.

Sierra and Max were stunned. "What happened to Obama?" they asked each other at the same time.

The Web gave them their answer a moment later. Obama was the 46th President of the United States, serving just one term from 2020-2024.

How this might have happened – how what they had done in the past might have caused this astonishing change – took a little time to discover. Max hit upon it late in the evening of their return to 2062 AD. "Ah, here it is." Max highlighted a few lines in the text on his screen and passed the phone to Sierra. The two thought of it as a phone, even though it had little resemblance to the phones they grew up with and had last seen and used in 2042. "It says here in Biden's autobiography that he was very taken by a book he read in parochial school as a kid – a treatise by Aristotle on good government and the dispensing of justice."

Sierra looked at the screen and nodded. "That was one of the texts we rescued from Alexandria and left with Mr. Appleton." The screen was on a stud Max had been wearing on his jeans. It was the size of an archaic postage stamp, which expanded to the size of his hand as he held it in his palm. They had picked one up for each of them, likely greatly overpriced, at a shop that catered to tourists on Fifth Avenue. They paid with their retina scans, still attached to their still active bank accounts from 2042.

"Biden said it taught him something about connecting to the people, which served him in good stead in the Democratic primaries in 2008, which he won." Max clucked his tongue. "Amazing. What else has changed?"

"No way to find out except by living here a little," Sierra said, profoundly shaken.

"And the reason why the two of us still remember our original reality?" Max asked, though he already knew the answer. But he found it reassuring to hear it, anyway, from Sierra, his partner in this something other than sanity.

"Because we came from Reality 1, in which Biden was Obama's Vice President from 2008-2016," Sierra replied. "Our actions in the past created Reality 2, but since we're still from Reality 1, we remember it."

"That makes sense," Max said, and breathed out slowly. "I guess the other big question now is what should we do about it?"

***

They awoke the next morning, legs and arms entwined, neither at first aware of where they were, except together in bed.

But reality came quickly upon them. "We knew something like this would happen," Max said, stroking Sierra's hair, kissing her, and arising from the bed. He reached for his clothes, crumpled on the chair.

"No," Sierra said, about the clothes. "We need something 21st century."

"Right, of course," Max said, and went for a suitcase with the new clothing they had quickly purchased at the tourist-trap store on Fifth Avenue yesterday. They had arrived there from the Millennium Club a few blocks up the street, about 10 minutes before the store closed. "But there was no point in rescuing the Aristotle scrolls from the Library," Max said, returning to his initial thought, "if we didn't want them to change our world in some way, with any luck for the better."

"I know," Sierra said, not particularly happy, but not unhappy either, just still in some kind of shock, Max thought. He enjoyed looking at her, enjoyed watching her pull undergarments and jeans and shirt out of the suitcase, enjoyed watching her put them on almost as much as he enjoyed her taking them off.

"You think Biden as President is a change for the worse?" Max asked her.

"No, it's not that," Sierra said. "At least, not from what I know of our original history, in which Biden was a good enough Vice President under Obama. It's . . . I don't know, it's the magnitude of the change. Biden rather than Obama as President is world-changing, or could have been. We'll have to see . . . . I guess I was just expecting, hoping, that the changes would be more subtle, more, I don't know."

"More under our control?" Max asked.

"Yeah."

"All right," Max said. "There's still a lot that's under our control. Our bank accounts from 2042 are live, we confirmed that yesterday. Let's get breakfast, get out of this hotel, and go to your apartment."

"Expenses are bound to be higher than in 2042," Sierra said.

"True, but our bank accounts have been collecting interest," Max said. "Look, there was an argument in favor of our going to 2042 not 2062, but I took your point about not wanting to run into Socrates or Thomas – Alcibiades – just yet."

"I'm not sure if I ever do," Sierra said.

***

They continued their analysis over breakfast. "It feels good to eat again in our own time, or close to it," Sierra said, sipping a gengineered sour-cherry orange juice.

"Yeah, it does," Max said, digging with zest into the scrambled mini-ostrich egg that he and Sierra were sharing. "You know," he said, savoring the taste but thinking about something else, "it's interesting that you brought a man into the future – Socrates – and he apparently had no effect on our world. But bringing a book into the future did."

"That's for two reasons, probably," Sierra said. "One, I brought Socrates to 2042, which kept him clear of almost all of our past. But the scrolls we rescued from Alexandria percolated through the entire 20th century – giving Joe Biden a chance to read at least one of them."

Max nodded. "And the second reason?"

"Mr. Charles told me that Thomas kept Socrates strictly under wraps," Sierra said, "likely to avoid triggering any changes in future history."

"And likely to keep Socrates to himself," Max added.

"True," Sierra said, and sipped more of her juice.

Max regarded her. The last thing he wanted to do was to start her thinking about Thomas aka Alcibiades. "If you think this new world in which Joe Biden was President is not in humanity's best interests, you could do a re-set, couldn't you?" he asked gently.

"No. I mean, yes, I assume my future self could still make that happen, but I don't think we want to go jumping around time changing history and then changing it back again if we're not comfortable with the results," Sierra said.

"I guess you need to be in closer touch with why you saved the scrolls in the first place," Max said. "If it was to make the world a better place, or the world as it should be, as it would have been, if the scrolls had not been burned, well, this is a beginning, isn't it? Better this than if we found no changes at all, right?"

Sierra wasn't sure she knew. Or, if she did know, and what she knew was that Max was right that surely a change like this was better than no change at all, she still didn't feel good about it, certainly not comfortable. Hadn't someone once told her that comfort was beyond the reach of the time traveler? Maybe she had said that herself. "Maybe this is what Heron was warning us about," was all she said to Max.

"Warning? Last time I checked, he and his legionaries were trying to kill us," Max replied, with some heat.

"To prevent disruptions in time," Sierra said.

"Because he wanted to protect the history and future that he had likely helped to create," Max said. "How do we know that *that's* the best timeline for humanity?"

"We don't," Sierra said. "And you're right, of course." She touched Max's hand. "I'll be ok, don't worry. This change in our reality just hit me harder than I expected. I just need a little time to adjust, I guess." But she also knew she needed to think a lot more about this.

***

Max left to make sure Sierra's apartment from 2042 was still available for them – Sierra had purchased the apartment at some point for a tidy sum she had acquired in the future further along the line, but you never knew when it came to apartments in New York City. Max was also instructed to buy some decent 2062 clothing for the two of them. Sierra knew that he knew what she liked.

Sierra wanted to relax in the hotel atrium with her phone. She could soak in some of what was new in 2062 ambience and do more research online into this new world she had unintentionally helped to create.

She discovered something about two hours later, about five minutes before Max returned. He approached her with two bags filled with clothing and his patented big smile.

"Ted Kennedy died on the day of Biden's first inauguration in 2009 in this reality," was her greeting to Max.

He sat next to her on the neo-wicker seat, designed to automatically hug the right parts of your body, as the digi-sign said. "Didn't he die around then in our reality?" Max asked.

"Yeah, but not on Obama's first inauguration day – Teddy survived until the following summer."

Max nodded.

"My grandmother was a big fan of the Kennedys," Sierra continued. "That was one of the reasons my mother chose Harvard over Princeton when she got her professorship in mathematics."

"Ok," Max said, "so–"

"Well, there's something even more interesting about this," Sierra said. "Ted Kennedy had some problem at the luncheon after Obama's inauguration and he was whisked away in an ambulance, and wrongly reported dead on Wikipedia."

"I don't recall that," Max said.

"You wouldn't," Sierra said. "But it was a big deal in our family. My grandmother always used to cite it as a reason you couldn't trust Wikipedia, even though Teddy's death then was also wrongly reported in other media."

"Yeah, took a decade or two for Wikipedia to achieve its vaunted status, I know that," Max said.

"The incorrect report of Ted Kennedy's death was a big deal in Wikipedia's history," Sierra continued. "I read about it in more than one text about the history of social media."

Now Max grew very thoughtful. "I'm beginning to see why you think this incident is so important to what's now going on with us and our travels."

"Exactly," Sierra said. "It's one thing that Aristotle's book changed history and got Biden elected President in 2008. That's earthshaking, as we've been saying. And the change in the date of Ted Kennedy's death is obviously important, too. But, what I'm wondering is why our reality, before we rescued the texts from Alexandria, had the wrong report of his death in January 2009 – why have any incident happening on that day at all?"

"It's almost as if, for some reason, part of the current reality leaked into our original reality," Max said.

Sierra nodded. "And does that suggest to you that maybe our current reality has some sort of priority or legitimacy when it comes to the date that Ted Kennedy died?"

"You mean the reality we're now in – Biden President, Ted Kennedy dying on Biden's first inauguration day, Obama elected President in 2020 not 2008 – is somehow the reality that was most meant to be?"

"Yeah, maybe," Sierra replied. "Though I'm not even clear about what exactly that means."

"Well, one thing is pretty clear," Max said. "There's not all that much difference between the two realities, if you look at them a certain way. I mean, Biden was Obama's Vice President, and Ted Kennedy did die in the first year of Obama's first term, in our original reality. Whatever exactly that may mean."

***

Sierra's apartment on 11th Street between 5th Avenue and University Place was fine. Automatic air systems had kept the rooms as fresh for 20 years as if the windows had been open the entire time on an early Spring day. And the neighborhood hadn't changed at all. "This is the first time we've been in this place together since that morning we flew to London, just a few days after you came over here that night in 2042. I had just begun reading the *Andros* dialogue," Sierra said, with a tingle of a tear in her eye.

Max smiled deeply. "And we had a very good time that night, if memory serves."

Sierra took his hand. "Seems like another lifetime, doesn't it?"

"Life may be like that, anyway," Max said. "People often say that when they meet someone they hadn't seen since college, and that has nothing to do with time travel."

Sierra nodded.

"What I find even more amazing than how fresh this apartment smells is how the financial system worked so well for us," Max said, "almost as if the banking system was designed to accommodate time travelers." He laughed.

"I guess people leave money in accounts, unattended, with nothing taken out or put in, all the time," Sierra said. "They passed some law in the 2020s about that, extending into perpetuity the time you could leave money in an account with no activity, just earning whatever interest. My parents were very happy about that, for some reason."

Max resisted saying maybe your parents knew you would go into time travel. He confined himself to saying, "Do you want to go see them?"

"I'm not sure," Sierra said. "They're both still alive and together – and content, as far as I know – but I don't know if I want to draw them into this."

"And attract Heron to them," Max added. "Yeah, I get it. You should think about it."

Max had been orphaned in 2040, a year before she and he had met, Sierra knew, so whether or not to meet his parents now in 2062 was moot. But there was always the option of trying to stop the train crash that took their lives, or getting them off the train, which would be easy, if she and Max decided to do that and went back to 2040. They had briefly talked about that in one of the rare quiet moments they had stolen in their run from Heron.

"I know what you're thinking," Max said. "You're thinking about my parents, and wondering if the Biden Presidency starting in 2008 and the big boost it gave to train travel didn't result in a safer train system, meaning the crash that took my parents didn't happen in this reality."

Sierra looked at him. Actually, that last part hadn't occurred to her at all.

***

They took a robo-cab back up to the Millennium Club. They hadn't been able to look at the library's classical holdings when they'd arrived the previous day, because the area had been undergoing a renovation yesterday. They wanted to see which of the texts they had rescued in addition to Aristotle's treatise on good governance had made it into this future.

Max had searched for his parents online. There indeed had been no train crash as in their original reality, but his mother had died anyway about five years later in a freak car accident in which a robotic automobile had gone awry. "One in a million," *The New York Times* story said, but it taught Max and Sierra something about the inevitability of death across time-lines – "at least fifty-percent of the time, that we now know of," Max had said, in a husky voice filled with shock, dread, anticipation, and other emotions Sierra could not identify. Max's father was now in Los Angeles, and Max had decided he'd wait at least a few hours to contact him, perhaps by phone, perhaps by flying out there to see his father in person.

Sierra stroked Max's hand in the cab. She understood some of what he was going through, because she had gone through the same unnerving blender of emotion when first she lost him in Londinium in 150 AD and then discovered he hadn't died after all. She tried so hard not to provoke paradox in her journeys, and yet Max was going through the whiplash of its loops right now. But he was right in what he had said to her last night – what did she expect, given their tampering with history by rescuing the scrolls in Alexandria?

The Millennium Club looked good in the noontime sunlight. It had basically remained unchanged in outward appearance since its construction at the end of the 1870s, a beacon of bygone Victorian culture in the neo-digital age. The doorman greeted them warmly with a British accent but didn't know them. Fortunately, both of their retinas were in the Millennium's databank.

"Looks like a younger version of Hudson from *Downton Abbey*," Max said about the doorman to Sierra, as the two walked up the stairs to the classics library.

"Carson," Sierra said, "from *Downton Abbey*. Hudson's *Upstairs, Downstairs*."

The classics library was now restored from yesterday's work and open to everyone in the club. It had all four of the Aristotle scrolls Sierra and Max had rescued, now translated by Benjamin Jowett and bound in the early 20th century green covers with gold embossing that Sierra had always loved. It had the *Andros* dialogue, right between the *Phaedrus* and *Cratylus*, in the four-volume *Dialogues of Plato*, also translated by Jowett. It had all the books known to have been written by Heron – his *Automata*, *Belopoeica*, *Dioptra*, *Catoptrica*, *Geodesia*, *Geoponica*, *Mechanica*, *Metrica*, and *Pneumatica* – and two thought to have been written by him, *Geometria* and *Stereometrica*. But there was no sign anywhere of Heron's *Chronica*.

There was no sign of Mr. Charles or anyone else they knew, either.

Sierra and Max took the four Aristotle books they had stolen from the ancient flames to a pitted maple table illuminated by a green banker's lamp that Sierra was sure was an original. "They used these in the early days of incandescent lighting to lessen the glare," Sierra said, "but they're beautiful in any case, aren't they?"

Max nodded, distracted.

"What's the matter?" Sierra asked him.

Max took a deep breath. "I think I'll call my father now," he said, "the tension is killing me."

"Of course," Sierra said tenderly and took his hand. "There's a men's room around that corner," she pointed to the far side of the room, "if you want some privacy. Or, we can leave these books for later, and we can go back to the apartment."

"No," Max said. "You should look at the books." He kissed her on the forehead and walked quickly away.

Sierra watched him and fought to keep her emotions in check. She carefully picked up Aristotle's treatise on good government. This edition had been published in 1933, the very year that what was left of Appleton's had merged with the Century Company to make the Appleton-Century Company. The first edition had been published by William Henry Appleton in 1898. That made sense – three years after she and Max had left the scrolls with him in his Wave Hill home, and a year before their beloved friend and protector was to die. Sierra turned the page and caught her breath. Here was something that made no sense at all.

The translator was Benjamin Jowett, who Sierra was sure had died prior to Max's and her visit with Appleton in 1895. She surreptitiously checked Jowett's bio on her phone – mobile devices were forever not allowed in the Millennium – and yeah, she had been right, Jowett had died in 1893. His last work had been a translation of Aristotle's *Politics*, so translating another four treatises by the philosopher fit right in, but how on Earth did Appleton get the manuscripts from 1895 to Jowett before he died in 1893?

Sierra shook her head and smiled. The answer should have been all too obvious to her. Appleton had assured her that he was going to retire from time traveling, and spend his last few years shuttling only between his home in the Bronx and his office on Bond Street in Manhattan, but of course he had changed his mind, traveled to London after she and Max had left in 1895, and taken a Chair back to 1890 or thereabouts to see Jowett–

She became aware that Max was standing next to her. There was something not right, judging by the expression and paleness of his face, but she couldn't tell just what that was.

"I spoke to my father," Max began.

Sierra stood, and got Max into a chair.

"It was a very short conversation," Max continued. "I couldn't say much, after he told me that he had just talked to me yesterday. I didn't want to disrupt his life or whatever the hell is going on in this reality, so I told him I was calling because I needed to check my recollection of something that happened when I was kid. I told him it was for an article I was writing."

"Ok," Sierra said, and put her hand gently on Max's shoulder. "And . . . what did he tell you about your other life here?"

"You and I are happily married and have two kids," Max said, with tears in his eyes and voice.

***

They held each other's hands for a long time, and said nothing.

"Are they an alternate version of us," Max finally said. "Or–"

"They could be actually us, you and me, the human beings sitting right here now at this table, just a little or whatever into our future, and we traveled back to be with your father and got married," Sierra said slowly. "I don't know . . . we need more information from your father."

"What do you think we should do?" Max said. "My father's in California, but I didn't ask him where our alternate Biden-as-2008-President selves may be – we could be right here in New York."

"And we don't want to bump into ourselves and the paradoxes that could hurl in our faces," Sierra completed the thought.

Max nodded. "We could travel to the future – a hundred or even two hundred years from now, to avoid running into ourselves with extended lifespans – or back into the past again."

"Or we could travel to another place right now – like London," Sierra said.

"The future sounds like a little more fun," Max said, with not much of a smile on his face.

CHAPTER 2

[Rome, 1615 AD]

R oberto Francesco Romolo Bellarmine – consultor of the Holy Office, head of the Roman College, Cardinal, former Archbishop of Capua – turned to his guest with a weary smile. "So, Maffeo, any words of wisdom about Galileo? He'll be in Rome next week, and we have arranged a visit."

Maffeo Barberini, scion of one of the wealthiest, most powerful families in Italy, a Cardinal, too – and one day to be Pope, Bellarmine was sure – removed a grape pit from his tongue. "Only what you already know – he is right."

"Pity more of our people cannot grasp that," Bellarmine said. "The nonsense that has been produced in our own College – that the moon is really pure, perfect, sublimely spherical as Aristotle held, and the mountains and craters seen through Galileo's telescope are but imperfections far below that heavenly invisible surface – you would think this was 615 not 1615 of our Lord, and Rome had just been sacked of all common sense and reason!"

Barberini chuckled. "As I recall, Galileo had a good answer to that feeble argument: if we accept that heavenly surfaces are invisible, then we could just as easily agree that the real surface of the moon, constructed of that same magical substance, actually rises in towering mountains ten times higher than his telescope has seen."

"He is clever," Bellarmine said, unsmiling. "And that is what makes him dangerous. I have tried to convey to him the thought that his mathematics, his observations, may be right – that we may welcome them, rejoice in them, as an improvement over Ptolemy's epicycles – but that the underlying, everlasting truth is just as it ever was."

"And what truth is that?" Barberini asked.

"That is no doubt the question that troubles Galileo," Bellarmine replied, "and why he sometimes gives the appearance of accepting our arguments, yet in his truest soul rejects them. He knows that we ourselves are unsure of just what the underlying, everlasting truth really is."

"As we have good reason to be," Barberini said. "But that is our burden – not the world's. And part of our burden is to keep the world – not only the physical world, but the souls of its people – stable."

"Which brings us back to the problem of Galileo," Bellarmine said, sadly. "His theories, his publications, presented to the world without our mediation, cannot help but sow confusion in the common soul."

"Have you implied to him anything at all of the Instruments?" Barberini asked, as delicately as he could manage.

"No, I have not. Therein lies the road that was taken with Giordano Bruno. And it did no good – it did worse than no good. In the end . . ." Bellarmine could not bring himself to finish.

"In the end, our Holy Church had to kill Giordano Bruno," Barberini said. "Still, the result need not be the same with Galileo. He is a different kind of man – more practical, more of a scientist than a mystic like Bruno. He may see a different kind of lesson in the Instruments."

"No," Bellarmine insisted. "I will not have it."

Barberini permitted himself the slightest of smiles.

***

"You are a stubborn man," Bellarmine said to Galileo.

"Stubbornness has nothing to do with this, Your Eminence," Galileo replied. "Truth is what this is about. I can say 'the Earth does not move,' as easily as the next man. But if, in truth, the Earth does move, then it matters not what I say. For in time others will make the same observations as I, and they will say that the Earth does move. And where will our Holy Church be then?"

Bellarmine was at least heartened to hear Galileo refer to the Church as 'our,' even if this plural possessive pronoun likely came with some measure of sarcasm on the astronomer's tongue. "You are stubborn because you assume that future telescopes, perhaps with power far greater than yours, will see the same things in the heavens as your device," Bellarmine answered. "But how can you be sure of that?"

"I am not sure of that," Galileo said. "Devices change, and so then does the knowledge they produce."

"Precisely," Bellarmine said. "The only thing constant in this world is the Lord's word, and the only constant path towards that is the Church's teaching."

"Yes, but if observations conducted through device A contradict the Church's teaching, then even though device A may be improved upon at some future time by device B, ought we not at least consider the evidence presented by device A at this time?"

Bellarmine looked away. "Devices," he said at last. "Believe me, there are more devices in this Universe than you with or without your telescope have ever imagined."

Galileo squirmed. "Are you referring to the Instruments? Do you seek to intimidate me by intimations of your Instruments of Torture?"

Bellarmine said nothing.

"I am a weak vessel," Galileo continued. "I might well sooner lie about what I know to be true than be subjected to your torture. But what would that gain you in the end? Do you suppose you can torture the whole world – impose your will on every human eye that looks at the heavens through a lens?"

"I was hoping you might be persuaded, not by torture, but by reason itself, to see the dangers in the way you proselytize your theories," Bellarmine replied. "I was hoping that once so convinced, we might even enlist you to help in our cause – explain to the world that, although science always progresses, always changes, the soul and its place in the Universe remains constant, remains forever, and our Holy Church is the only reliable guide to that."

"Forgive me, Eminence – but I fear it is the Church that is treading on the domain of science here, not vice versa, in your insistence that the Earth is the unmoving center of the Universe. And you have no evidence that the Copernican theory, which my telescopic observations support, is wrong."

Bellarmine sighed. "Suppose I showed you evidence."

Galileo scoffed. "Where, in the Holy Bible?"

"No," Bellarmine said very quietly. "In Instruments perhaps ultimately not unlike your telescope – Instruments that offer vision far deeper than your telescope. Dangerous Instruments – far more dangerous than your telescopes." He wrung his hands. "I had hoped not to have to speak to you of this. But I see there is no other way."

Galileo shuddered. "You are speaking to me again of torture? Of burning out my eyes?"

"No, not of torture – at least, not of physical torture, I assure you," Bellarmine replied. "I would invite you to accompany me on a journey."

"To the torture room?" Galileo asked, still not convinced.

"To the city of Socrates, Plato, and Aristotle," Bellarmine replied. "To Athens."

***

Galileo complained every hour he was awake, which was most of the seven-day voyage by sea from Rome to Athens. "I don't like this kind of travel at this time of year," he said to Bellarmine after he had thrown up his latest meal overboard, "but I fear my life depends upon it."

"I am bringing you to Athens to learn," Bellarmine replied. "You of all people should welcome that."

Their ship entered the Port of Athens without incident. It bustled with international trade under Ottoman rule. Galileo was still complaining. "The Turks have telescopes, but to them they are just toys. They have no idea what they are looking at when they point them at the sky."

The two disembarked with Bellarmine's servant Ruggero – a priest about thirty with the build of a Swiss Guardsman who had accompanied them on the voyage. He carried Bellarmine's and Galileo's belongings, as well as a number of knives.

The weather was mild. "Our destination is about ten minutes on foot," Bellarmine said.

Galileo nodded. "I would welcome a walk on solid earth after all of those days at sea."

[Athens, 1615 AD]

They arrived at Hakam's coffee house about fifteen minutes later. Galileo had stopped several times to divest his sandals of pebbles. "They serve a wonderful heated beverage they call *kaweh* – which means 'vigor'," Bellarmine explained. "The taste is delicious, the aroma is from heaven, and it will indeed strengthen your constitution and sharpen your intellect."

Galileo smiled fully for the first time in a week.

"They name many of their coffee houses after Hakam, and their proprietors take his name," Bellarmine continued. "Someone by the name of Hakam is said to have opened the first coffee house in Constantinople about sixty years ago."

Ruggero walked into the coffee house alone, while Bellarmine and Galileo waited outside. The servant came out a few minutes later, and pronounced Hakam's safe to enter.

The three walked into a dimly lit room, vivid with tobacco smoke and coffee and a cascade of Greek, Turkish, and Arabic voices. Galileo's eyes watered with pleasure. Bellarmine said something to Ruggero, who nodded and approached a well-dressed Ottoman on the far side of the room.

"Would that be Hakam?" Galileo asked.

"Presumably, or his assistant at very least," Bellarmine replied.

Ruggero returned with Hakam, who smiled, bowed extensively to Bellarmine, and ushered the three to a table. Ruggero thanked Hakam and passed him some coins.

"I took the liberty of procuring a cup of *kaweh* for you," Bellarmine said to Galileo.

"Thank you," Galileo replied. "It looks to be a very expensive beverage, judging by what your priest paid the proprietor."

"Only a small part of that payment was for the *kaweh*," Bellarmine advised.

***

Galileo insisted on a second cup of coffee, and wanted a third.

"Too much at one time is not good," Bellarmine said. "It will not get you intoxicated like wine, but it will disaffect your humor."

Galileo started to object–

"And we have only a limited amount of time to see the room behind that wall." Bellarmine gestured to the wall against which Hakam was standing, sipping coffee himself, and alternately watching Bellarmine's table and a colorfully, scantily clad young woman who was slowly undulating her body.

"I can see why he would find her of interest," Galileo said, appreciatively.

Hakam, noticing Bellarmine's gesture, approached their table.

"Is the room ready for us?" Ruggero asked Hakam, in Turkish.

Hakam nodded and led the three to the far wall. He pressed his hand against a panel, which opened to reveal a key hole. Hakam produced a key and applied it to the hole. He pulled a door open, and waved Bellarmine, Galileo, and Ruggero into the room.

"I will await outside, here with you," Ruggero said to Hakam, who nodded.

***

Bellarmine and Galileo entered the room and closed the door behind them.

The room was well lit, but Galileo could not locate the source of the light. It was not sunlight or flame, Galileo was reasonably sure. There was a chair in the center of the room, glistening with all kinds of metallic and reflective elements.

"This is the Instrument of which you spoke," Galileo said, "which you wished to show me?" He shuddered, easily imagining how he could be tortured in such a chair.

"Yes," Bellarmine replied. "And this is one of the things the Instrument produced." Bellarmine picked up a bound book from a table near the glistening chair and gave the book to Galileo.

The astronomer sat in one of two plain wooden chairs at the table. He stroked the book, narrowed his eyes, and gasped. The title read, *Dialogo sopra i due massimi systemi del mondo*. It was indicated as published by the presses of Landini, in Florence, in the year 1632 AD – 17 years in the future.

Its author was Galileo Galilei.

***

"Clever forgery!" Galileo exclaimed, half in anger, half in admiration. "Your scribes at the College seek to publish some confusing document under my name, and therein mislead the world about my real contentions!"

"I think it is not a forgery," Bellarmine said, "or, at least, something not as simple as a forgery. I think you will agree, if you continue reading."

But Galileo turned away from the text, and focused instead on Bellarmine. "It is a *Dialog about the Two Chief World Systems*, purportedly written by me, except I did not write it. Therefore, it is a forgery."

Bellarmine shook his head no. "I think you would do better to say not that you did not write it, but you did not write it yet."

"Preposterous," Galileo said. "How could you possibly know that?"

"Would it surprise you to know that I read your *Sidereus Nuncius*, produced via that very Instrument at which you have just been staring, in 1599, the year Clement VIII made me a Cardinal – a good decade before you would even make the observations with your telescope that would form the basis of that essay you published in 1610?"

"Produced as in printed, as by Gutenberg's marvelous press?" Galileo asked.

"No, not printed by this Instrument per se," Bellarmine said. "But the Instrument made your printed books possible for me to read, by a process far more marvelous than the press."

"Forgive me, Eminence – but none of this makes sense. It cannot be true that you read a text of mine before I even wrote it!"

"I assure you it is," Bellarmine said. "You see, I have been an admirer of your work – albeit secretly – for quite some time. Perhaps even longer than you."

Galileo harrumphed, and returned his attention to the book. "Why did I need to travel to Athens with you to see this? Not that I minded the hot beverage and other things in that room outside." Galileo smacked his lips. "But you obviously have been here before, knew about this book – why did you not just take this book back with you to Rome? Surely it would be more safe there in your keeping than here."

"It is not permitted. The books must stay in this room."

"Not permitted by whom?" Galileo asked.

"I do not know with any assurance," Bellarmine replied. "I met him three times.   He said to me at one point that he was St. Augustine. At another that he was Heron of Alexandria."

Galileo's eyes widened. "The author of *Catoptrica*, about reflecting surfaces?"

"I believe so. Yes," Bellarmine said. "He also spoke of Ptolemy, but of meeting and knowing him, not being him."

Galileo shook his head in disbelief. "I would suffer even your instruments used for torture in return for a conversation with Ptolemy, were that in the remotest sense a real possibility. But your informant is clearly a lunatic."

"There is no way I can conclusively prove at this instant what I am telling you," Bellarmine allowed, "not about seeing *Sidereus Nuncius* in 1599, eleven years before you wrote it, not about the legitimacy of your authorship of the *Dialogo* that you see before you now, which apparently requires seventeen more years before it comes into being in the world outside of this room. And not about the Instrument you also see before you, and the man who claimed to use it to bring those and other books to me."

"Other books from the future?" Galileo asked. "I still do not believe that."

"Yes, from the future," Bellarmine replied. "But they are no longer in this room. He is concerned about leaving them here, for the same reason he does not want them to leave this room. He wants to avoid 'contamination of the future' – those were his very words."

"But he had no concern about me seeing this *Dialogo*," Galileo said.

"No concern," Bellarmine said. "In fact, he wanted me to bring you here, to show you this book."

Galileo raised an eyebrow.

"He has a plan for you," Bellarmine said—

The conversation was interrupted by a flashing light and a strange sound in the room.

"We must leave," Bellarmine said. "The light and the sound are a signal that we must vacate the room."

Galileo looked again, very intently, at the book on the table. He had opened it to the first page, and he turned now to the second.

"You cannot take that with you," Bellarmine reminded Galileo. "If you do, Hakam will stop you."

Galileo looked at the second page another minute, then nodded and closed the book. "I understand. I needed to make sure this book was really written by me – I know my own thought and my own writing."

"And was it?" Bellarmine asked, also wanting the answer to that question.

Galileo rose. "It is impossible. But I believe it was."

***

The two opened the door. Hakam bade the two to leave the room, which they did. Hakam closed the door behind them and locked it with his key.

Ruggero and Hakam had been joined by two tall men of rugged build, armed with swords. They stood on either side of Hakam, with their backs to the door, and their eyes fixed on Galileo, Bellarmine, and Ruggero.

"Did we commit some offense?" Bellarmine asked Ruggero in Italian, which he reckoned was the least likely of his tongues to be understood by Hakam. The armed men and Hakam stood impassively – whether in courtesy or lack of understanding of Bellarmine's words, it was impossible for him to tell.

"I do not believe so," Ruggero replied in the same language. "I think Hakam only wants to insure that you do not enter the room at this juncture. He says it is a question of your safety."

"I understand," Bellarmine replied. He looked at Hakam. "May we sit at a table and have more of your delicious *kaweh*?" Bellarmine asked Hakam, in Turkish.

"Certainly," Hakam replied, and pointed with a smile to an open table on the other side of the room. Hakam beckoned another man, of average height, and instructed him to show his honored guests to the table across the room and bring them more *kaweh*. The two armed men stood by the door, expressionless.

The four reached the table, and Hakam's man bowed with a flourish and receded.

"Yes," Bellarmine told Galileo. "You can have one more cup of coffee."

Galileo smiled broadly.

***

"Why is it unsafe to stay in the room with the Instrument," Galileo asked, after their coffees arrived.

"From what I understand, the signal was telling us that another Instrument was soon to arrive, to materialize, in the room," Bellarmine replied. "And that arrival greatly disturbs the air in the room – charges it like a bolt of lightning – with the consequence that anyone inhabiting the room at that moment is put at risk."

"I should like to see that," Galileo said.

Bellarmine said nothing.

Ruggero's eyes were fixed on Hakam and the two men with swords, still standing by the door.

"Will this new Instrument be conveying more fictitious books, or perhaps the man who claims to be Augustine?" Galileo asked.

"Impossible to say, at this point," Bellarmine replied. "But I think you already know in your soul that the book you held in your hand was not a fiction – even though it has somehow, contrary to all sense and reason, not yet been written by you."

"Tell me about the other books from the future," Galileo said. "I assume they were not all written by me?"

"That is correct," Bellarmine said, "and I wanted to talk to you about one in particular–"

"Forgive me, Excellence," Ruggero said to Bellarmine and pointed to the door. Hakam had opened it, and he and the two men were walking inside.

***

Bellarmine, Galileo, and Ruggero walked to the door, which was now bolted shut. Ruggero put his ear to the door and shook his head. "I hear nothing," he said.

The door opened about five minutes later. Hakam bid Bellarmine and Galileo to enter, and gestured to the table near the glistening chair. There were now two books upon it. One of them was in a binding Galileo had not seen before.

Hakam and the guards left the room and closed the door, leaving Galileo and Bellarmine within. Galileo went to the table. He picked up the book with the strange binding and started to read.

"This is the other volume from the future that I spoke of," Bellarmine said to Galileo after a few minutes. "It is from the very far future, hence its unusual binding. You'll see that the pages are also numbered. Your works are discussed beginning on page 27, and on many subsequent pages."

Galileo was too engrossed to speak, except to mutter, "Yes, yes," several times, as he devoured the words in the book, written in Italian. "There is much that I do not understand here," he eventually said.

"Of course," Bellarmine said, soothingly.

"How long will I be permitted this time, to read this book?" Galileo asked.

"For my part, you can stay here with me, as long as you like," Bellarmine replied. "But our host or this Instrument may say otherwise."

Galileo nodded, almost absently, and turned his attention back to the book.

Bellarmine sat at the table in the other chair, and picked up the other book, the *Dialogo*. He had read this more than once in its entirety, but it still thrilled him to read it.

"Do you not find it peculiar that you wanted me to read this book, but it was not here, but when we returned to this room less than an hour later, this book was here?" Galileo finally came up for air, almost two hours after they had reentered the room.

Bellarmine, still seated at the table, expanded his hands. "Your question touches on the essence of this Instrument. It apparently travels through time in much the same way as a vessel traverses the sea. If that is so – and I have seen ample evidence that it is – then if I had indicated at some future time the desirability of the text you are now reading being situated in this room, at this very time, then someone from the future might well have sought to fulfill that desire and traveled back to this time with the volume which is now in your hands."

Galileo shook his head in amazement, confusion, and just a glimmer of understanding. "I suppose that is no more incredible than what I have been reading here about how my theories have been revised by this Albert Einstein."

Bellarmine nodded. "Yes, the Jewish genius in the future who will overturn everyone's understanding of the Universe, just as you seek to do with your own observations now."

Galileo let out a great sigh. "I think I can see that the notion that the sun is the center of our system is . . . a relative thing, not as absolute as first I thought. We must take care not to make the same mistake with Copernicus as the world has been making for lo these fourteen centuries with Ptolemy."

"My faith in your power of reason has not been misplaced," Bellarmine replied.

Galileo read for about another hour, then rose. "The *kaweh* has apparently excited not only my mind but my digestive system. I must—"

"Of course." Bellarmine rose, and the two left the room.

***

Hakam, who was talking to Ruggero outside the room, accompanied Galileo to an indoor facility.

"The armed guards left a while ago," Ruggero informed Bellarmine. "I believe I heard them speaking in Latin, in a dialect not familiar to me."

Bellarmine raised an eyebrow.

Galileo returned with Hakam a few long minutes later. "I think I have read enough," Galileo said, with fatigue.

"Good," Bellarmine replied. "Back in Rome, I am sure that your friends are thinking we have been torturing you, or have killed you, or are threatening to do one or the other if not both. It would be helpful if you could show your face and assure everyone that you are unharmed."

"But I am not unharmed," Galileo said. "My intellect has been stretched to the breaking point, perhaps beyond. I will never be the same."

"This is the price we pay for knowledge, is it not? This is the price you want the whole world to pay – a world of people with intellect far weaker than yours – when you offer your theories, which you are so sure are true, about the Earth and the heavens. Except, you are not so sure now, are you."

"No, I am not," Galileo admitted.

"Let us take our leave," Bellarmine said in Turkish to Hakam. "We are grateful for your kindness and hospitality."

Hakam nodded. Bellarmine, Galileo, and Ruggero left the coffee house. They walked five minutes towards the port, retracing their steps, and stopped at an inn. "This is a good place for a quiet repast and a good night's sleep," Bellarmine said to Galileo.

***

They boarded the ship for their return voyage to Rome the next morning. Galileo and Bellarmine talked about nothing other than what had happened the previous day at Hakam's coffee house.

"You need not worry about the survival of your soul," Bellarmine said softly to Galileo. "Others before you have seen those Instruments and their wonders, and survived quite well."

"Others? Who?" Galileo asked.

Bellarmine pondered for a moment. "Leonardo da Vinci saw those Instruments. I suppose there is no harm in telling you that."

"Yes, I could believe that," Galileo said. "He is rumored to have made sketches, extraordinary, of flying devices, and of machines that could live under the sea."

"The rumors are true," Bellarmine said.

"And where did the Instruments come from? You mentioned Heron, St. Augustine? How long have those Instruments been in Athens?"

"That I am unable to tell you, not because I do not want to, but because we honestly do not know," Bellarmine said. "Not everyone in the Church believes the St. Augustine account – even though it was given to me by a man who claimed to be St. Augustine, and at another time Heron of Alexandria, as I told you. But some of my brethren say Marco Polo brought one of the Instruments back with him from Cathay. I do not believe that. I suppose they are not too heavy for transport across land or sea, but there is nothing I have seen in the Instruments or what they have conveyed that suggests a provenance in the Orient."

"Which of your brethren know about this?" Galileo asked.

"Mostly Jesuits," Bellarmine answered, "and a few others."

"And how long have these Instruments been in Athens?" Galileo asked.

"Unknown," Bellarmine replied, "we believe many hundreds of years. The first definite record we have of them here is in

1357 AD. I have scrutinized the works of Aquinas from the century earlier but so far I have no indication that he knew of any future books or any conveyances like the Instruments. The first Churchmen who attempted to read the books could barely understand what they read. They of course were conversant with some of the references to the Ancients. But when they came upon you – Galileo Galilei – they had as much comprehension of you as you do of Albert Einstein."

Galileo trembled. "I understood not much of Einstein – most of his mathematics is far beyond me. But I grasped some of Isaac Newton, and from that vantage point, and what little of Einstein I could comprehend, I can see that my work is . . ."

Bellarmine nodded sympathetically.

"So much knowledge to be had there, in that room in Athens," Galileo said, rubbing his eyes. "Will I be permitted to return?"

"Perhaps," Bellarmine said. "We shall see."

"I must renounce my views of the cosmos? That is the price for my return to Athens? I would not necessarily be averse to that, given what I have seen, or what I think I have seen, of what the future thinks of my work."

"It is far more complicated than that, and the choice will not be mine alone," Bellarmine said.

"But even if I renounce what I have said, even if I publish not another word about my telescopic observations and their support of Copernicus, that will not stop others from following in the path I have started," Galileo said. "Even the Church lacks the power to erase what the printing press has already placed in the hands and minds of the world, or at least its scholars!"

"We do not want you to renounce anything – not now," Bellarmine replied. "Word of course eventually will indeed spread about your discoveries and your theories. We know that from the Instruments. We cannot stop that. Nor do we want to. What we want is to make sure, as much as possible, that word reaches the people at the right time, in the right way – when their souls are ready to accept it."

"But how?" Galileo asked.

Bellarmine put his hand on Galileo's shoulder. "Leave the details to us. You can continue writing and publishing as you have been doing – but try to take care to make sure you distinguish between science and its explanations, which change throughout history, and faith and its explanation of the way things truly are. In time, you will write your *Dialogo* – you have already read it, so you will have an advantage." Bellarmine smiled a beatific smile. "Who knows, perhaps some of our very discussions in the past few days will find their way into that fine book. But also take care not to include anything you have read from the future, because that would—"

Galileo nodded. "Yes. I understand."

"Do not worry," Bellarmine said. "We will provide you with instructions – detailing just when you should write your treatises, just when you should appear obstinate, just when you should give in. Leave it to us."

"Yes," Galileo said, still not trusting Bellarmine or the Church completely, still wary that all he had experienced in Hakam's coffee house was not somehow some ruse by the Church to control him, but vexed deeply enough by the Instruments and the books to accede to Bellarmine's requests at least for now.

[Rome, 1615 AD]

"A fine wine," Bellarmine said, and offered a glass to Barberini, the night after he, Galileo, and Ruggero returned to Rome.

"And a fine journey, too, judging by your countenance,"

Barberini replied. "I take it all went well with Galileo. I told you the Instruments were the best way to proceed."

"We must beware the deceptively easy wisdom of hindsight," Bellarmine said. "Our brethren showed Bruno the Instruments too, and his reaction was very different from Galileo's. He was uncontrollable. He had to be burned, as you know. Just a year after I became a Cardinal. That was sinful, I am sorry to say. It should never have happened. It must never happen again."

"But you seem sure that Galileo is on the right path," Barberini said.

"I am as sure as I can be of anything pertaining to the Instruments," Bellarmine replied.

Barberini looked at him with just the slightest quizzical expression, and bid his brother cardinal a good night. "You should sleep," Barberini told Bellarmine, "even successful journeys take their toll on the body and spirit."

Bellarmine closed his eyes after Barberini left, but his sleep was soon interrupted by Ruggero at the door. "Sorry to disturb your respite, Your Eminence," Ruggero said softly. "He wishes to talk to you."

Bellarmine nodded. He knew who the 'he' was. Ruggero left and Heron entered the room.

***

Bellarmine managed a smile and bid his visitor to sit. "Something to drink?" he asked, out of basic courtesy, though he had never seen Heron drink a drop in his presence.

"No thank you," Heron replied and sat. "But do not let me stop you."

"I have had enough for the evening," Bellarmine replied.

"Well, then," Heron said. "I came to inform you that your trip to Athens with Galileo apparently went very well."

"Apparently?" Bellarmine knew just what Heron was saying, but wanted to hear it from the time master's mouth.

"What Galileo read in Athens will temper his exuberance," Heron replied. "He will still put forth his telescopic evidence in favor of the Copernican system – which is, after all, an improvement over Ptolemy's *Almagest*, which had its usefulness – but Galileo will present his views in a more gradual way, which will not overly disturb the people, and will give your Church time to make this revolution in such fundamental thought a little less disruptive."

"And you know this because you have seen the results in the future," Bellarmine supplied the last line of this strange confession.

"Yes," Heron said.

"We owe you a debt of gratitude," Bellarmine said, truthfully.

"Might we discuss a way in which you could repay it?" Heron asked.

Bellarmine tried not to look surprised or put off. This was something he had not expected. "Of course."

"There is a woman at large who is bent on undoing all that I – and now, you – have done," Heron said.

"A woman?"

"Yes," Heron replied, "as dangerous to me as Joan of Arc was to the powers she opposed."

Bellarmine looked Heron in the eye. "Joan of Arc was found innocent, wrongly executed, and is a martyr to our Church, as surely you know."

"I invoke her name as an analogy of what one woman can do," Heron said, "not as someone equal in all respects to the woman who plagues me and my work. This woman also has no army at her command. But she is cunning and dangerous. I thought she died in 415 AD. But I have come to see I was wrong in that belief."

Bellarmine lowered his gaze, looked up at the ceiling, then back at Heron. "How can I help you?"

CHAPTER 3

[New York City, 2062 AD]

Sierra joined Max at a table near the edge of the main library in the Millennium Club, shaking her head no.

"Heron's work," Max said, darkly. "He's the only one with the power to do this, other than you, in the future – as far as you know."

Sierra now nodded, sat, and poured water for herself from a pitcher that kept the liquid at the precisely the best temperature for human consumption, regardless of the temperature in the room. She had attempted to set the sleek, time-bounding Chairs to 2262 AD, 200 years in the future, and several nearby times, somewhere she and Max could be for however long without running into themselves or anyone who knew them. But the Chairs wouldn't take those settings. "If I'm the one who blocked the Chairs from going to the future – from wherever I may be now in the future – that's even a better reason for not going anywhere near that time," she said.

"On the grounds that your future self knows better than you do now? That assumes that you're actually learning as you go along," Max added with a sarcastic chuckle. "The more we do this, the more I think Dylan was on to something literally true for us in 'My Back Pages' – I knew more when we started this than now."

"We've been at this three days," Sierra said, trying not to lapse into the self-pity that was always on the verge of being the time traveler's companion. "If we keep waiting for the line to the far future to open up, we may find the Chairs gone."

"Or additional Chairs in the room, with their passengers hunting for us in 2062."

"Exactly," Sierra said.

"So we go to the past?" Max asked.

"Let's wait one more day, and if the future is still blocked, yeah, we go to Mr. Appleton in 1896, a year after we left, and see if we can do anything to make this 2062 less . . . disconcerting than it is."

***

Sierra and Max climbed the spiral staircase to the room with the Chairs the next day. The two in which they had arrived a few days earlier were still glistening in the center of the room.

"I called my father one more time this morning, when you were sleeping," Max said suddenly. "I guess my way of saying goodbye."

"I'm glad you did," Sierra said, "but it's not necessarily goodbye."

"I know," Max said, hoarsely. "Nothing's definite about anything. He thought I was playing some kind of joke on him. Apparently my other self called him yesterday, and of course had no recollection of my call to my father a few days ago. My father asked me to stop it."

Sierra put down her bag with 1890s garb and took Max's hand. "That's part of why it's a good idea that we get out of this time, one way or the other."

She squeezed Max's hand, walked to one of the Chairs, and ran her fingers lightly over the inlaid digital controls. She shook her head no. "The future is still blocked. Should we try 1896?"

Max nodded, gave Sierra her travel bag, and sat in the second chair with his. The two decided on a specific time and date in 1896. Sierra synced the two Chairs, Max confirmed that the sync was engaged, and Sierra tapped the key on the control that would send the two chairs back to arrive at precisely the same time in 1896.

Bubbles ascended around each of them, they each had the sensation of a snowflake on their lips, and the bubbles receded.

[New York City, 1896 AD]

They took their time dressing in their 1890s clothing, appropriate for a couple in their late 20s in the Millennium Club. They helped each other with the hooks and buttons. Max gave Sierra an encouraging kiss on the neck and stepped back. "You look lovely, my dear," he said, with a reasonably good approximation of 1890s cadence.

Their plan was to get a room in the hotel they had stayed in the last time they had been here – just a week ago in their lifetimes – then call Appleton on one of those brand new spanking old phones to see if he was home, and, if he was, take a train from Grand Central, just down the block, up to Appleton's home in Wave Hill.

But they caught sight of his familiar moustache and bowtie as they walked near the edge of the dining area. He looked up and saw them, smiled broadly, and gestured them grandly to his table.

"I had hoped the two of you would find some peace in the future," Appleton said, "but it always delights my heart to see you! It has been well more than a year in my life since last we met!"

Max shook his hand, Sierra squeezed his shoulder, and the two sat.

"Tea?" Appleton lifted a cup. "The Millennium has some new flushes from the Orient, quite good."

"Whatever you have that's black and strong would be good," Sierra said.

Max nodded.

Appleton summoned a waiter and gave the order. He turned to Max and Sierra as the waiter receded. He grew more serious. "It wasn't easy," he said, quietly. "Jowett was not at his peak. His focus was diminishing. He managed to complete the translations of the Aristotles before he died, but never made much progress on the *Chronica*." He nearly whispered the name of the Heron text. "Science was never Jowett's strong suit. But I think I may have someone who can help with this." He touched a stack of papers – under which, Sierra realized, was a book.

"That's not—" Sierra began.

"No, no, of course not," Appleton said. "I would never bring the *Chronica* like this to the club. And it is as yet still in the scroll form in which you entrusted it to me, and the one manuscript copy that I gave to Jowett and then retrieved when it became clear that he could not do the job. But here," Appleton took a book with a blue grey marbled cover and gold embossing out from under his papers and handed it to Sierra. "It's by Jack Astor. Do you know it?"

Sierra took the book, nodded slowly, and tensed.

"*A Journey In Other Worlds* by John Jacob Astor," Max leaned in to get a better look. "No, I don't think I know it."

"It is a scientific romance. The air vessel that leaves the Earth makes its departure from Van Cortlandt Park in the borough of the Bronx, just a few miles from my home!" Appleton said, triumphantly. "How could I resist publishing it?"

Appleton and Max both became aware that Sierra was frowning. "Oh, of course not," Appleton said to Sierra. "I know better than to ever reveal to him any hint of that."

Max looked at Appleton and then Sierra. "You want to fill me in?"

Sierra and Appleton both began talking, but Appleton deferred to Sierra. "John Jacob Astor IV is one of the most famous people to lose their lives on the Titanic," she said. "He was thought to be one of the richest men in the world."

"I admit, I looked at the passenger list of the Titanic, in the future, as soon as I learned of its sinking," Appleton said. "I had to know if any of my children or my family were upon it. And of course I immediately recognized Jack's name. But I know what it could do to history if I told him about that."

Sierra had opened the novel. "It says Appleton's published this in 1894 – that's two years ago. Is it just coincidence that you brought the book to the Millennium here today?"

Appleton looked at her with concern. "You seem more suspicious – of me – than the last time we met. Did something go awry in the future?"

"In a manner of sorts, yes," Sierra replied. "That's why we came back here now, to talk to you. But about the Astor novel—"

"You are right," Appleton said. "It is no coincidence that I have his novel with me now. I was just talking to him, before you arrived, about how he might help with finding a translator for the *Chronica*. He is a very wealthy man, as you said."

"That's very dangerous—" Sierra began.

"Of course it is," Appleton said. "Everything we are doing in this time travel business is dangerous. But you risked your lives, and others perished, in obtaining Heron's scroll. What was the point of doing that if it languished, untranslated and unread, in a dusty cubbyhole in my desk? And anything that Jack Astor may guess about what we're doing will go down with him on the Titanic, won't it?"

"That is almost 20 years from now," Sierra said, "a long time to keep a secret."

The waiter approached with their teas. Behind him was a thin man, also with a moustache but a cravat not a bowtie, and much younger than Appleton. "Jack!" Appleton rose. "Did you leave something here?"

"I had an additional thought," John Jacob Astor replied, and smiled at Sierra and Max.

"John Jacob Astor, Sierra Waters and Maxwell Marcus," Appleton intoned the introductions.

***

Astor kissed Sierra's hand, shook Max's, and told the waiter who was still hovering that no, he wouldn't be staying more than a few minutes, and wouldn't require anything more to imbibe.

"Call me Max, please," Max said to Astor, with a smile.

"Of course," Astor replied. "And my friends call me Jack – please do."

Appleton explained that Sierra and Max were part of the team that had acquired the newly unearthed scrolls by Aristotle and Heron in Egypt the year before and were here in New York for a consultation. Fortunately, Sierra and Max both were well versed in the circumstances of the real discovery of two leaves of Aristotle's *Constitution of Athens* in Egypt in 1879 and the longer text in 1890, and had no difficulty appearing knowledgeable about the subject to Astor.

He beamed at both of them, especially Sierra. "It is gratifying to see such a comely woman making such a contribution to our store of knowledge. Who knows what other treasures of the past and its intellect are waiting in the sands of Egypt!"

Appleton nodded. "Jack and I were talking about the problem of obtaining a suitable translator for the *Chronica.*"

"Poor Jowett's of course no longer with us," Astor said. "I had an idea about contacting Frederic Kenyon – he translated *The Constitution of Athens* for the British Museum – but they are being very peculiar about that, as William knows."

"Something shady about how they got the papyrus codex out of Egypt, is my guess," Appleton said. "My contacts at the Museum refuse to discuss it, and they are discouraging Kenyon from having any discourse about translation of ancient texts. I am not sure Kenyon has the requisite science for it, either."

"Which brings me to the reason for my unscheduled return to the Millennium," Astor said, with a flourish and a loud whisper. "I was walking up Fifth Avenue, and I saw one of Samuel Clemens' books in Brentano's – his wonderful *Yankee in King Arthur's Court*. He has a keen interest in the miracles of science. He knows about time traveling, of course—"

Sierra tensed slightly at the mention of time travel, and hoped it didn't show – at least, not to Astor.   She couldn't help thinking that Mark Twain was buried in Woodlawn Cemetery in the Bronx, not very far from the grave of Socrates . . . and that he would live in Appleton's beloved Wave Hill for a few years after Appleton died.

Appleton winced slightly for different reasons, thinking that if he had been better tending his publishing business in

1889, he would have made more of an effort to talk Clemens out of publishing this book with his own damned Webster company, and cast his lot with Appleton's instead. He looked for a moment at Sierra, thinking it was her mentor Thomas – who was actually so much more – who had diverted his best attention from publishing for most of that year. But in all fairness to Thomas, Appleton in 1889 had still not gotten completely over the loss of his beloved wife Mary just five years earlier. He grieved for her still. He always would.

Astor continued, apparently oblivious to Sierra's and Appleton's demeanors. "But Clemens is abroad and bankrupt. He is $100,000 in debt – I offered to help but he is a proud man. And in addition to all of that, he's taking the death of his daughter Susy very hard—"

"An inflammation of the meninges, she was just twenty-four," Appleton said, gravely. "Truly tragic."

"Yes," Astor said. "And then I thought – there may be someone better than Clemens, someone with the necessary training in Greek, in science, and the possible science of time travel, even more so than Samuel Clemens. He came out with a book just last year – a scientific romance, much better than I could ever write – *The Time Machine*, do you know it?"

Now Sierra smiled, not only to hide the turmoil within but in appreciation of the absurdity, by any rational standard, of this conversation. "Yes, by H. G. Wells, of course!"

***

Astor briefly made the case for Wells. "He is young – just thirty years of age, two years younger than me. His writing is vibrant. He clearly is energetic, more so than a man of Clemens' age, and— Oh, forgive me," he said to Appleton, "I didn't mean to suggest—"

Appleton waved away the apology. "No offense taken. I am sure Mr. Wells does have more energy than Samuel Clemens, than I do, and certainly more than Mr. Jowett." He chuckled at his own joke.

Astor smiled, stood, reached across the table and clapped Appleton on the shoulder. "So we're in agreement that we should contact Mr. Wells about this translation? I can telegraph him as soon as I leave." He gave a quick, perfunctory look at Sierra and Max.

"Yes . . . ," Appleton said slowly, also looking at Sierra and Max. "He is apparently a man of the future, which would make him ideal to translate Heron's strange book."

Sierra looked at Max, and realized there was no point in opposing Wells, certainly not now, and maybe not at all. She nodded her head yes.

Max did the same. "Makes sense to me."

"Good!" Astor beamed and started to take his leave. "Where are the two of you staying, if I might be so intrusive as to ask?" he suddenly asked Sierra and Max. "I have the perfect place for you," he said, before either replied. "The William Waldorf Astor, my cousin's hotel – just a hop, skip, and a jump from here, on Fifth Avenue and 34th Street. I'm building a better one, right next to it, but it's the best you can do right now." He pulled a fountain pen from a pocket on one side of his jacket, and a little writing pad from the other side. He tore a piece of paper from the pad, scribbled upon it, and handed the result to Sierra. "Just present this at the front desk. You'll be shown a highly comfortable room."

Appleton nodded, seeing the extent to which Astor was enjoying playing the host.
Sierra nodded as well. She still had misgivings about being

too close to Astor and his fate on the Titanic, but putting up too much resistance at this point would make Astor even more likely to take notice of her and Max.

"Thank you," she said with mustered brightness.

***

Sierra was in Max's arms later that night, after the two had said goodbye to Appleton for the day, after Astor had left.

"I don't know," Sierra said, softly. "I feel like ever since we saved those scrolls, everything's been moving too quickly, spinning out of our control. First Biden in our future, now Astor and H. G. Wells back here. Those two are wild cards."

"But what's the alternative?" Max asked, and stroked her hair. "If we hadn't taken the *Chronica*, that would have left Heron free to shut off the time travel completely, to control it in any way he wanted, whenever he pleased. It would exist just in novels and movies, or only in Heron's hands, and we would have no way of improving the world."

"I know," Sierra said. "It's just, so far, I'm not sure that anything I've done, we've done, has improved much of anything." She stretched up to Max's lips and kissed them. "Except maybe me and you."

"Thanks." Max laughed and slapped her gently on her naked backside.

"This hotel is beautiful," she said. "It's right where the Empire State Building used to stand."

"Yeah," Max said, more interested in gliding his fingers slowly down the middle of Sierra's back.

"That doesn't make you feel a little weird?" she asked.

Now his lips grazed her side. "I gave up feeling weird about any place I've been with you a long time ago," he murmured. "But I'll tell you something about John Jacob Astor. Maybe it would be good to have someone who's richer than God in our corner for a change, to bankroll whatever we have to do to stop Heron."

***

Max found an envelope under their door late the next morning, after they had awoken from a long night's sleep that had begun well after midnight.

"A bill?" Sierra asked. "Maybe Jack Astor is not so generous."

"It's from Astor, but it's not a bill," Max said. "It's an invitation – to join him for lunch in about . . . " He scooted over to his night stand, which had the pocket watch he had been carrying with him for several years now. He looked at the watch . . . "that would be about 20 minutes from now. Can we make it?"

"Do we have a choice?" Sierra asked, sarcastically, and eyed the bathroom, which contained a bathtub and a shower. "I will say this for him – this hotel has all the mod cons."

Max laughed. "Do the Brits say that now?"

"I don't think so," Sierra replied. "It's from the psychedelic era, the 1960s, if the course I took in 20th century popular culture had it right."

She rose from the bed and walked to the shower.

Max took in the view, and wondered if they had time—

"We don't have the time," Sierra said, as she entered the bathroom, correctly reading Max's mind as she usually did in these situations.

***

The two found Astor waiting for them at a sumptuously

appointed table in the hotel's restaurant. He stood up, beamed, and motioned Sierra and Max to join him.

A waiter brought a bowl of olives a moment after the three were seated.

"Do you like olives?" Astor asked Sierra and Max. "These are from Greece, from the Kalamata Mountains. A fellow by the name of Monopati imports them, then cures them in olive oil, salt, and vinegar made from his own wine on his farm in Sandwich, Massachusetts, on Cape Cod. He makes them the ancient way. I assure you, if you never tasted an olive like this, once you have, you'll never go back to those clumsily spiced Roman kind."

He passed the bowl to Sierra, who had indeed enjoyed olives like these, many times, over dinners with Alcibiades. She speared one with a small narrow fork and passed the bowl on to Max. She placed the olive in her mouth, bit into it, and her eyes began to water.

Astor gently put his hand on hers. "It's ok my dear. Your secrets are safe with me. I only want to help." His gaze included Max.

Sierra withdrew her hand, though she didn't mind the feel of Astor's on hers. "What secrets would those be?" she asked Astor, coldly.

Max moved his chair back from the table, and started to stand. "Maybe this lunch is not such a good idea."

Astor stood, and urged Max to sit. "Please," he said. "I only want to be of assistance to you. What you are endeavoring to do, what you are doing, must be a Herculean task indeed, if I am understanding correctly."

Max slowly sat. Neither he nor Sierra spoke.

"I know William very well," Astor continued. "He has not betrayed you. But I can put two and two together – it isn't too hard to guess how he suddenly obtained this wealth of manuscripts."

Sierra decided at that instant that there was nothing to gain by continuing to play this so coyly. "Most people would think anyone who claimed to travel through time was either lying or insane," she said, quietly.

Astor nodded. "Do you know the philosopher Charles Sanders Peirce – spelt P, e, i, r, c, e, but pronounced 'purse'? I met him at a lecture William James was giving, several years ago."

"A silk purse from a sow's ear?" Max quipped. "Yes, of course we know of him – he is also a disciple of John Dewey, the pragmatist, is he not?" Max was taking care to use the present tense as well as converse in as old-fashioned a way as he could manage, in case Sierra needed to say that she was just playing games with this Astor with her remark about time travel.

"Good," Astor replied. "I'm gratified that his work has survived into your future. He speaks of fallibilism – that everything, including the keenest rationality, has its flaws and its limits. So, yes, most rational minds would think time travel was impossible, but that does not mean they would be right."

Again, Sierra and Max said nothing.

Astor continued, looking with a penetrating gaze at Sierra. "I had dinner at the Millennium Club with your mentor, Thomas, a few years ago. He told me about the wondrous things the two of you are doing. He told me how William was helping you. He asked me to keep on eye on William, who of course is no youngster. He wanted a younger man, back here, to know what has happening. I was honored that he chose me."

"Thomas O'Leary?" Sierra was barely able to speak the name.

"When did you have this dinner with him?" Max asked.

"Several years ago, as I said," Astor replied. "I have not seen him since."

The waiter approached to take their order, and with a written message for Astor. He read it quickly at looked up and Sierra and Max. "Business calls, but it's just as well – I do not want to overwhelm you. We shall speak again, soon." He stood, bowed slightly, and walked away. Then he turned around and came back to the table. "Dvořák – Antonin Dvořák – do you know him?"

Sierra nodded.

"Will you join me tomorrow – as my guests? His *From the New World* symphony is being performed," Astor said, "on West 25th Street. It's a marvelous work! Do you know it? Of course you do – it's a masterpiece that will survive for millennia! I'll leave details for you at the front desk, this afternoon." Astor turned again, walked away, softly whistling the theme from the Symphony's Second Movement.

***

Max and Sierra ordered a lunch of cheese, fruit, and breads and consumed it quickly. Neither said a word about Astor, operating on the unconscious futuristic assumption that, who knew, this dining room and their conversation could have been bugged.

Sierra finally said something about being recorded by Astor as the two walked out onto Fifth Avenue in the early autumn sunshine and began to stroll north.

"That's logically not very likely," Max said, "certainly not with equipment that could pick up what we were saying. The phonograph is still very weak, and can't record very clearly at a distance. Though – Astor did say that logic has its limits."

Sierra stopped walking. She turned to Max. "Look, the question for me is can we work with him, get to know him as we have William, and not tell him about his appointment to drown on the Titanic?"

"We'll need to think about that," Max replied, "but that's not the only question."

"Ok," Sierra said, not sure where Max was headed. "What's the other one?"

"I saw your face when Astor mentioned Thomas's name," Max said.

"He might be a good person to talk to," Sierra responded, "as a check on what Astor says Thomas told him. For all we know, Astor could be working with Heron."

"Appleton seems to have confidence in Astor, but fair enough," Max said. "Still, that's not the only reason you'd love to see Thomas."

Sierra began walking, then reached back to take Max's hand and pull him along.

"I know you still love him – Alcibiades," Max said, softly. "I can't compete with that. But I thought—"

"Alcibiades made his decision when he decided to leave me in the past, and live in the future as Thomas," Sierra said, with a husky voice. "I don't know what I could do to change that, and at this point I really don't want to."

Max squeezed her hand. "I'm not trying to wring a commitment out of you— All right, let's talk about John Jacob Astor."

Sierra smiled. "You know, this whole thing started with

our attempt to save Socrates.   Now we're about to consider whether we should try to save John Jacob Astor from his fate.   I guess not exactly the loftiest progression."

***

The two continued north on Fifth Avenue.   "Are we going to the Millennium Club?" Max asked.

"I'm not sure," Sierra replied.   "You know, I always loved Dvořák's *New World Symphony* – my mother took me to a Philharmonic concert when I was a kid, and they gave it a rousing rendition.   Come to think of it, I'm sure I heard it at least once, playing in Thomas's office, when I went in to see him about my dissertation.   He was leaning back in his chair, dangling that long pen in his fingers like a plastic cigarette – God, that seems like more than one lifetime ago.   Maybe Thomas heard the symphony when he was back here on one of his trips, with Dvořák sitting right next to him in the audience. You think Astor talking about Dvořák to us now is a coincidence?"

"Probably not," Max replied.   "Time travel strings together events that otherwise would be taken as coincidence."

"Time travel makes a mockery of coincidence," Sierra agreed, then drew Max's attention to a man across the street, walking briskly on Fifth Avenue, in a white suit.   "That's not Samuel Clemens, is it?"

Max tried to squint without being too obvious.   "No – same shock of hair, but no moustache.   He always had a moustache, didn't he?   And Astor said he was overseas now."

"You're right," Sierra said, "not Clemens.   But that gives me an idea.   Why don't we continue to the Millennium Club, and see if we can take a pair of Chairs ten years forward, to 1906.   If that movie I saw about Clemens when I was in high school was right—"

"*The Belle of New York*?" Max asked.

"Yeah. According to that movie, Clemens was a fixture on this avenue in 1906. And if we don't run into him here, we can visit him at his townhouse, also on Fifth Avenue."

"What about Astor?" Max asked.

"The Chairs are much more precise now – someone must've made some adjustments in the future," Sierra said. "We should have no trouble getting back here just a few moments after we left, regardless of how long we stay in 1906."

"And if the Chairs are gone?"

"Then Astor will just have to wait for another meeting with us," Sierra replied. "I don't trust him completely, not yet. And another ally – Clemens – that we bring into this, rather than thrusts himself upon us, could be good for us."

***

They were at the Millennium Club on West 49th Street off Fifth Avenue in a few minutes.

A familiar face greeted them at the open door. "I know better than to ask where the two of you have been," Cyril Charles said with a big smile, "far too complicated. So I'll confine myself to inquiring if the two of you are well, which you appear to be."

"We are, Mr. Charles, thank you," Sierra said and returned the big smile. She decided not to hug him, because he seemed a little younger than usual, which meant she couldn't be too sure about the status of their father-and-daughter-like relationship at this point, though judging the age of these Millennium guys was always a challenge.

"Will you be relaxing in the lounge or using the room

upstairs?" Charles inquired.

"Upstairs," Sierra replied.

Charles nodded. "I believe there is only one Chair there at the moment, but by all means go up and see for yourselves," he said, and pointed to the first set of stairs, wide and gradual, that would bring them to a floor with the bar, the dining room, and a second set of stairs, also wide and gradual, which led to the floor with the main part of the library. In the corner of the main library was another set of stairs, not as wide, which led to the classics library, all of its books in Greek and Latin – decreasingly visited as the years progressed – and a final set of stairs, narrow, steep, and winding, which led up to the room with the Chairs. "You know the way," Charles said, "but allow me to unlock the door for you."

"Thank you," Sierra said.

"Who used the second chair," Max said quietly to Sierra, as to the two slowly walked up the stairs to the library floor, then to the second library floor, about half a staircase behind Cyril Charles. "We haven't been here that long, since we arrived with the two Chairs."

"Very good question," Sierra said.

The three climbed the final, winding set of stairs. Cyril Charles opened the door to the room with the Chairs. "I shall leave you to your business," he said, in his courtly way. He bowed and walked back down the stairs.

Sierra and Max entered the room, which indeed contained only one Chair. "I suppose you want to take the one Chair to 1906 and Mark Twain," Max said. "I'm not happy with leaving you alone again."

They both knew that the first time he had left her alone had been when he had been killed – or, almost killed, depending on how you looked at it – on the shores of the Thames in Londinium in 150 AD.

"No, I'm much more interested now in who took the second chair," Sierra said. "And I agree that it's not a good idea for us to split forces in these circumstances."

"So maybe we should have a drink in the bar after all," Max said, "and see if anyone arrives."

"That could take years," Sierra said, "but a drink is a good idea."

Max pointed to the weak incandescent bulb that lit the room. "I wonder if they have a way, back here, of knowing if a Chair has arrived in the room – they seem to already have some kind of primitive electrical wiring."

"Could be," Sierra said. "We can ask Mr. Charles."

"Hell, we can ask him who took the Chair," Max said.

"He won't tell us – they don't usually talk about those things."

The two walked out of the room and closed the door.

"Was that bulb flashing?" Max asked. "I just caught a glimpse."

Sierra re-opened the door. The incandescent bulb was indeed flashing. "Could be an alert for an arriving Chair," Sierra said.

She closed the door and they both walked a little down the winding stairs. They both knew that standing in too close proximity to an arriving or departing Chair could be lethal.

They slowly walked back up the stairs after a few minutes. They heard noise in the room within. The door opened.

"Fancy meeting you two here," John Jacob Astor said, beaming, and extended his hand for a handshake with Max and a squeeze of the hand with Sierra.

***

Sierra knew this changed everything with Astor, instantly making him less and more dangerous. He had not only heard about time travel from Thomas, he was doing it himself. So he was less dangerous in terms of knowing their secrets, but more so in terms of what he might be doing with these Chairs.

Sierra also noted that Astor was wearing the exact same clothes as when they last saw him, little more than an hour ago.

Astor caught the meaning of Sierra's appraising expression. "I went back to 1881 to help Bell with the funding for his telephone device – marvelous invention," Astor said. "Most people back then don't yet see that – William Orton, God rest his soul, President of Western Union when the telephone was patented, declined to invest. He was under the misapprehension that the telephone would never be more than a scientific toy."

Sierra nodded.

"In any event, I'll leave you two to your business with these Chairs," Astor said jovially and winked. "You don't yet know me well enough that I would presume to ask where you are going. I'll see you tomorrow night at the concert." He tipped his hat – which Sierra for the first time noticed he was wearing – and walked quickly down the spiral stairs.

"Maybe we should postpone the visit with Mark Twain," Max said, "and see if we can find out more about this Astor guy."

"My thoughts exactly," Sierra said. "And I'm regretting as always that our digital devices don't survive our travels with the Chairs – Heron's doing, I once brought back a little digital dictionary to Alcibiades."

"They have libraries back here," Max said. "Maybe we should visit one and see what the newspapers have to say about Astor."

Sierra laughed, ironically. "If I'm not mistaken, Astor's grandfather or great-grandfather founded the New York Public Library in the 1850s. But I don't know where the main branch is now – we didn't pass it as we walked up Fifth Avenue and 42nd Street."

"I think that's a few years away from being constructed there," Max said. "Cyril Charles would know where the closest, decently-stocked branch is now."

***

They encountered Cyril Charles as expected at his post in the vestibule. He knew better than to ask them whether they had traveled somewhere and returned, or had decided not to travel through time at this point at all.

Max smiled and shook his hand. "Do you know the address of the closest branch of the New York Public Library?"

"That would be the Lenox Library, up on 70th Street and Fifth Avenue," Charles answered, immediately. "There's also the Astor Library to the south – but that is a bit further away, below Washington Square Park." He smiled slightly, knowingly, at the name Astor.

"Thank you," Max and Sierra said, ignoring the smile. They walked to Fifth Avenue and turned north.

"Do they have microfiche in use yet?" Sierra asked Max.

Max scrunched his face. "It's been invented already, for sure. But I don't think it's in common use in libraries as yet. But they should have copies of the newspapers themselves that we can look through."

Sierra looked up the Avenue. "The Library's about 20 blocks north – should we walk it?"

"Those horse-drawn carriages look like fun," Max said.

"We could probably walk faster," Sierra said, gesturing to a slow-moving carriage that now stopped and discharged a passenger.

"Where's your sense of adventure?" Max asked, playfully.

"Ok, we'll take the damned horse," Sierra said, and waved to the driver, who nodded back at them.

"Wait," Max said. "Did you take any money with you from the hotel?"

Sierra shook her head no, and waved the driver off. He nodded again and continued north with his horse-drawn carriage.

"How much is the fare?" Max asked Sierra. "A penny?"

"Doesn't matter," Sierra said. "It's a penny we don't have."

"We should have asked Astor for some cash," Max said, "a time traveler's per diem." And the two began their walk up Fifth Avenue.

***

The walk was the longest the two had taken in the 1890s, and filled with everyday history come to pulsating life. They encountered boys and girls selling newspapers in the middle of the Avenue – "no child labor laws back here," Sierra mentioned – and vendors of all ages, raucously hawking their wares on the sidewalks. "Bootblacks," Max looked at a row of men polishing shoes and boots against a wrought-iron railing, and then at his own footwear. They were a pair of nondescript shoes from the future that didn't look too out of place in 1890s, and never needed polishing.

They encountered someone far more interesting as they crossed 60th Street. Sierra gestured to a man walking towards them, very thin, well dressed, about 40 years of age. His black hair was parted in the middle and he had a moustache, like many men in this city at this time, including John Jacob Astor, except Astor's hair was lighter and his moustache a little longer.

"I'm pretty sure that's Nikola Tesla," Sierra said, and slowed down to a halt.

"Should we talk to him?" Max asked. "How can we not?"

Sierra agreed. "This time and place has more famous people walking around than Ancient Athens or the Library of Alexandria," she said.

The man was in nodding distance. He caught Sierra's eye and smiled.

"Nikola Tesla?" Max asked and extended his hand for a handshake. "We're—"

Tesla took the hand and widened his smile. "I know who you are, and I'm pleased indeed to meet you."

CHAPTER 4

[Rome, 1615 AD]

Heron had an instinct. He would not find much else of use to him in this time and place. He had brokered the potentially disastrous conflict between science and the Church, with neither side fully understanding what had happened. Science would progress and the Church would continue. He'd had more than his fill of those longwinded sanctimonious Church fathers. He believed in no God, except what was in himself, and he knew that the Church and all dogmatic religion did plenty of damage to humankind. But he also believed that humanity was always in need of some moral guidance, especially in this age, as the Renaissance was about to move into full gear.

He also had concluded that Sierra Waters or whatever she now called herself was not here. Heron had come here in the first place because his erstwhile colleague in 150 AD Alexandria, Claudius Ptolemy, had been concerned that Sierra Waters might have come to this early Renaissance time to coax Galileo in his Copernican, anti-Ptolemaic ideas. But Heron could find no sign of her here.

He thought she was no longer in the further past, either. There was nothing left of Alexandria now, had not been for nearly a millennium, and if she had been back there even earlier – had traveled back there after she had feigned her own horrible death as Hypatia – then he would have known about it. There would have been some sign of her. What he did know, or at least strongly suspected, is that she had taken his *Chronica* before the Library has burned – the book he had foolishly written in his vain youth, teaching her and all the world about the mechanics of time travel, and, worse than that, what could be done with it.

But if she was neither here nor in the past, that left just one time – the future. But where? He had at one time installed a tracking device on all of the Chairs, which would have told him where and when Sierra Waters was now. But she had apparently disabled that, some time in the future, as she had done with so much of his work.

Heron sighed. There was one man, that puttering nuisance William Appleton, who might know the whereabouts of Sierra Waters.

Heron booked passage to Athens. He had toyed, many times, with setting up a portal here in Rome, but had always concluded that the convenience was not worth the danger. The Vatican had too many priests with too much time on their hands. Sooner or later one of them would stumble onto the room with the Chairs, and that could create complications Heron did not want to engage.

[Athens, 1615 AD]

The sailing voyage to Athens was smooth. Hakam was fortunately right inside his coffee house.

"The business with the Cardinal and the scientist was concluded to your satisfaction?" Hakam asked, after the formalities of greeting had been concluded.

"Very much so," Heron replied, and gave Hakam a pouch of silver. It was much in excess of what Heron usually paid for this work, but he had come to rely on Hakam's efficiency.

Hakam gestured to the room beyond the room. "All is ready for you," he said.

Heron thanked him again, entered the room, and locked the door. He looked at himself in the small mirror on the wall. He had had his face DNA-fashioned to look like St. Augustine, but that had not been needed for his sojourn here in the early 1600s. He knew exactly what the real Augustine had looked like – he had conversed with him, long into the night, enough times – but Bellarmine and these priests hadn't the vaguest idea. The surviving pictures of the saint looked nothing like the man.

Heron sat in the Chair and set it for the future, 2087 to be exact, where the technology for precise facial reconstruction was readily obtainable. His first step would be to set his face to someone recognizable as a friend of Appleton in the 1890s. Then he would travel back to 1899, shortly before Appleton's death, and see what he could wring out of the man in the last months of his life, when he would be too weak to travel anywhere to sound the alarm on Heron's visit, if somehow Appleton were to realize who Heron was.

Heron lowered the go lever and the bubble ascended. He stroked his upper lip with the second knuckle of his right hand. He would need to grow a moustache.

[New York City, March, 1899 AD]

The new face and the flight to New York City in 2087 were easy. The trip back to 1899 – or what Heron hoped to do there – would be more difficult. Fortunately, speaking English in a way that did not attract attention would be no problem. Heron was a polymath when it came to language, and the melting pot par excellence that New York City was in the 1890s would provide suitable cover for anything he said that might have differed from the usual dialects heard around town.

Heron walked down the winding flight of stairs with his new face in the Millennium Club, nearly a year before the 20th century, depending upon how you counted it. Whichever way it was categorized, Heron knew the century ahead would be pivotal for humanity.

Cyril Charles, the unctuous dope, was in the vestibule of the club. These doormen – Heron thought of them as doormats – traveled through time more frequently than Heron, and apparently owed allegiance to no one but themselves. Heron had long been intending to do something about them, but was always caught up in matters more pressing.

Charles greeted Heron in his disguise with a smile and a bow. Heron had a small band of people back here who know who he was, and upon whom he could rely. He was glad Mr. Charles was not among them.

Heron walked out onto Fifth Avenue. The remnants of the huge snowstorm that had hit the entire East Coast last month, including New York City, were still on the street. He supposed he could have come back a month or two later. But Appleton was due to die in October, and with Heron not wanting to interfere with that, he didn't want to cut this too close. He had a firm policy of interfering as little as possible with the natural course of events.

Of course, that begged the question of what was the natural course? Heron often considered that the history as he had encountered it was not the natural course of events, but as some other manipulator in time had made them happen. That manipulator could have been Sierra Waters, or a later version of himself, or someone he had no knowledge of at all.

Heron shivered. It was colder here in March 1899 New York than he had expected. Or maybe he was more vulnerable to the cold than usual, having spent so much recent time in more temperate climates. Fortunately, he spotted a men's apparel shop across the street. And he had come prepared with plenty of 1890s American coin. He quickly purchased a woolen overcoat, which fit well over the woolen waistcoat he was wearing, and walked back out onto Fifth Avenue.

He headed south, to Grand Central Terminal, where he would place a call on a public telephone to one of his minions. Several men on the street nodded at him as he proceeded. Possibly they recognized his new face. That didn't matter. In this day and age, communication had not yet progressed to the point at which everyone knew where famous people were, by virtue of their ubiquitous little messages on tiny telephones. Likely no one on the street personally knew the true possessor of Heron's current face, so the chances were slim that someone who attempted to converse with him would realize that he wasn't who he appeared to be.

He reached Grand Central Terminal and made his call. "Let's meet at the seafood restaurant in 20 minutes," Heron told his associate, who said he would be there shortly. Heron had developed a taste for seafood in Alexandria. He knew the Oyster Bar would be opening in Grand Central Terminal in a little more than a decade. In the meantime, the current establishment would have to do.

Heron left his new coat on the back of the chair he was shown to, in a quiet corner of the restaurant. Coat checks were a good few decades away.

He ordered an unflavored seltzer water, to start. He needed a clear head. "Very good, sir," the waiter responded. "And good to see you back here again!"

The waiter returned with the seltzer and a copy of *The New York Times*. "And may I say you were very right to back this in 1896 – this is the best newspaper in New York City. I read it every day!"

"Thank you," Heron said. His newly adopted lookalike had indeed financed Adolph Simon Ochs' purchase of this newspaper in 1896. Heron was mildly surprised that this was known by his waiter – but, here in New York City for the next few centuries, actors and actresses and authors and all kinds of people who were trying to become important took up restaurant work in their lean times.

Heron's man approached. He was in his twenties, had the same style of hair as Heron – parted a little more in the middle – and a moustache, too. "Good to see you, J. P.," he said to Heron, with a little wink.

"Mr. Porter," Heron motioned his associate to take a seat and got right down to business. "I need you to find out something very specific about William Henry Appleton," he said.

"The publisher?"

"Yes," Heron replied. The waiter arrived with a menu and a request for a drink order from Heron's associate. "I'll have a scotch whiskey, your best single malt, no ice," Porter said.

"Very good sir," the waiter said and left.

"You expecting me to pay for that?" Heron asked Porter.

"I—"

"I'm only joking," Heron said and laughed loudly. "Of course I will! It supports my impersonation of J. P. Morgan!"

***

The two dined on raw oysters. Heron smacked his lips. "So the key is the *Chronica*," he said to Porter, who was on his second scotch. "I've scoured every catalog well into the future, and there is not a sign of it. Which means, if Appleton has it, he has not yet been able to publish it."

"Is it possible this Sierra Waters never got it out of the pyres of Alexandria?" Porter asked.

"I would not rule that out. But I have learned the hard way not to underestimate the intelligence and the talent of that woman," Heron said. "The safest course of action is to assume that she indeed took the *Chronica*."

"Perhaps she gave it to someone other than Appleton," Porter suggested.

"Yes, that's of course possible, too," Heron said. "But as far as I know, the only one in Sierra Waters' circle in a position to get anything published is this Appleton. So he would be a good place to start."

Porter nodded. "Is Appleton fluent enough in Greek to do the translation? And, for that matter, does he command the mathematics? From what I have seen of your work, the equations are well beyond the average general publisher."

"Good questions," Heron replied. "I assume he is not. So that raises the question of whom would he entrust with such a momentous task. See if you can find that out from Appleton, too."

"I shall do my best," Porter said.

Heron stood, signaling that this meeting was over. "I know that you will, Mr. Porter."

***

Edwin Stanton Porter was currently in the employ not only of Heron, but of Thomas Edison and his associates. Porter sometimes suspected that Edison knew Heron, but never dared to ask either man. Being in league with a man from the future would certainly explain Edison's outpouring of inventions – not only in moving pictures, Porter's specialty, but in recording of sound, electrical lighting, and the like. His primary employer, Edison, was at this point probably the greatest inventor in history. The only possible competition might be Leonardo – but he had only sketched most of his great inventions, not brought them into physical being and usage as had Thomas Edison. Other inventors in this century – Morse, Daguerre, Bell – had just one great invention to their credit, in contrast to Edison's dozens.

Porter hopped on a southbound motorized carriage on Fifth Avenue. He spotted Mark Twain walking north, resplendent in his white suit.

Porter had an appointment in a café on Broadway with another of Edison's photographers – erstwhile, for the past few years – William Dickson. He was 10 years older than Porter, and was widely considered the real brains behind Edison's kinetoscope moving-picture machine. He had the same moustache and sideburns as Porter, who considered Dickson an older brother. Perhaps Dickson could be of help with how to best approach William Henry Appleton.

Dickson rose to greet Porter with a firm handshake and big toothy smile. "Good to see you again, good to be back in New York," Dickson said in his Scottish accent. "As much as I love London, I miss the energy of New York!"

Porter sat and the two ordered pints. After catching up with each other's doings, Porter told Dickson about the job Heron had given him. Porter may have suspected that Edison was in league with Heron, but he knew for a fact that Dickson had done many things for the strange man over the years.

Dickson considered. "Mary Anderson," he said after a few moments. "Take her with you to see Appleton. I had a delightful time with her in London last year – almost talked her into making one of my 'What the butler saw' little photo-plays. You know what those are?"

Porter nodded and grinned broadly. "Scantily clad aristocratic women further undressing, usually by the sea shore! A true milestone in photography!"

"Yes," Dickson said, and chuckled appreciatively. "And I learned that Miss Anderson has an abiding interest in Hypatia – which, as everyone knows, is one of Appleton's consuming devotions."

"I heard she's preparing for a performance as Hypatia in the play of the same name, based on Charles Kingsley's novel," Porter said.

"Well there you go!" Dickson said, and ordered another two pints.

***

Porter paid Mary Anderson a visit the next morning. She was staying in a small hotel north of 59th Street. He thought that Dickson's idea was brilliant. Mary would be a perfect entrée to Appleton. Not to mention that she was deliciously easy on the eyes. She was forty years old, but looked at least a decade younger.

The carriage stopped across the street from Mary's hotel. Porter climbed down, walked up to the hotel, and announced himself to the doorman. Mary came down a few minutes later. "What a pleasant surprise!" she said, with a radiant smile.

"Can I buy you a cup of coffee, or something stronger?" he asked.

"It's a little too early for something stronger, but that never stopped me before," Mary said. "The café is very nice." She pointed to a little restaurant down the street.

"How are the rehearsals proceeding?" Porter asked her, when they were seated, and had placed their orders for drinks.

"Very well, thanks for asking," Mary said. "It's a wonderful part. Such a tragic story!"

"Yes," Porter replied.

"And how go your photo-plays?" Mary asked.

"Quite well, too," Porter said. "And that is what I wanted to see you about."

"I've never acted in a photo-play," Mary said, coyly. "I don't share the low opinion that many in the theater have of the photo-play. It's just that I have never been offered a suitable part. But they may well be the way of the future. They can be shown on the screen a myriad of times, and the actors and actresses never tire!"

"I'm gratified you feel that way," Porter said. "I was thinking you might want to reprise your performance of Hypatia in a small photo-play I am contemplating making about her."

"I've seen some of the Lumière Brothers' work – *L'arrivée d'un train en gare de La Ciotat* is my favorite! Magical, wonderful, stunning! In addition, of course, to the work done by Mr. Edison's company!"

"Yes, I hope to make some photo-plays for him, someday soon," Porter said, and bowed his head modestly.

"But those photo-plays are quite short – less than a minute," Mary said. "How could you tell anything of poor Hypatia's story in that short a time?"

"There is no reason the moving picture cannot be longer," Porter replied.

***

The two made a plan to attempt a visit with William Henry

Appleton at his Wave Hill home in Riverdale, if Porter could secure an appointment. He kissed Mary gallantly on the hand and decided to walk south on Fifth Avenue.

He thought it was a good plan. Appleton was a patron of the arts, and would be flattered that Porter sought his advice for a moving picture about Hypatia. Who knows, Appleton might even provide a little funding. If Porter could develop a relationship with the publisher, he would be in a better position to find out about this *Chronica* .

Appleton was reputed to have a weakness for the fair sex, so bringing Mary Anderson along should further soften the old man. Porter reflected that he himself had a weakness for women, as well. He was married, so he had to behave himself, but they couldn't stop a man from dreaming. He envisioned not leaving Mary at the door of her hotel, but accompanying her up to her room at her invitation. "Just a moment, please, let me change into something more comfortable," he heard her say, in his imagination, as she went behind a screen on the side of her room. She emerged in a diaphanous negligee, easily seen through. He saw her breasts, her nipples, and the luxurious hair between her legs. He wondered if that was what the original Hypatia looked like. She certainly had looked that way in the Charles William Mitchell portrait of her from the 1880s. He wondered who had posed for it. Mary Anderson would not have been too young.

Now that would be a photo-play! A story of Hypatia, played by Mary Anderson, all in the nude!

He knew that Edison, the prude, would have no part of it. Indeed, Porter had had to disguise his true nature and lustful leanings from the inventor, as no doubt Dickson had done before him. Porter pretended to be interested only in his work – more interested in machines than people, was the word about him. But he was actually quite the opposite, which was the one of the reasons he had allowed himself to be recruited by Heron.

A mad man? A time traveler, as he claimed? Perhaps both, because Heron had told him things about the near future, a few years ago, which had become true.

***

Porter met Mary two days later at Grand Central Terminal. Demolition of the main house had just begun – a stately new terminal was to be erected here – and the two could barely hear themselves talk until they were comfortably settled in their New York Central train, which they were taking to see William Henry Appleton in the Bronx.

"I didn't know you knew J. P. Morgan, Edwin!" Mary gushed and touched his arm.

Porter felt electricity. "I—"

"I saw the two of you finishing a conversation when I arrived at Grand Central."

"Yes, he could be a valuable patron," Porter said.

"Indeed!" Mary said, and this time touched his shoulder. "I had no idea you had such friends in high places!"

As much as Porter loved trains, he regretted that he and Mary were on one now, given this wonderful touching. But the journey should be worthwhile – Appleton had agreed to see them.

He contented himself with a pat of Mary's hand. He looked out the window as their train exited a tunnel. He did love trains – they were exhilarating, the perfect place for adventure, the exciting things in life.

He looked as the trees sped by outside, newly green with

the early Spring. The fabric of motion fascinated him. He had come to realize that Heron was attempting to do with history and the future what he was seeking to do with images, arranging them to tell his story. He had always believed his own work was of momentous import, but one of the things that attracted him to Heron was the greater portent of his strange work. If Porter were a religious man, he could believe that Heron was the Devil. Surely nothing could compete with that.

Porter became aware of Mary's hand, lightly resting on his. Well, perhaps there were some things that could compete.

***

Their train pulled into the Riverdale station in the Bronx. It would be a stiff hike up to Wave Hill.

He started walking with Mary to the horse-drawn carriages assembled by the station.

"I can make the walk up to see Mr. Appleton – can't you?" she said with a smile.

"Absolutely," Porter replied.

The walk up the hill was invigorating. The two stopped right outside the entrance to Wave Hill and looked out at the Hudson. "They just opened an amusement park on the other side of the river," Porter said and pointed south. "The palisades are just as striking from that view, too – as if an ancient civilization cut them out whole with some kind of powerful blade."

"You have a potent imagination," Mary said, "as a maker of photo-plays should."

The two walked up to the front door of Appleton's splendid residence and knocked.

A man with a pinched face, not Appleton, answered.

"We are here to see Mr. Appleton," Porter announced, "as per our appointment."

The face grew more pinched. "My name is Geoffreys," he said quietly. "I am afraid Mr. Appleton will not be receiving any visitors today. But you may enter if you like, and I can provide some libation for your walk back to the train."

"But, as I told you, we have an appointment," Porter objected.

Mary took Porter's arm, and made to enter. "Is Mr. Appleton here now?" she asked, softly.

Geoffreys nodded. "He took suddenly ill, just an hour ago." Geoffreys pulled a pocket watch out of his woolen vest. "The doctor will be here any moment. I thought he was you when you knocked on the door."

The two entered and sat in the vestibule. Geoffreys returned a few minutes later with tea service for two. There was a loud knock on the door.

"Dr. Stanley, thank you so much for coming." Geoffreys ushered the doctor in, who indeed looked like a doctor, Porter thought, replete with the black medical case and all. Geoffreys and the doctor nodded at Porter and Mary, and walked off into the house.

"This looks like it isn't the day for us to talk to Mr. Appleton about making a photo-play," Mary said to Porter.

"You're right, of course," Porter said. "Should I find Geoffreys and tell him we're leaving?"

"I think not," Mary said, and the two finished their tea, left the Appleton residence, and walked back down to the Riverdale station on the Hudson.

"Fortunately not as tiring as the walk up," Mary said with a smile, clutching Porter's arm, as they reached the station.

***

Porter explained it all to Heron, still looking like J. P. Morgan, in the seafood restaurant in Grand Central the next day.

"It's my fault," Heron said. "I know Appleton is supposed to die in October, 1899, but I should have checked on his health earlier in the year – with a doctor attending him, as you said, there might well have been a record of this somewhere. Assuming Appleton wasn't feigning it."

Porter suppressed a shudder for the revulsion he felt for this man's cold-blooded ghoulishness, but it was a mixed shudder, because he also felt a deep, inchoate admiration for Heron, too. To take on one's shoulders the burden of changing the world, literally, or keeping it safe from those who would change it! "What will you do now?" Porter asked.

"I am not sure," Heron replied. "I could travel back to a time a little earlier, of course – before Appleton grew ill – even as close as last week or a few days ago. But that could create other problems."

"Such as, if you contacted me last week, why do I not recall that now?" Porter asked.

Heron nodded. "You're a quick study – they say that in the theater, yes?"

Porter nodded. "You could enlist someone other than me."

"Yes," Heron replied. "Or I could try to contact Appleton myself, a week ago, as J. P. Morgan."

"But would that not lead to complications for you, in your own mind?" Porter asked.

"Yes, it could indeed," Heron replied.   "But I have considerable experience accommodating these complications and contradictions in my mind . . . . Did you bed her?"

Porter was taken aback. "Who? Mary Anderson? You ask a lot of questions!"

"I give far more in return," Heron said.

"No, not yet," Porter replied, evenly. "On the matter at hand, what about just waiting a few days or a few weeks, and seeing if Appleton recovers, or least improves enough for me to see him? That would engender no complications, right?"

A waiter approached to take their order.

Heron rose and put coins on the table. "Order whatever pleases you," he said to Porter. "You have more than earned it.   I'm off to untangle this mess.   I will try to alert you to what I do, if it is not already apparent."

CHAPTER 5

[Foster Square Facility, Brewster, Massachusetts, 2096 AD]

A woman sat at a console. Actually, she wasn't a human woman, she was a female android, but few humans could tell the difference.

Sierra Waters had left her very specific instructions. But she was not bound by them. She had free will. Still, the ethics of her situation required her, as much as an ethical dictate could, to certainly be guided by Sierra's instructions. After all, Sierra was in large part responsible for her very existence.

Whom should she save? She had reversed the death of Synesius several times, but maybe this was the time to let him rest in peace. She had reversed Max's death in 150 AD on the shore of the Thames, and in 2042 AD in the Parthenon Club in London, along with Synesius then, too. Everyone agreed that reversals or re-sets, every single one of them, risked tearing apart the immensely complex tapestry of time. She had an obligation on that score, too – if not to Sierra Waters, then to humanity, or even existence itself.

One thing she was sure of: an android's death almost never warranted a re-set. Many humans believed androids were not fully alive. Ironically, many androids agreed with them. She did not, mainly because she felt truly alive inside. But she agreed completely that re-sets should be few and far between, and if ruling out an android's death for a reversal limited the number of re-sets, she was all in favor of that.

Her thoughts returned to Sierra Waters. She thought she understood this human woman – not surprising, since she had known all along that so much of her own mental architecture, her patterns and penchants of thinking, were based on Sierra.

Sierra Waters had tried to improve human existence by literally saving some vital parts which been lost in original history – assuming, of course, that the world and the history which Sierra had grown up with was the original, and not the creation of another time traveler such as Heron. Sierra had attempted to save Socrates from the hemlock and the philosopher's own stubborn nature. She had attempted to save some volumes from the flames that at three times different times in history had engulfed parts of the magnificent, ancient Library of Alexandria. Ironically, the ancient Library burned was the very history Sierra had grown up with, but she had come to believe that the conflagrations were the work of Heron.

And Sierra Waters had achieved something of both lofty goals, after a fashion, for Socrates and the Library -- though the life of Socrates, after she had saved him, did not amount to very much for the world, and she had managed to save just a fraction of the ancient Library's immense holdings.

But one of the scrolls Sierra Waters had saved was Heron's *Chronica*, which he had wanted burned, and now Sierra Waters was out to save the process of time travel itself -- or its recipe, contained in the *Chronica* -- lest Heron keep it from everyone but himself. Heron wanted to keep the instructions and equations of the *Chronica* and its usage suggestions about time travel from the world at large, which Sierra might agree was a good thing. But keeping them from Sierra herself was something Sierra would not think was good.

Why had Sierra entrusted so much responsibility in this quest of hers, this fight to keep humanity on the best course, to an android? Debates raged as to whether the androids were more or less than human, but all agreed, including Sierra Waters, that they were not human.   So why did Sierra trust her?

The answer was that it was not so much that Sierra trusted an android, the android realized, it was that Sierra did not trust humanity.

But androids were not completely trustworthy.   Heron had some access to them, too.   And he had constructed androids with faces and bodies that looked like those loyal to Sierra. One had killed Synesius and Max and many others in the Parthenon in 2042, probably the most horrible event which Sierra had requested her to re-set.

How could Sierra be sure that she, this android sitting at a console with a true-view of Cape Cod Bay right now, was not true to Heron?

The answer was Sierra could not know that for sure.   But in her android brain, she believed with every ounce of her being that she was trying to do the best for Sierra and humanity, just as her sister androids had done.   They had sacrificed their lives for Sierra, whatever that meant, and she knew, or believed she knew, that she would do the same if necessary.

She got little reassurance from the fact that, if she was now in existence, and Sierra Waters had created her, then that meant Sierra Waters had survived.   Time travel had a way of leaving the most logical reasoning in tatters and shreds.

CHAPTER 6

[New York City, 1896 AD]

Max and Sierra joined John Jacob Astor IV and Nikola Tesla in front row seats at the National Conservatory of Music. Astor had reserved the seats for them at the Dvořák concert.

"The music will be beautiful," Tesla said to Sierra and Max, "but I keep telling Jack that we best repair to 1899."

"We'll get there soon enough, the old-fashioned way," Astor responded, genially. "I'm no expert, but it strikes me that traveling in those Chairs incurs a lot more risk to everyone than even riding in a one of Ford's quadricycles! Have you seen it?"

"I try to steer clear these days of anyone associated with Thomas Edison," Tesla replied, stiffly.

"Of course," Astor replied. He turned to Sierra and Max. "But surely the two of you would agree on the inadvisability of time travel except when absolutely necessary."

Sierra nodded. She and Max were still trying to absorb all they had learned in the past few days, in particular the discovery that at least some people more or less famous from this part of history had knowledge of time travel – in Astor and Tesla's cases, not only knowledge but actual experience in the Chairs.

Although Appleton, trustworthy as always, had presumably not divulged a thing, apparently his publication of the

Aristotle texts Sierra had rescued from the doomed Library of Alexandria, as well as his attempt to find a translator for the *Chronica*, had brought into being a group of people back here all too conversant in time travel. Some were already known to Sierra and Max, like Astor and Tesla. Others likely were not.

For all Sierra knew, these people might have learned about the Millennium Club and its room with the Chairs even if Sierra had not saved a single scroll from the flames. Appleton had told her that Thomas, after all, had contacted Appleton before the venerable publisher had met Sierra. But it seemed a safe bet that Sierra and Max's expedition in Alexandria was for some reason what had brought most of this out. She regretted not having checked her history in 2062 AD more carefully before rushing back here with Max. Joe Biden elected President in 2008 might well be the least of the changes in history, with these scientists and financiers knowing about time travel back here.

William Arms Fisher, Dvořák's student and now conductor at the Conservatory, took the stage and indicated that the performance of the symphony was about to begin. It occurred to Sierra, as it occasionally did, that music was a kind of psychological time travel itself. When you heard it, you could be instantly transported to the last significant time you heard it – a trigger of how you felt at the time, whom you were with, even the smallest details of that moment. The auditory nerve had tendrils in the deepest memory centers of the brain.

She squeezed Max's hand. She had no association of the *New World Symphony* with Max or anyone else in her life, other than that time in the office with Thomas. She wondered if Astor or Tesla or anyone else here did – the symphony, after all, was less than three years old, not much time to build up deep associations. She and Max had looked up Dvořák, Tesla, and Astor when they had finally arrived at the uptown library yesterday – they found nothing of apparent significance to anything they were doing here.

But the nearness of the *New World Symphony*'s creation in 1893 to where she and Max were right now made her realize something about time travel which was easily overlooked: you could gain as much from a leap a few years forward or back as you could from one far forward or way back in time. A small leap forward was precisely what she had had in mind about Mark Twain.

The mellifluous, beautifully sad harmonic of the symphony began.

***

The symphony ended with the crescendo of every horn, string, and woodwind in the orchestra. Then a heartbeat of silence . . . and everyone in the audience rose and applauded.

Sierra, grasping Max's hand again, found she had been crying. This was the first symphony she had heard in its entirety since she was a child.

Astor, who had been seated next to Sierra and was now standing with her, leaned over and spoke softly in her ear. "Do you know why I invited you here?" he asked.

Sierra, still moved by the music and not wanting to speak, shook her head no.

"I wanted you to meet someone," Astor said.

"Who?" Sierra managed, and looked around.

"You," Astor replied.

Sierra whirled around—

"No, no," Astor assured her. "I didn't mean it literally – though given who you are, I can well see why you would think that.

Apologies," he said sincerely, "I didn't mean to startle you." He lowered his voice. "What I was saying was, with all of this *traveling* you have been doing, you need to take a bit of time to reflect on who you are, what you really want. There is a very good book by Sigmund Freud, a Viennese physician--"

Max, who had been listening to all of this, interrupted. "We know who he is. Sierra doesn't need a psychoanalyst!"

Tesla, who had been staring off into the distance, but also apparently listening, joined the conversation. "Freud thinks we all do," he said, with a touch of derision, though about Freud or what Max had said, was not clear. "Should we repair for coffee? I know a perfect place!"

"I've always loved that word," Sierra said, and the four left the concert hall.

***

All four ordered alcohol in the café. Astor raised his glass in a toast. "These 1890s are the grandest time in human history, would you agree?"

"I have not traveled enough to other times to render an informed judgment," Tesla replied, "and, in truth, neither have you," he said to Astor, but met his glass with a loud clink.

Sierra and Max did the same but said nothing.

"I've seen enough of other times, past and future, to know," Astor insisted, after a long sip of his single malt scotch. "The two of you should think about settling down here, after all of this unpleasant business with Mr. Heron is finished."

"It may never be finished," Sierra said.

"Tell me more about Heron," Tesla asked Sierra and Max. "He was one of the great inventors, a Da Vinci of his time, yes?"

Sierra nodded and considered. Even in the worst-case scenario of these two being in league with Heron, it couldn't hurt to tell them what Heron already knew she knew. "I first met him in 150 AD. There are multiple possibilities as to who he was and is, when and where, and at this point it's not safe and probably not even possible to find out more. There might have been an original Heron back then, and our Heron, a genius from the future, took his place at some point – either before or after I met him in Alexandria in 150 AD. You know, in the future, even further from where Max and I were born, it's very easy to create faces—"

"You mean, masks?" Astor asked.

"No, faces," Sierra said. "In our future we know the codes – the ingredients – that can be used to create living things, such as cells, organs, and complete organisms."

"Codes . . . as in, what Charles Babbage was working with?" Tesla asked.

"That's right," Max said.

"But back to Heron, please," Tesla requested.

"So there might have been an original Heron, whom our Heron replaced at some point," Sierra said. "Or, our Heron may have been the original Heron, who somehow invented time travel —"

"But how, specifically, was Heron able to do that?" Astor asked. "We have all time traveled, of course, but how? Even in our own enlightened time, the mechanism of time travel is a firm denizen of fiction."

"Yes, I have traveled to the past with Jack," Tesla said to the questioning gazes of Max and Sierra, "though I grant that time travel is a lot more complex than the steam-powered doors and persistence-of-vision devices that the real Heron or whoever invented."

"I think that's correct," Sierra said, not really surprised that Telsa had used the Chairs, given that Astor had taken Telsa into his confidence.   But she saw no reason, at this point, to spell out to Tesla – and to Astor, if he didn't already know it – that the entire blueprint for time travel was in the very *Chronica* that she was seeking.

"But please, go on about Heron," Tesla asked Sierra again.

"Well, the third possibility is that there never was a Heron in the past, until our man, a time traveler and inventor from the future, went back to ancient Alexandria for some reason and created a life and identity as Heron."

"Which do you think is the most likely?" Astor asked.

"I honestly do not know," Sierra said, truthfully, "probably an original, ancient Heron replaced by ours, but all three possibilities have factors in their favor."

Tesla stroked his moustache.   "Tell me, do you think it is possible for a man – such as I, or Jack, or Max – to travel to the future, and take on Heron's appearance?   What impact do you think that might have on your attempts to stop him?"

Sierra sipped her brandy. "I never thought of that."

***

"Why do you trust them?" Max asked Sierra about Astor and Tesla, as she lay in his arms in their bed at their hotel, after the two had made love, and then again.

"I don't know," Sierra said. "I don't – not completely. But something about the music tonight, and the brandy, made me feel, I don't know, better about them.   I guess I drank too much."

"I'm not complaining about the music or the brandy," Max said, and kissed her softly on the forehead. "They made it easier for me to take advantage of you."

"Like you have to work so hard when there's no music and I haven't had a drop to drink," Sierra said, and kissed him on the side of his neck.

Max chuckled and closed his eyes. "You and I are changing roles now, aren't we," he said, eventually. "I'm the suspicious one, seeing the glass half empty, and you're seeing it half full or more." He became aware that Sierra was softly snoring, and kissed her even more gently on her head.

One thing that did appeal to Max about the conversation with Astor and Tesla, however, was the idea that he could travel into the future and put on Heron's face. Well, it wasn't a full-fledged idea, it was just a toss-away thought, but still. He as Heron would certainly put a crimp into whatever Heron was doing, and maybe permanently derail his plans. But . . . what did Heron look like now? Sierra was sure he changed faces whenever needed, and Max had a vague recollection of Synesius or Jonah or someone telling him at some point that Heron was looking like Augustine – was Tesla aware of that, aware that there was no specific Heron face that Tesla or Astor or Max could make themselves look like? Max sighed. This was the nub of the problem. For all he and Sierra knew, Tesla or Astor was Heron, and they had been talking to Heron right across that table, as Sierra sipped her brandy and Max his rum.

Could the DNA facial reconstruction make the recipient look much younger? Of course it could, that's how this surgery had started in the first place, and was still by far its most frequent usage in the 21st century. Could it change the face of the recipient enough to make him or her look like a different gender? This was no doubt done for some number of people, too. But following through on what your new gender could do obviously would require a different kind of surgery.

Sierra had turned over in her sleep, and her hand was now resting right below his abdomen. He thought about waking her up, for a third go. But she needed her rest, and she was sleeping so peacefully. No, not tonight.

Maybe he wasn't as young as he used to be.

But her hand felt so good where it was. He carefully swiveled around, and glancingly kissed her sleeping lips. Hell, he still felt younger than most of the people in the world, in this or any time.

***

Sierra found a note under the door the next morning. She woke Max.

"He wants to meet us for breakfast in an hour," she said.

"Who?" Max rubbed his eyes and sat up. "Astor?"

"Yep."

Max got out of bed. "You showered yet?"

Sierra nodded.

Max walked into the bathroom, left the door open, and started to shower. "One thing I don't like about this guy is he yanks us around like puppets on his string," he said loudly.

"If we believe he's on our side, his wanting to see us so often could be a good thing," Sierra said, right outside of the bathroom door.

"You've softened your attitude about Astor," Max said. "Surely the symphony wasn't that persuasive."

***

The two joined Astor for breakfast. He was already seated at the table, and rose to greet them.

"I have news that might interest you," he said, after the waiter took their orders.

'Tell us," Sierra said.

"I have a report from one of my contacts that Heron may now be in 1899," Astor said. He lowered his voice. "Whatever 'now' may mean in this context." He laughed loudly.

"How did your contact come to tell you this?" Sierra asked.

"Traveled from there – 1899 – to where, or when, we are now," Astor replied. "All of this is happening in New York."

"And you're not going to tell us who your contact is, right?" Max noted with a frown.

"Not until I know the two of you a little better," Astor replied. "Let me be honest with you." He put out his hands, open palms, on the table. "I told you that Thomas O'Leary and I spoke. He was very thorough. He explained to me that the face he had when we were speaking was not his original face. He told me automata in the future can be fashioned with faces that look like specific humans. I won't pretend to you that I understood it all. But I comprehended enough to understand that the two of you may not be who you seem to be. Don't get me wrong – I believe that you are Sierra Waters and you are Maxwell Marcus. Certainly William Henry Appleton believes that, and he's in a much better position than I to know. But I just can't yet be 100% sure, and the stakes, as you know, are awfully high."

"I guess we should be grateful that we've found a champion like you," Sierra said, "especially with William declining. And I don't mean that the least bit sarcastically."

Astor bowed his head slightly. "Thank you. But I wasn't fishing for compliments."

"What do you think Heron is doing in 1899," she asked Astor, though she knew the answer.

"To wring what he can out of William," Astor replied, sadly, "including the *Chronica*, if it's not already under translation in other hands. Heron must know that William does not have many days left in 1899."

Sierra nodded, and thought again, does Astor know he himself will die on the Titanic in 1912? She controlled an urge to blurt this out. Unless Astor already knew about his death, telling him about this now would only pitch this whole conversation and whatever help Astor was trying give into wild disarray. But she didn't know how much longer she could keep this out of her mind and her speech.

"You're suggesting we travel to 1899, to protect Appleton?" Max asked.

"Yes," Astor said, "all three of us. He's certainly no match for Heron on his own, especially in his deteriorating health. By the way, William has been thoroughly briefed since 1896 about my knowledge and use of the Chairs, so you need not be concerned on that account."

***

"One good thing about short leaps into the future or past is that you needn't worry about time-appropriate apparel," Astor said to Max and Sierra as the two met him in front of the Millennium Club a few hours later, to take their trip to 1899. It was his way of saying he approved of what Max and Sierra were wearing.

"How far into the future or past have you traveled?" Max asked

Astor.

Sierra shot Max a look which she hoped Astor didn't catch. She fervently hoped Astor hadn't traveled anywhere past April 15, 1912, the date of the Titanic's sinking.

"Not very far," Astor said, cheerily. "I'm trying to first develop my time-travel legs."

Sierra smiled. "You've confirmed that the room at the top of the spiral stairs has three Chairs?" She knew that he had, but wanted confirmation anyway.

"Oh yes," Astor replied. "Cyril Charles told me in fact that there were four Chairs up there, not more than an hour ago."

Max and Sierra both started to speak—

"Yes, I know," Astor interrupted. "This raises the question of who arrived here and when in that surplus of Chairs. But if we decide to wait here, until we find out who arrived, well . . . if the people who arrived mean us harm, then waiting is the strategy of sitting ducks, which surely we do not want to be."

"I agree," Sierra said. "Let's proceed with our plan."

Max looked a little less positive about this, but did not raise any objections.

The three entered the Millennium Club. "Good afternoon, Mr. Astor," the man inside said, and smiled courteously at Sierra and Max.

"These are my guests, James," Astor said.

James nodded. "Of course."

Sierra and Max returned his smile and proceeded with Astor.

"I've never seen him before," Sierra said to Astor.

"He's new here," Astor said, "a lot younger than the usual, as you can see."

The three walked up the first, second, and third flights of stairs to the second floor of the library, then up the winding set of stairs to the room with the Chairs.

Astor put a key to the door and it opened.

Sierra looked at Max. Astor apparently had an authorized key, she thought. More evidence that he was truly on their side? No – because Heron's people apparently had such keys as well.

There were indeed four Chairs in the room.

"What specific date in 1899 are we headed to?" Max asked Astor.

"My contact says Heron was spotted in March 1899," Astor said. "We probably should aim for the end of February, to be safe."

"Are we dressed warmly enough?" Max asked.

"Probably not," Astor replied. "But we can see to proper overcoats after we arrive. I know some very nice shops."

The three sat in the Chairs. "I'll do the honors," Sierra said. "I'm setting our arrival for February 25, 1899, at 10 o'clock in the morning."

"Sounds good," Max said, and Astor nodded.

Sierra lowered the go lever. Transparent bubbles arose around each head. The cosmos kissed them and the bubbles receded.

[New York City, February, 1899 AD]

"One thing I need to be especially careful about is not running into myself here in 1899," Astor said. "You two are no doubt aware of the problem. I could be having a drink right now at the bar downstairs."

"We won't stop at the bar," Sierra said, "and the likelihood of encountering yourself as you walk down the stairs is slim."

"Of course," Astor said, and the three left the room.

They encountered no one of note as they proceeded downstairs to the Millennium Club's entrance, at which Mr. Bertram was standing.

"I have seen him at the Club," Sierra told Astor. "Max knows him, too."

Astor nodded.

"Hello," Bertram said to Max and Sierra. "Mr. Astor, I do not believe we have met. My name is Reginald Bertram."

"The pleasure is all mine," Astor said with a bright smile, and shook Bertram's hand.

"You're not going out there like that?" Bertram said, a little appalled. "We had a blizzard here 11 days ago – 'The Snow King,' it's being called – 16 inches in Central Park, and one of the coldest days on record."

Max had already opened the front door. A frigid face-numbing blast confirmed what Bertram was saying.

"Where can we get some warm clothing?" Sierra asked and shivered.

"The Club has a nice selection of overcoats," Bertram replied. "I don't know if they'll suit your style, but they're well packed wool, and you can borrow them for as long as you like."

"That would be wonderful, thank you," Sierra said.

"Would you like to come with me?" Bertram asked. "Or, it might be faster if I just pick three coats out for you." He eyed

Sierra, Max, and Astor. "I have a good eye for size and fit – I was a haberdasher in London, before the Parthenon Club hired me away!"

"You choose, by all means," Sierra said. Max and Astor nodded agreement, and Bertram left to get the overcoats.

"One of the hazards of temporal travel in intemperate climates," Sierra said. "We never had such problems in Athens or Alexandria."

A group of men entered. One, with a moustache, thick head of hair, and a pair of spectacles attached to his vest with a silver chain, instructed a younger man who was holding the door open while he scraped the snow off of his boots. "Shut that door, man – you'll make it feel like Siberia inside the Club!"

The man apologized and complied.

"J. P.!" Astor said with delight and pumped the extended hand.

"Jack," J. P. said more sedately. "You look younger every time I see you."

Astor laughed. "These are my friends, Sierra Waters and Maxwell Marcus, just returned from Egypt."

"I ought to go there one of these days," J. P. said, shaking hands with Max and gently squeezing Sierra's. "I have business upstairs, even though no business is allowed in the Club," he said and he took his leave.

"J. P. Morgan," Astor whispered to Sierra and Max. "He financed Thomas Edison a few years ago – actually, more than a few years ago, now. Tesla was *furious*."

Bertram appeared with the overcoats. "I think this greatcoat should suit you," he said to Sierra, and graciously dressed her in a deep beige coat with a cloak. "This should keep you warm as toast."

"Thank you," Sierra said.

Bertram did the same to Max, who received a stylish dark grey greatcoat.

Astor looked on approvingly, beaming at Sierra and Max. He put his arms through the black greatcoat Bertram extended to him.

A man appeared with three hats. "Thank you," Bertram said to the man, then to Sierra, Max, and Astor, "I can't let you go out into this cold with bare heads."

"Thank you," Astor said again, and took the black hat, with wide brim and flat crown, offered to him. Max did the same.

Sierra's was even more stylish, and mauve.

"Return all of this whenever convenient," Bertram said, and left with the hat bearer.

Sierra, Max, and Astor said thanks again, and walked out into the street. The cold hit their noses, unprotected by the greatcoats and hats.

"Let's proceed up to Wave Hill," Astor said, his breaths forming visible puffs in the icy air. "The trains from Grand Central run frequently."

"Should we call first?" Max asked.

"Not necessary," Astor replied. "I'm sure William will be happy to see us."

***

Astor professed to find the seven-block walk south to Grand Central Terminal invigorating. Sierra was happy that most of the snow had been cleared. But all three had to walk as close to the buildings and as far away from the street as possible, "lest we be splashed in the face by one of those horses or horseless carriages," Astor advised, grumpily.

They checked the schedule inside the Terminal. "Good timing," Astor observed. "There is a train to Riverdale in 20 minutes."

"Do you think we'll be able to make the climb up to William's house with all of the snow?" Max asked. "There's likely to be more of it in the Bronx, right?"

"Yes," Astor replied. "But we won't need to hike it. Did you notice the electrical hansom cabs in front of the Terminal? If they haven't made it as far as the Bronx as yet, there should be a few old-fashioned horse-drawn carriages readily available."

The train left at its posted time. The ride was smooth. There indeed were no electrical vehicles at the Riverdale station. Astor summoned a horse-drawn hansom cab, as promised. "Wave Hill," he instructed the driver, after helping Sierra and Max up into the cab.

"Very good, Guvnor!" the cabbie replied.

"Are you from the other side of the pond, England?" Sierra asked.

"Yes, I am indeed, Miss," the cabbie replied, and coaxed the horse to start its journey.

"Commerce has increased between New York and London in our decade," Astor said to Sierra, "not only economic, but intellectual. Transatlantic cable has been commonplace for a while, and the ocean liners are faster and more reliable than ever."

Sierra nodded, and again put the Titanic out of her mind.

"Visiting Mr. Appleton?" the cabbie inquired of his passengers. "He hasn't been in the best of health of late – I brought a doctor up to see him, just last week, if I'm not speaking out of turn."

Sierra thought that he was, but didn't object, because she valued the information this cabbie might convey more than chiding him for the impropriety of talking about Appleton's health. "What was the purpose of the doctor's visit?" she asked the cabbie.

"Can't rightly say that I know," the cabbie replied. "But a visit from a doctor when the moon is out can never be good."

"Well, it could be," Astor said, "if the purpose of the visit, for example, was to see to a woman with child. Fewer things in this world than we suppose are one-hundred-percent bad or good."

The cabbie grunted his presumed agreement and was silent for the rest of the ride.

The cab soon arrived at Wave Hill. "Will you be long?" the cabbie inquired. "Shall I wait to provide a return ride to the train?"

"Not necessary," Astor said, and paid the cabbie generously in coin.

The three approached the door of Appleton's residence. Astor applied the knocker.

Geoffreys opened the door. He knew all three callers. "Here to see Mr. Appleton?" he inquired.

"Yes," Astor replied. "Is he fit to see us?"

"He was indisposed a little while ago—"

"But I'm quite fine now," Appleton appeared, with a big smile and a slow, labored walk.

Sierra rushed up to him and hugged him. "How are you, old

friend?" She kissed him on the top of his head, which was now even balder than the last time she had seen him in 1896 – just a few days ago for her, three years ago for Appleton. His moustache was also whiter, and although he was still a little portly, he was less so than the last time the two had been together at the Millennium Club.

"I'm 86 years old – I'm feeling as well as I can for anyone that age." He winked at Sierra and whispered, "actually, I may even be a little older, considering all the time I spent out of time with you. But do not be concerned. I'm happy. I'll be back with my dear bride before too long."

Sierra blinked back tears.

Appleton, still hugging her, turned to Max and Astor. "I assume you're here because there is some kind of important business afoot that requires my attention, wavering as it may be?"

"We believe Heron is in this year," Astor said.

"And if he hasn't already, he may come to see you," Max added.

Appleton let go of Sierra. "Come," he said to all three. "Let us sit by the fire."

They walked into an adjoining room. "Can Geoffreys get you something?" Appleton inquired.

"Tea," Sierra said. "Thank you."

"Tea for me, too," Max said.

"Well, then, let's make it tea for all three!" Astor said.

Geoffreys, who had been standing close by, nodded.

"And I'll have a cognac," Appleton said.

Geoffreys nodded and went to get the beverages.

"I had at least one unpleasant conversation with Heron, in Alexandria while you were away, if memory serves," Appleton said to Sierra. When it came to this business, Appleton had learned that memory was decidedly not a reliable servant – and, alas, it was not the kind of servant one could educate for improvement.

"He may not look like that anymore," Max said.

"Back to that again," Appleton said and coughed. "This face changing is almost as disconcerting as the time travel." He looked again at Sierra. "You fooled a lot of people, looking like Hypatia in Alexandria!"

"Yes, not quite my finest hour – too many good people died," Sierra said.

"Too many good people always die," Astor observed.

"Indeed," Appleton said. "By the way, I'm gratified that the three of you have apparently taken each other into your confidences. We need all the help we can get."

Astor nodded vigorously, Sierra nodded slightly, and Max not at all.

"What do you suppose Heron wants from me?" Appleton asked.

"To intercept the *Chronica*, would be my best guess," Astor replied.

Appleton laughed, coughed, and waved away help from Geoffreys, who had arrived with the tea and brandy and placed the tray on the table. "It's too late," Appleton said, when he recovered his voice. "But I guess you wouldn't know that, because you came from?"

"1896," Sierra replied.

"Ah, yes, then," Appleton started coughing again.

"Perhaps Mr. Appleton would like to rest a little," Geoffreys offered in quiet but firm voice.

Appleton glared at him.

"Of course," Astor said. "But just one question, then – what did you mean that it's 'too late' for Heron to obtain your copy of the *Chronica*?"

"It is already out of my hands," Appleton replied, serenely, "and under translation, as far as I know."

"May I ask by whom?" Astor asked.

"It's safer for none of you to know, wouldn't you agree?" Appleton responded. "Safer to let that knowledge die with me – knowledge of the translation of the *Chronica* – until the book takes its proper place in the world. Neither should be too long now."

"You still have some time," Sierra said, voice rough with emotion. She stood and put her hand on Appleton's shoulder.

He put his wrinkled hand over hers. "No point in pretending, my dear. We both know I haven't much time left in this Earthly realm. I only hope I've done well enough to merit a better place, though it would be difficult to find a place better than this, in your company, and the honor and joy it has brought me to know you. In many ways, you have made my life."

Now Sierra couldn't hold back the tears. Max's eyes were moist, too.

Appleton squeezed Sierra's hand with surprising strength. "The translation is assured," he said. "These kinds of things cannot be rushed. But I am confident that Heron will no longer maintain a monopoly on his time traveling."

***

Geoffreys called for another cab, which arrived in ten minutes.

This cabbie had a thick Irish brogue. "Down to the train station by the river, is that right?"

"Yes, please," Astor said, as he, Sierra, and Max settled into the cab.

"Do you share William's confidence about the translation?" Astor asked Max and Sierra.

"Not with Heron out and about in these parts, not with him time traveling. No, I don't," Max said.

"What should we do about it?" Astor asked.

"Do you feel comfortable enough with us now to reveal the name of your spy?" Sierra asked. "William revealed a great deal of our work to you in that conversation we all just had."

"I have an appointment with my source at Grand Central in two hours," Astor replied. "Would you care to join me?"

"Yes, we would," Max replied.

CHAPTER 7

[New York City, March, 1899 AD]

Heron decided as soon as he left Porter's company that he needed someone more high-powered to get the *Chronica* from Appleton. Even if Porter's failure to see Appleton was not his fault this time, the point still held. Heron should have realized this all along.

He walked as quickly as could up to the Millennium, gambled that the real J. P. Morgan was not standing in the vestibule, and almost lost.

"Mr. Morgan," a man who looked and sounded like a British butler from the early 20th century greeted Heron with a smile. "You're back again! Welcome!"

Heron nodded, grunted, and hustled up all of the stairs to the room with the Chairs. He needed to clear the air, clear his head – see a little more clearly, perhaps, how his present predicament had come to be, and maybe set something in motion to change it – and nothing provided as good an opportunity for that as a little trip to the past. He timed this one to be about two months before he was now.

[New York City, January, 1899 AD]

He found a public phone at Grand Central, away from the seafood restaurant and any possibly prying eyes. Yes, it was time to bring in reinforcements, with someone whom he trusted about as much as Porter, which was to say not that much at all, but who had had much greater impact on the world, in large part due to information supplied by Heron. That would be Porter's boss.

Heron had his phone number committed to memory.

A groggy, gruff voice answered the phone. "Hello?"

"Mr. Edison?" Heron looked at the clock on the far wall. It was 2:45 in the afternoon. This lunatic was likely taking his famed afternoon nap. "Did I wake you?"

"Yes, you did," Edison replied. "Do I know you?"

"Your phone number is not widely available, so likely you do," Heron replied.

"Your voice does sound familiar," Edison said.

"I need to see you," Heron said. "This afternoon."

"That sounds more like an order than a request," Edison said.

"When you realize who I am, you'll understand," Heron said.

"I'm in West Orange, New Jersey," Edison said.

"I'd prefer we meet in Grand Central Terminal in New York, in about two hours. Is that satisfactory?" Heron asked.

Silence. Then, "I know who you are – yes, I'll meet you at Grand Central in two hours – the train and ferry service is frequent at this time of day, but still not as efficient as it could be," Edison said.

"Good," Heron said, and told Edison to meet him at the seafood restaurant. "One other thing – I'll be looking like J. P. Morgan."

***

Edison sat down at Heron's table in the restaurant. "You

look like J. P., but you certainly didn't sound like him on the telephone. That was apparent to me even with my partial deafness."

"I could have undertaken a vocal chord reconstruction, but I won't be staying here as J. P. Morgan very long," Heron replied, "and you likely would have thought I was J. P. Morgan not me on the telephone, whatever I said to the contrary, if I had J. P. Morgan's voice." Heron knew about Edison's hearing impairment, but, like the rest of the world, was unclear about its extent. Heron did know that Edison told at least half a dozen stories about what had caused his hearing loss, ranging from ear infections to being smacked on the side of his head by a train conductor.

"J. P. Morgan has been one of my financers," Edison said. "I know him well. I'm not very comfortable with you having taken his face." Edison rubbed the stubble on his own unshaven face.

Heron was always slightly surprised by Edison's unkempt hair and appearance, and that he smelled like someone from the mostly unwashed Middle Ages. "Are you comfortable with the many designs for inventions I have given you?" Heron asked.

The waiter appeared.

"I'll have a plate of shrimp," Edison told the waiter.

"I'm fine," Heron said.

"Your designs have served me well," Edison said to Heron, as the waiter departed. "That is why I am here. Do you have something new for me?"

"As a matter of fact, I do," Heron said, and favored Edison with one of his rare smiles. "It concerns time travel."

"Time travel?" Edison repeated, with a touch of ridicule. "Isn't that the stuff of scientific romance?"

"So was the use of electricity to illuminate cities, until I gave you a copy of *Babylon Electrified*, brought back through time from 1889, to where you were in 1879, still perfecting your carbon filament light bulb, which I grant you was your invention entirely."

Edison nodded. Acknowledgement of his genius independent of Heron placated him, as Heron hoped it would. "That's certainly true," Edison said. "And I'll freely admit – to you – that your advice about the recording of moving images enabled me to get the jump on the Lumière Brothers in France and Friese-Greene in England both."

Heron smiled through J. P. Morgan's moustache again. "I have been working towards such wheel-of-life inventions for a very long time." He thought it best not to tell Edison that he had given similar advice to the Lumières and William Friese-Greene, whom he had found much more convivial than Edison.

"I'm still not convinced, however, that time travel is possible," Edison said. "You may have received the information you gave to me about new inventions not from the future but from other sources alive in the world today, who are known to you but not to me."

Heron considered and reached another decision. "I shall prove it to you. I'm going to leave right now. I'll be back in a moment and certainly before your plate of shrimp arrives – back with information obtained from your future self, which I could obtain only through time travel, and not from someone unknown to you now."

Edison shrugged and nodded. "I'm always in the market for a palpable demonstration."

Heron rose and walked to the door of the restaurant. Their waiter was standing there, talking to the maître d'hôtel. "I'll be back in just a minute," Heron said to them.

He hustled again up to the Millennium. Mr. Bertram, another Brit in service to the Clubs with too much time on his hands, was now at the door. He merely nodded at Heron, looking like J. P. Morgan, and said nothing about Morgan's being or having recently been in the club. Good.

Heron set the Chair to March, 1899, for a few days after his meeting with Porter, whom he did not want to cross paths with in this trip to demonstrate time travel to Edison. There were three other Chairs in the room, but he didn't have the time to figure out who had brought them there.

[New York City, March, 1899 AD]

The weather was warmer. Heron walked to Grand Central, and again called Edison in New Jersey, from a public telephone. He insisted as before on Edison coming into the city and meeting him at the seafood restaurant. Edison grumbled, cursed, and agreed.

Edison arrived two hours later, still annoyed.

Heron bid him to sit, which Edison did, still muttering.

"I apologize for this inconvenience," Heron said, honestly. "It is on behalf of an important cause, which you will understand when this pair of meetings – this is just one of two meetings we are having – is concluded.

Edison rolled and closed his eyes, then opened them. "I'm listening."

"I need you to tell me something you experienced in the past two months – something no one other than you would know about," Heron said.

"I rescued a dog in the blizzard we had last month," Edison immediately responded, "at the beginning of the big storm. But I didn't bring it home.   It jumped out of my arms before I could bring it to a shelter. I haven't told anybody about that – I have a reputation as a dog-hater, because I electrocuted Dash and a few other mutts to demonstrate the dangers of AC electricity.   But I have nothing against dogs, and I didn't want to tell anyone about the dog I rescued which got away because I didn't want anyone to think I had harmed the animal."

Heron took it all in.   "Thank you – that is perfect for my purposes." He stayed with Edison over cups of soup, which both professed to enjoy, only Edison truthfully, and the two then walked out onto 42nd Street.

"Thank you, again," Heron said, and walked north, once again, to the Millennium. His luck was apparently getting better and better. No one was at the door at all, this time.

But as Heron proceeded up to the room with the Chairs, he thought he caught sight of that fool Cyril Charles, on the second library floor, in the periphery of his vision.   Charles might have noticed Heron, but Heron couldn't be sure, and he didn't have the wherewithal to deal with this now.

[New York City, January, 1899 AD]

The British butler was of course at the door, as he had been when Heron had arrived in January. "Important business bids me to leave," Heron said to the Millennium doorman.

"Have a good day, Mr. Morgan," the doorman replied.

Heron walked down Fifth Avenue to the seafood restaurant, where Edison was still seated.

"You beat the plate of shrimp," Edison said to Heron with a harsh laugh.

"As I said I would," Heron said.

"What have you to tell me?" Edison asked. "What can you tell me that I won't know until sometime in the future?"

"You will rescue a dog in a big snowstorm in New Jersey in February," Heron replied.

"That is very specific," Edison replied.

Heron nodded. "That should make this proof more convincing."

"But how do I know you are not now just giving me the idea of rescuing a dog in the snow, which I will do next month only because we are having this conversation?" Edison asked.

"Because if were that so – that I don't know the future and I am just introducing this idea to you now – there is surely no way that I could make a dog materialize for you in a blizzard," Heron replied. "Further, the information your future self just gave me is that the dog escaped from you before you had a chance to bring it to a shelter. When the storm comes and you have the dog in your arms, try to hold on to it, and see what happens. It will no doubt escape, however hard you try to not let that happen." Heron also knew he was changing history with this conversation, and the Edison he had talked to the month after next had had no recollection of this conversation, which had not yet happened in his reality.

"Tell me more about the time travel," Edison quietly said, very seriously, "and what you want me to do. I am inclined to give you the presumption, for now, that you have indeed just time traveled – it certainly tickles my fancy, as they say. Tell me what you want me to do. And if your prediction about the dog in the snowstorm comes true in February, I may endeavor to help you."

Heron now had to be exceedingly careful. He did not want Edison to attempt to create a time traveling Chair. There was insufficient collateral technology in this age for Edison or anyone to do that now, in 1899 or even 1999, anyway. But if Edison made the attempt, and received publicity about that – which he would, given his stature, and lots of it – that could get other inventors interested. Who wouldn't want to invent a time machine? And that could result in a discovery of the Chairs. "There is a book I wrote," Heron said.

"Yes?"

"It was stolen from me," Heron said. "I need your help in reacquiring it." The *Chronica*, Heron hoped, was still in the ancient Greek in which Heron had written it as a vain young man, nearly two millennia ago. Edison was an autodidact – famously self-educated, with some courses at Cooper Union, and Heron was all but certain none of them included reading of ancient Greek. So if Edison could get the *Chronica*, and Heron could take it from Edison before the boorish genius could bring it to a translator, Heron would get what he needed.

"Who stole it from you?" Edison asked.

"That is not relevant," Heron replied. "What matters now is who has it."

The waiter appeared with Edison's plate of shrimp.

"Anything else?" the waiter inquired.

Edison brushed him away, dug into the shrimp, and belched his appreciation. "And who would that be?"

"William Henry Appleton," Heron replied.

"The publisher?" Edison asked.

"Yes."

"I don't know him," Edison said. "I did build the first hydroelectric plant in Appleton, Wisconsin – named, I believe, after a Samuel Appleton. Any relation?"

"I don't know," Heron replied. "Samuel's family came from New Hampshire, as did William's. They could be distant cousins – I haven't investigated it further."

"Curiouser and curiouser," Edison grunted and laughed through a mouth of shrimp.

"There was a house built in Appleton, Wisconsin called the White Heron," Heron said. "I'm sure that is total coincidence." Heron didn't believe in coincidence, but he didn't want to make this too convoluted for Edison.

"I'm sure it is," Edison said, and laughed again. "How do you suggest I approach William Appleton? I'm not exactly known as a man of letters."

"Tell him you're thinking of writing an autobiography," Heron said. "And you can also mention your work in Appleton, Wisconsin – that could attract William's interest as well." Heron again expected it could be helpful to stroke Edison's ego, as the quickly emerging psychologist, Sigmund Freud, might say. In fact, one of the reasons Heron had thought to contact Edison for this task was the inventor's Appleton, Wisconsin connection.

**

The two passed by another pair of men standing about half a block from the restaurant, dressed in black, with full facial hair, conversing in a language Heron did not recognize.

"That's Yiddish," Edison said, "a mongrel tongue of a mongrel people, Jews. You know of them?"

"One of my best students was a Jew," Heron said, thinking of

Jonah. "He was highly intelligent, and he was very loyal, until —"

"He knifed you in the back?" Edison broke in. "That's the way it is with those people, loyal only to themselves and their money."

Heron chose not to contest the point, but noted that this celebrated inventor was not only a boor but a bigot. "Please attend to the Appleton matter as soon as you can, timing is everything in this business we are in."

Edison bristled at being directed so explicitly what to do, and about being in any kind of business with a man as bizarre as Heron. "And if I'm too late with Appleton? If he no longer has your book?"

"Then I might have to go further back in time and have this same conversation with you, all over again for me, first time for you," Heron said.

"And I wouldn't be remembering it now, because?" Edison asked.

"Because even though it would be happening to you earlier than now, it would not have happened to you yet, if that makes any sense," Heron replied.

"It gives me more of a headache than anything else," Edison said.

***

The two parted company on Fifth Avenue. "I'm taking the ferry to New Jersey -- I have work to do in Menlo Park. I'll see to your Appleton assignment first thing tomorrow, if that's ok with you," Edison said and headed west on 42nd Street, without waiting for Heron's answer.

Heron walked north on Fifth Avenue. He thought again about

Porter's failure with Appleton. Enlisting Edison's help was only a part of what Heron intended to do about this.

Heron didn't believe in bad luck – or, if it happened, he believed its occurrence was far less frequent than most people thought. When plans did not proceed as intended, it was usually not because of bad luck but bad planning, which hadn't foreseen that someone might interfere.

Appleton was already ill, Heron was willing to concede, on his way to dying in October. But already too ill to see someone who wanted to make a movie – or whatever it was called in this time and place – about Hypatia, whom Appleton had struggled so hard to protect when she was Sierra Waters? This Don Quixote Victorian tilting so nobly at time was still the better part of a year away from his deathbed. The more Heron thought about it, the more he doubted that Appleton had refused to see Porter because Appleton was too ill.

But if not ill, then why? Had Appleton been warned by someone about what Porter was really after? If that was the case, who had warned Appleton?

Heron had an idea, but he was not completely sure. In any event, this was not something he could do on his own. He had legionaries or their future equivalents in most of the eras he frequented. In 1899 New York City, they would be in the building on Mulberry Street, putting in its final decade as Police Headquarters –before the New York City Police Headquarters, serving the newly unified multi-borough city, opened at 240 Centre Street in 1909.

Heron had walked enough to reach a decision. The Millennium Club was across the street. He walked in. No one was at the door. He walked quickly up the flights of stairs to the Chairs, took one to March 1899, then walked out again onto the street where he boarded a noisy motorized public transport vehicle south. He was tired of the freezing weather, anyway.

[New York City, March, 1899 AD]

Heron's original legionaries were utterly reliable. They had started as literally Roman legionaries, whom Heron had hired away from Rome's employ with the promise of adventure, money, and the chance to really influence history. And there was nothing inflated in those goals -- all were attainable.

Once recruited, the former Roman legionaries were taken to one of Heron's camps, in the late 21st century, where they were trained in the arts of combat with weapons that did not exist in Roman times, as well as given intense practice with knives and swords and weapons they already knew.

These legionaries were eventually situated in many times and places. They had served Heron well in Athens in the time of Socrates and in Alexandria in the time of Hypatia. But these men were not invincible, and, sooner or later, most of them perished in battle. Since there was not an inexhaustible supply of true Roman legionaries, Heron had been obliged to look elsewhere for replacements, and for trustworthy people to post in new positions. With the human population constantly increasing, there naturally were more candidates in the future than the past.

The disadvantage was that they could not be easily deployed in the ancient world or the Middle Ages – not without lengthy training in the relevant culture. And they were not as blindly loyal as the original legionaries, whose punishment for disobeying orders in ancient Rome was usually far more severe than in the military or the police of the United States of America, for example.

But the advantage of recruiting a legionary from the 20th or 21st century is that he or she – there were some women in Heron's employ, though not as many as men – would already be well versed in guns, explosives, and, in the case of the 21st century, laser weaponry. Often they came from law enforcement, but sometimes not. In the United States of America, guns were in abundant supply throughout the populace until the middle of the 21st century.

James Flannery had been with the New York Police Department in the 1990s – still was, in fact, a Lieutenant with "Giuliani's finest," as Flannery put it, when he wasn't working for Heron a century earlier, under cover of working for the 1890s New York police. He was well versed in the firearms of this era, and had no problem fitting in with his Irish ancestors, who were just a few generations closer to the Emerald Isle than was Flannery. Heron had provided him with extensive, forged documentation of a career with the Boston police that Flannery never had, which made it easy to get hired as a Lieutenant in the 1890s New York City police.

Now Flannery waited to meet Heron in front of the police headquarters on Mulberry Street, ruddy cheeks and Phillip Morris cigarettes imported from London in hand and mouth.

Heron was punctual to a fault. Flannery didn't have to wait long.

"Let us walk," Heron said to Flannery, as to the two exchanged nods of greeting.

"Lieutenant," several rookie cops paid their respects as Flannery and Heron walked down the street. He gave a curt smile in response.

"I have a task for you," Heron told Flannery, when they were clear of the police headquarters and any cops who might overhear.

Flannery nodded. "Something I can do myself, or should I

assemble a team?"

"You should be able to do this yourself," Heron replied. "It is a simple apprehension, questioning, and, if necessary—"

"I understand," Flannery replied. "Do you have a name?"

"Mary Anderson," Heron replied.

"That's a very common name," Flannery said.

"She's an actress," Heron said.

"*That* Mary Anderson? I've seen her picture in the paper – she is one fine looking woman."

"Will that be a problem?" Heron asked. "Do you have qualms about doing your job when beautiful women are involved?"

Flannery laughed. "Of course not. I assume you want to me to question her as soon as possible."

"Always," Heron replied. "She and Edwin Porter attempted to see William Henry Appleton last week – that might be a good place to start."

"Porter the film pioneer?" Flannery had flirted with being a film major when he'd been a student at New York University in the late 1970s.

"Yes," Heron replied, "though they're still referring to it as 'photo-play' back here."

Flannery nodded. "I gather Porter and Anderson were unsuccessful in their attempt to see Appleton? Why was that?"

"Illness," Heron replied, "or so Appleton's man said."

"You think he was lying?" Flannery asked.

Heron made an I-don't-know gesture with his hands. "That's

why I'm bringing you into this."

"Ok – you'll hear from me soon," Flannery said. "Anything else I should know?"

"No," Heron replied.

"Good," Flannery stopped, turned, and walked away from Heron, back in the direction of police headquarters.

Heron watched Flannery walk away, and thought about the fact that, having hunted someone who was acting as Hypatia in ancient Alexandria, he now was doing the same for an actress who would soon be playing Hypatia in a turn-of-the-century theatrical production in New York City. This seemed strange, even to Heron.

***

Flannery had no love for this Heron, or whoever the hell he was. But he liked Heron's money – with his wife's father in and out of the hospital needing heart-bypass surgery not covered by Flannery's insurance at the end of 20th-century America, a lame-brained son who couldn't hold down a job, and a daughter knocked up when she was 19 and who knew who the father was, Flannery had need of money. And Heron had this time travel timed just right. Flannery could spend as long as he liked or was needed back here in the 1890s, and when he went back to the 1990s, he'd have been missing just the hour or so it took him to get back and forth between One Police Plaza on Park Row and the Millennium Club uptown. He could even snip that hour if it mattered, by setting his return for an hour earlier. Sweet deal.

And from what he understood of Heron's motives, Flannery agreed with them. Heron wanted to keep the world as it was. That made sense. Because even if someone stopped a terrible thing from happening, like the assassination of John F.

Kennedy, who knows what unexpected bad things Kennedy's survival might bring into play. Like that Ray Bradbury story he'd read as a kid in high school.

Flannery stopped at his secretary's desk when he reached his office. "Juliet, please have Detective Woodruff come in to see me." She was an attractive woman, but her long skirts drove him crazy. To her, they were provocative, because they showed some ankle. To him – well, Juliet reminded him of an Amish woman in that Weird Al Yankovic send-up of "Gangsta Paradise," flirting and sexually suggestive in a dress that went down to her mid-legs. These women in the 1890s had a lot to learn.

"Of course," Juliet said and smiled at him.

There was a knock on his door a few minutes later. "Come in," Flannery said.

Oliver Woodruff entered. He sported sideburns, a moustache, and a nice suit.

"I need you to find out what you can for me about Mary Anderson, an actress – her current whereabouts, home address, anything of interest," Flannery said.

"Very good," Woodruff nodded and left.

Flannery had made a decision by bringing Woodruff into this. Whatever Heron had meant by "if necessary," Flannery would not be making Mary Anderson disappear. He was a hired gun, yes, but he was no murderer.

***

Woodruff returned two hours later. "She wrote a book," Woodruff said. "I purchased this in Brentano's." He gave the book to Flannery.

Flannery looked at the cover and opened the book. "*A Few*

Memories," he read the title from the front pages, "by Mary Anderson. Published by Harper and Bros, 1896."

"She's staying at this hotel, on 65th Street, off Fifth Avenue," Woodruff said, and handed a piece of paper to Flannery with the address written upon it.

Flannery looked at it and nodded. "Very good. Anything else?"

"She fainted on stage in 1889," Woodruff replied. "The newspaper report said it was 'nervous exhaustion'. It was during a performance in Washington, DC. She announced her retirement with great fanfare shortly after. But my friend in the theater thinks she's due to come back soon, possibly in a play about Hypatia that's been in rehearsal on and off for years. She's an ancient Greek woman, right? – or maybe Egyptian, I'm not sure."

"That's very helpful," Flannery said. "Thank you, Detective."

Woodruff left, knowing better than to ask Flannery what all of this was about, if the Lieutenant had not volunteered the information.

***

Flannery called Mary the next morning. She was amenable to seeing him on short notice. "March is beginning to go out like a lamb," she said. "Does a walk in the park appeal to you as venue for our interview?"

Flannery told her that it did, and they met in the park, across the street from Mary's hotel, about an hour later.

He had been briefed by Heron about his goals, including retrieving the *Chronica*, when Heron had recruited him in 1990s New York City.

Mary took his arm as they walked in the park. At forty years old, she was ten years his junior, but to Flannery she looked much younger. He was glad there was no way his wife could see this stroll.

"We're investigating some threats that were made against William Henry Appleton, the publisher, based upon some long-standing grievances. I understand that you and Edwin Porter – the, photographer, I believe he is – tried to see Mr. Appleton earlier this month?"

"Yes," Mary replied.

"May I ask the reason for your visit?"

"Mr. Porter wanted to make a photo-play based on Charles Kingsley's *Hypatia*. Mr. Appleton apparently has a great interest in her – it is said he fell in love with her historical personage, and deeply regretted that his company, Appleton's, was not the publisher of the Kingsley novel. Mr. Porter thought Mr. Appleton might be ripe for an appeal to support the making of Porter's movie."

"I see," Flannery said. "And your role in this?"

"Why Lieutenant Flannery," Mary batted her eyelashes, "I was to be suggested as an actress who might portray Hypatia in the photo-play – I'm preparing right now for that part in a stage play of that story adapted from the novel by G. Stuart Ogilvie."

"I'll make sure I have a front seat for that," Flannery said.

"I shall look forward to it!" Mary replied.

Flannery smiled. "Has anything more come of Porter's idea for a photo-play?"

"Not that I know of," Mary replied. "We haven't spoken since last week. Perhaps he decided to pursue the idea with another actress." She pouted slightly, with a twinkle in her eye.

"I doubt that," Flannery said. "But to return to Mr. Appleton –

he was unable to receive you?"

"Yes, he was indisposed – actually, ill might be a more appropriate word," Mary said.

"Did you actually see him? Did you believe him – perhaps he was just making an excuse?"

"I think not," Mary said. "Indeed, a doctor came to the house."

"Did you catch his name?" Flannery asked.

Mary furrowed her brow. "Dr. Stanley, I believe it was. Not the explorer," she added. "I met him once at a dinner in London!"

Flannery chuckled. "Thank you – that's very helpful. One more question, if I may, for now?"

"Of course," Mary said.

"Do you know Sierra Waters?"

Mary furrowed her brow again. "I don't believe I do. Is she an actress?"

"I don't believe she is," Flannery replied.

The two walked back to Fifth Avenue. As they started to cross the street, a motor car came towards them. Mary, making a point to Flannery, didn't see it. Flannery did. He made a split-second decision. Heron might well have wanted him to not pull Mary out of the way. For all he knew, Heron might have hired the driver. But that wasn't Flannery's style. And, besides, he liked Mary, and the fantasies he had been having about her as they walked in the park. He yanked her back, out of the way of the car, at the very last minute.

"Slow down, you mo--," he screamed at the car, one of those Duryeas, if Flannery was right. It didn't slow down a bit. It was only going a little faster than 15 miles an hour, Flannery reckoned. The turning point for likely pedestrian death by automobile was 35 mph – 2 out of 10 dead at 30, 5 dead at 35, 9 out of 10 dead from being hit by a car moving at 40 mph, Flannery knew -- but even 15 miles per hour was fast enough to badly hurt and possibly kill someone on direct impact.

"Sorry about the language," he said to Mary. He turned back to the receding car, waving his hand and gesturing to the sidewalk. "Pull over," he shouted, then realized the driver was out of earshot. He touched his chest then reached into his pocket for his radio, to summon police help, and found nothing -- of course not, walkie-talkies were more than fifty years away from becoming standard issue! He had a whistle, but there was no way the driver could hear that now. He turned back to Mary.

"Don't be sorry," she said, and kissed his cheek. "You saved my life!"

He brought her back to her hotel, and asked if he could see her again if further questions arose about Appleton.

"Of course," she said, and thanked him again.

Flannery watched her walk into the hotel and thought, she's a good actress but I'm a better cop. He was sure she was lying when she said she didn't know Sierra Waters.

***

Flannery took a Fifth Avenue motorbus or whatever they called this contraption downtown. He enjoyed looking out of the window. There was an optimism in this 1899 which was lacking 100 years later. Maybe it was the two world wars, maybe it was the atom bomb, who could say? But people were more cynical in the time he came from, and more innocent now. Heron had told him things would get worse in a quick hurry in the 21st century. Flannery had asked him what he meant, and Heron had refused to answer. Maybe it was better that Flannery didn't know.

He also wondered if he really had saved Mary's life – if she would have died from the impact – and what that would have meant to history if he had let her die. Henry Bliss, as every traffic cop knew, was the first person to lose his life in New York City due to being struck by a motorized vehicle. That would happen in September of this very year, on the other side of the park, on West 74th Street. But if Mary Anderson had just been killed, what would that have done to the history books, to his memories – this time travel stuff was mind boggling beyond belief! For that matter, he could now make sure that he was standing on West 74th Street at the crucial moment when Bliss was hit – Bliss was exiting a trolley car on 8th Avenue in the evening – but saving Bliss could also up-end history. Heron had strictly warned him not to interfere with any historically recorded events.

Flannery's big decision now was how much to tell Heron about Mary Anderson. If he told Heron that he believed she was lying about not knowing or knowing about Sierra Waters, that could amount to a death sentence for Mary. Because if Heron believed that Mary was working with Sierra, and Flannery refused to kill the actress, then Heron could find another way. Heron was obsessed with Sierra Waters.

On the other hand, bald-facedly lying to Heron about this – which is what leaving out a crucial piece of information, probably the most crucial in the interview, would amount to – could result in Heron severing their relationship and his paycheck, which would leave his family at bay a century from now.

Flannery was not one to ponder things too long. When Heron called him, shortly after he returned to police headquarters, he told Heron what he suspected about Mary Anderson. He didn't tell Heron about her near collision with a motorcar, and how he had saved her. "What would you like me to do next?" Flannery asked Heron. He didn't believe in waiting for the other shoe to drop – he preferred dropping it himself.

"This is very useful information – Mary Anderson responding to the name Sierra Waters – we can use it to our advantage," Heron replied.

"So you don't want me to—"

"Not at this point, no," Heron interrupted. "I believe you have the wrong impression of me – I don't like taking human life. I once even saved Sierra Waters herself, back in the ancient world, in what we today call Asia Minor, many years ago in my lifetime." *If only I'd known more back then*, Heron thought.

"Good," Flannery said, and exhaled quietly in relief. "Why do you suppose Edwin Porter asked Mary to come along with him to see Appleton? Is he part of this cabal to get your *Chronica* out to the world, too?"

"He is attracted to her, certainly, as no doubt are you, too," Heron replied, "but I doubt that is the reason he included her on his visit to Appleton. He likely knew of Miss Anderson's preparation to play Hypatia, and this made her appealing to take along to see Appleton, given the publisher's great interest in the woman." Heron tried to control himself from saying Hypatia with obvious venom, and wasn't sure he succeeded.

"Just coincidence, then, that Porter took Mary Anderson along to see Appleton, and she is on your radar?" Flannery asked with a little sarcasm. He knew from their discussions that Heron didn't believe in coincidence. "You know what 'radar' is? Yes – of course you do."

Heron nodded and ignored the jibe about coincidence. "Who knows how long Mary Anderson has been attracted to Hypatia.

Kingsley's novel was first published in 1853 – it's been widely read. His story has little to do with real history, of course, but it's made Hypatia an object of desire for men and a heroine to be admired and emulated by many women. Sierra Waters and Mary Anderson no doubt came upon Hypatia in very different ways, but their attraction to her is no coincidence. The more I think about it, Sierra Waters contacting Mary Anderson, once she heard about Anderson's interest in Hypatia, makes perfect sense."

"And what does that mean for us?" Flannery asked.

"It means the problem we need to most address is not Mary Anderson but Sierra Waters," Heron replied. "She's the one who needs to be stopped, as she always has been. But I've been attempting to do that for so long, with so little success, that I am beginning to think she is protected by some fundamental law of the universe of which I am unaware." Or the next closest thing, Heron thought, something in the distant future that he knew too little about.

CHAPTER 8

[New York City, February, 1899 AD]

"To whom do you suppose William entrusted the translation of the *Chronica*?" Astor asked Sierra and Max, when the three were comfortably seated on the train back to Grand Central.

"One thing I love about you people back here is the precision you have with the language," Max observed. "It's degenerated a bit in my and Sierra's time."

"Thank you," Astor said.

"We already discussed Mark Twain and H. G. Wells with William in 1896," Sierra said. "Chances are if the translator was either of them, he wouldn't have been so cagey."

"You think he was being cagey?" Astor asked. "You don't take him at face value when he says he thinks it's safer that way?"

"Oh, I agree it's safer," Sierra said. "But I guess after all we've been through, I don't quite believe that William wouldn't tell us the name."

"He was trying to protect us?" Max asked.

"Yes, always," Sierra said. "But by not telling us who the translator is, William is preventing us from giving that translator *our* protection, which could be very important, too."

"He may also think the opposite," Astor said. "Keeping the translator's name secret may be the best way of protecting the translator."

Max nodded. It occurred to him that maybe Appleton didn't reveal the translator because he didn't fully trust Astor. He wondered if that's what Sierra was trying to signal to him now, with the upshot that he and Sierra needed to be careful about what they said to Astor. Max was sitting by the window, and looked out of it now to gather his thoughts without Astor's eyes on his face. So far, Astor had done nothing untrustworthy, and he'd had ample opportunity to hurt Sierra if that's what he'd wanted. If Astor was working with Heron, he could have easily arranged to have Heron's legionaries meet them at the National Conservatory of Music – he and Sierra would have been easy targets in that front row.

"Possibly it is the translator who doesn't want his name known," Astor spoke up, "and insisted upon that anonymity as a condition of his employment by Appleton."

"That makes some sense," Max said. "The translator would be on Heron's hit list."

Astor gave Max a quizzical look.

"On a list of people Heron would want to kill," Sierra provided a translation of the future jargon.

"And you would be at the top of the list," Astor said to Sierra, softly, with concern.

"Yes," Max replied. "We think Hypatia's horrible death in ancient Alexandria was orchestrated by Heron. He had good reason to think Sierra was Hypatia – we gave him good reason."

Astor was silent for a few moments. Sierra said nothing.

Astor spoke. "I have money, as you know. I can protect you," he said to Sierra.

She shook her head no.

"Protecting her and safeguarding the *Chronica* are mutually exclusive," Max said.   "Appleton understands that, I understand it, you probably understand that now, everyone understands it, except—" he looked at Sierra.

"I understand it," Sierra said, "but there's nothing to be done about it. Unless we want to abandon the field and give it all to Heron. And even then, he wouldn't be content with any of us alive, including you now, Mr. Astor."

"Jack," he said.

The conductor walked through their car and announced they would soon be arriving at Grand Central.

The three left the station and walked south to 39th Street, where Astor's source was waiting for him in a small tavern.

Astor's source rose, and smiled especially broadly through his moustache when the three walked through the door and he saw Sierra.

Astor made the introductions.   "William Kennedy Dickson, meet Sierra Waters and Maxwell Marcus."

***

"This is the honor of a lifetime," Dickson said to Sierra, when all were seated and ordered their libations, as Dickson had called them.   "It's rare indeed that one person can do so much for civilization, and be as beautiful as you," he said to Sierra, and looked appreciatively into her eyes.

"You come from Scotland," Sierra observed.

"Yes, born in France, raised in Scotland, did lots of work here at Edison's Black Maria before heading back across the Atlantic," Dickson said.   "I made the *Edison Kinetoscopic Record of a*

CHRONICA

Sneeze."

Max was impressed. "*Fred Ott's Sneeze*! Five-second movie. First motion picture copyrighted in the United States – I saw it a hundred times in Shanahan's undergrad film class at Fordham University! It's an honor to meet *you*!"

Dickson turned to Max, deeply appreciative for a different reason.   "I'd heard about that – through the time travel grapevine – that my work is venerated in the future. But it's nonetheless immensely gratifying to hear it from someone who hails from the future!"

"How did you find out about us?" Sierra asked, with a smile, but still wanting very much to know.

"Jack's a great fan of the photo-play," Dickson replied.   "He sought me out and recruited me, as it were, last year in London."

"There are Chairs in the Parthenon Club in London, as you know," Astor added.

Sierra was again surprised about how much Astor knew – and was doing. It still made her uncomfortable. But she apparently needed to get used to it. "William Henry Appleton told us that Heron's *Chronica* is already deposited with a translator," Sierra said to Dickson. No need to keep that from him, since Astor already knew it. "Any ideas about whom that might be?"

Dickson tilted his face and considered. "Are you certain that Mr. Appleton was talking about a translator? Maybe he vested the book in someone's else keeping, in the expectation that such a person could in turn arrange for a translation."

"Come to think of it, he didn't use the word 'translator'," Max said. "He spoke only of 'translation'."

"Who could arrange for a translation?" Sierra asked. "Another publisher, with more suitable connections?"

"That could have appealed to Appleton," Max said, "given his knowledge of his own impending death."

Dickson couldn't suppress a shudder. "It's things like that that give me reason to think maybe the world was better off without time travel."

"Trust me, there are lots of reasons," Sierra said to Dickson. "I'm glad to have you with us," she added, partially truthfully. "What have you learned about what Heron is doing back here?"

"He's trying to get the *Chronica* for himself, as you know," Dickson replied, happy to switch from Appleton's impending death to what Sierra had asked. "He's been working with my former employer, Thomas Edison, for years, and now with Edison's new golden boy, Edwin Porter."

"That is why I approached you," Astor said, "to get a friend into that nest of photographer vipers."

Their beer arrived.

"Edison's far more than a photographer, I know," Astor said, "but—"

"That doesn't make him any less a viper if he's working with Heron," Max said.

"More than working with him," Sierra added. "Who knows how many of Edison's inventions were suggested by Heron. That's one of Heron's specialties."

***

Dickson got on an uptown trolley car when the meeting ended – to Mary Anderson's rooms in the little hotel north of 59th

Street.

She was expecting him, and opened the door in a negligee. They kissed. He soon removed her negligee and she his clothes.

He kissed her on the neck and ran his hand over her stomach as they lay in bed.

"Do you like me better than women of the future?" she asked him, with her patented slight pout.

"I don't know – I've never had any," Dickson replied, and moved his hand lower.

"Jack Astor told me they shave their private parts," Mary purred. "Would you like me better if I did that?"

Dickson touched her nipple with the tip of his tongue. "I like hair. It's nice to run my fingers through," Dickson replied, and demonstrated to Mary what he meant.

She moaned softly, put her arms around his neck, and kissed him passionately.

He was soon inside her. She wrapped her legs around his lower back. He came loudly. She came softly, soon after.

"It's a good thing that I'm too old to have children," Mary murmured, still in Dickson's arms. "I'm a devout Catholic, and the Church thinks contraception is a sin."

"I know," Dickson said. "I'm happier without a condom, of course, but if push came to shove, there's a fine one made of intestine that does the trick."

"Is there a joke somewhere in that?" Mary said, and laughed.

"No, I just like playing with words," Dickson said.

"You play very well," Mary said, and cuddled close to Dickson.

"Appleton says the *Chronica* is already out of his hands," Dickson said, eventually. "At least, that's what he told Jack Astor."

"You don't believe him?" Mary asked.

"I'm not sure," Dickson said. "What would you do with it if it fell into your hands?"

Mary had already delicately cupped one of her hands under Dickson. "The *Chronica* is unique," she said. "If I misplace a script, I can easily get a duplicate. What would happen if the *Chronica* were lost or destroyed? If I had it in my hands, the first thing I would do is figure out how to make a duplicate."

"Maybe by some kind of mimeograph?" Dickson said. "Believe it or not, a bloke by the name of Albert Blake Dick got the patent on that – based on Edison's autographic printing."

"Dick and Dickson," Mary said, "has something of a ring to it."

"I was thinking about 'dick' in the sense the military boys use it," Dickson said, "if you know what I mean."

"I know exactly what you mean," Mary said, and the two stopped talking, as she extended her body completely over his.

***

Sierra and Max were back in Astor's hotel, slightly different than the one they had enjoyed in 1896. A year later, in 1897, Astor had completed and opened his own hotel adjacent to his cousin's, connected by a corridor. "And superior in many ways," he had explained. Astor had graciously insisted that Max and Sierra stay in his accommodations again. Their room had a fireplace. Max started the fire, and the two sat close to it, enjoying the crackling and the warmth.

"Beats that cold outside," Max said, and rubbed his hands. "This room's even better than the one we had in 1896."

"It is," Sierra agreed. "But I'm thinking we may need to move to later in the year – another way to get out of the cold."

Max nodded. "Agreed.   That's likely the only way we can find out more about what Appleton was talking about. You're thinking, what, a week, a month? And do we tell Astor?"

"We shouldn't talk about him in his room," Sierra said, raising the same point that had concerned her three years earlier. "The phonograph's now been around more than twenty years, so everything we say here could conceivably be recorded. But . . . I don't know, for some reason, I'm beginning to trust him more."

A log ignited and gave itself totally to the fire.

"I noticed," Max said, his face and Sierra's bathed orange in the big flame. "Why do you think that is?"

"You jealous?" Sierra asked with a smile.

"Absolutely," Max said, "of every guy who looks at you. But Jack Astor is a tough one to figure. I supported him more than you did, at first, as you know. And he's done nothing but help us since then – including this fabulous room and this wonderful fire. But . . ."

Sierra looked at him.

"I guess he's too enthusiastic," Max said. "And that's a ridiculous criticism, I know. We need all the help we can get. I don't know – I guess we have no choice but to trust him, he's too far into this with us to suddenly cut him loose."

"Look, we don't owe him any itinerary of where we're going, including through time," Sierra said. "He certainly hasn't done that with us. We can be allies without confiding in him everything we do." She looked at the little silver-plated pocket watch she had purchased here and wore around her neck. "Why don't we leave right now – the fire's inviting, but what else do we really have here that's better to do?"

Max thought for a second, and nodded. "That'll also allow us to end our mooching ways and return these coats," he pointed to the Millennium overcoats, now draped on an ornate armchair. Then he doused the fire.

Sierra stood, took her coat, and put it on. "Too bad about that," she said. "I was getting to like these coats – you look great in your greatcoat."

***

The two arrived at the Millennium about 20 minutes later. "Looks like the guy we saw here in 2062," Sierra whispered to Max, as the doorman opened the door and they walked in.

Max looked a little concerned. "Presumably they don't have any retinal IDs back here."

"Doesn't matter," Sierra continued her whisper, "as he long as he recognizes us."

He apparently did. He nodded and asked if Sierra and Max were looking for anyone at the Club.

"Not today," Sierra replied.

"Very good," he said in his crisp British accent. He bowed slightly and walked away.

The two left their borrowed coats in the cloakroom, with a note that said thanks. They ascended the necessary stairs and entered the room with the Chairs. There were two of them.

"Who took the third—" Max began.

"Doesn't matter," Sierra said again. "All we can do is speculate. If it's Heron, and he's waiting for us at the time we're going to, we'll find out about that soon enough."

Max agreed and unconsciously touched the hilt of the knife he always carried in his belt.

Each sat in a Chair.

"I'm setting it for one month from now," Sierra said.

"Works for me," Max said and threw her a small kiss.

Sierra set in the dates and initiated the go sequence. Bubbles ascended. The cosmos blew kisses.

[New York City, March, 1899 AD]

Sierra's bubble receded. She got out of her Chair.

"Max??!" She realized she was the only person in the room. "Max???" she shouted again to the empty room.

What the hell had happened? The two had jumped in sync dozens of times now, and it had worked just right every time. Had she done something wrong with the setting? No, she was sure she had done that correctly.

What should she do? Get back in her Chair and travel a month back – that's where Max would be if his Chair had malfunctioned. She felt a deep gnawing in the pit of her stomach – if the Chair had not worked right, Max could be in a lot worse shape than just a month earlier in time. What should she do? She felt more panicked now than in all the battles with Heron and his men.

She had to think clearly. There was an explanation for this—

She heard something in the air – the sound when a Chair was

imminently arriving. Her first instinct was to stay in the room, so she could see if Max was in the Chair and all right. But that could be fatal to her. She left the room, and closed the door behind her.

She was shaking and was glad no one was there to see it.

She heard something in the room. She took a deep breath. It could be Heron in the Chair or someone else bent on killing her. She heard a muffled voice through the door. It sounded enough like Max that she opened the door.

"Hey," Max said, as Sierra rushed over and flung her arms around him. "What's the matter?"

"You weren't here," she said. She was still shaking but it was subsiding. "What happened?"

"Nothing different, on my end," Max said. He stroked her face and tried to comfort her, seeing how upset she was. "Everything's ok."

"Well, something happened," Sierra said, regaining most of her equilibrium. "Something went awry in the syncing."

"Could Heron have done that?" Max asked.

"I don't know," Sierra said.

"Let's get out of here and up to Wave Hill to see Appleton," Max said. "If there's something not right with the Chairs, something dangerous could still happen in this room."

***

Sierra was still not quite herself as they reached Grand Central. The Chairs working as expected was one of the few facts of her existence she relied upon, in this insane life she had chosen for herself, and which Max had joined.

"You sure you can't remember anything different?" Sierra asked Max, for at least the fourth or fifth time.

"No, nothing different," Max said. "It was instantaneous, like it always is."

"All right," she said as they boarded the train up to Riverdale. "Let's see what we can learn now from William about where the *Chronica* is." She tried to clear her head some more, with only partial success.

The two hiked up the hill to Appleton's home. Max knocked on the door.

Geoffreys opened it with a face more dour than usual. "I'm sorry, he's sleeping now," Geoffreys said. "He's a little better than the day before yesterday, when Mr. Porter was here, but the doctor gave me strict orders not to let Mr. Appleton see anyone, until he's up and easily walking about."

"Porter?" Max asked.

"Oh, yes," Geoffreys replied. "A Mr. Edwin Porter – he paid a call with the actress, Mary Anderson. They were quite disappointed when they couldn't see him."

"Is that Edwin Porter, the film maker? *The Great Train Robbery*?" Max asked.

"I'm sorry, I don't follow," Geoffreys replied. "Is *The Great Train Robber* a novel?"

"*The Great Train Robbery*," Max said, "though, wait, maybe it's a little too early for you to know that . . . it was made in, 1901? . . . Ok, never mind. I was talking to myself, about ... moving pictures. You know, photography, but the images move?"

"I still don't understand what you're saying, but, no, I do not frequent the arcades," Geoffreys said.

Max nodded.

"And you are sure we cannot see Mr. Appleton, even for a brief minute?" Sierra asked, almost pleading.

"I wish it could be, my dear," Geoffreys said, softly but intently. "I'm afraid I have no choice but to follow the doctor's orders. Perhaps next week? The doctor says there's every chance Mr. Appleton will regain at least some of his strength."

***

The two trudged dejectedly back down the hill to the train station. "What was Edwin Porter doing here?" Sierra asked.

"Didn't Dickson mention something about Porter this morning – last month?" Max asked. "Maybe Dickson enlisted Porter in some kind of plan to find out the whereabouts of the *Chronica*."

"I need to stop for a second," Sierra said, breathlessly.

"Are you ok?" Max asked, concerned.

"I don't know," Sierra said, and reached out to touch Max's face. Then she pulled it towards her and kissed him, putting her tongue in his mouth, and moving it round and round with his. She pulled away, and kissed him again on the lips.

"Wow," Max said, now slightly out of breath himself. "That was, for what? You liked my analysis of Dickson and Porter?"

"Yeah, and we should see how Thomas Edison figures into this, since both of them worked or still work for him," Sierra said.

"And we need to find out what Mary Anderson has to do with all of this," Max said. "It's not just an accident that she showed up with Edwin Porter to see Appleton."

"Maybe Mary, whoever she is, was the one who made the decision to see William, and she was the one who brought

Porter along," Sierra said. "Who is she?"

"Geoffreys said she's an actress," Max said, "does that do anything for you? I never heard of any actress by the name of Mary Anderson."

"It may ring a slight bell," Sierra said. "I'm not sure."

They resumed walking and soon reached the station.

"Why did you kiss me back there?" Max asked.

"Do I need a reason?" Sierra said, and tried to smile.

"I know you," Max said. "You don't just kiss me out of the clear blue sky for no reason."

"I'm sorry," Sierra said.

Max laughed oddly. "You don't have to apologize for it – I'm just wondering—"

"I had to make sure it was you," Sierra said.

"We back to that again? I thought you tested me back in ancient Alexandria," Max said. "That was fun, too. Though, sometimes, a kiss like the one you just gave me on the hill can be the best thing of all."

"I was just worried," Sierra said.

"About what? That because my Chair arrived a few seconds late, that I was no longer me, and was some fucking duplicate that Heron sent in?"

"I'm sorry," Sierra said again. "I know now it's you – no one else moves their tongue exactly the way you do." Now she was able to smile. "But stranger things have happened. You know that. I wasn't wrong to be concerned."

"Ok," Max said, and took her hand.

The train arrived clacking at the station. Sierra and Max boarded, and Sierra thought, well, I know it's you, but I still need to know why that glitch in the sync, if it was a glitch, happened. She squeezed Max's hand and kissed him softly on the neck.

***

Sierra and Max walked out into the bright, cool late March sunshine outside of Grand Central Terminal.

"That's J. P. Morgan and Thomas Edison," a man dressed all in black said to another man, dressed the same as him, in a thick accent Max and Sierra instantly recognized as Yiddish.

Sierra and Max turned to see two older men walking quickly ahead of them and the men dressed in black on the street. The name J. P. Morgan meant little to Sierra and Max. But Edison of course they amply knew all about.

Max looked as if he wanted to run up to Edison.

Sierra put a restraining arm on his shoulder. "From what I remember reading, he's not the most sociable," she said to Max. "If we want to see him, we'd probably do better to contact him beforehand and arrange a meeting, rather than just accosting him like this on the street."

Max nodded. "By the way, we've haven't discussed this yet, but I assume we're headed back to Astor's hotel, after having been a gone a month, from his point of view."

"I can't see the harm in it," Sierra said.

The two proceeded to the hotel on Fifth Avenue and 33rd Street. The concierge walked briskly up to them in the lobby. "Mr. Astor was looking for you," he said. "May I tell him you're here?"

"Of course," Sierra said, and the concierge went off to get Astor.

"I'm going to use the facilities in our room," Max said. "Don't say too much without me."

She touched his face. "You've really got the jargon down pat now."

Astor approached a few minutes later. "Did you have a good time in whatever time you were in?" he asked, jovially.

"We went directly here, to this time, March 1899, to see Mr. Appleton," Sierra replied. She thought about telling Astor about the slight problem with Max's arrival, but decided she needed to think more about what had caused that before she told anyone else, including Astor.

"And I assume you found out nothing more about the whereabouts of the *Chronica*?" Astor asked.

Sierra shook her head no. "He's still too ill to see any one."

Astor nodded. "He loves you very much, you know. Not in the same way as Thomas did, of course, but—" Astor looked around. "I wanted to tell you that, but didn't feel comfortable talking about Thomas and you in front of Maxwell."

"Did you see him – Thomas – while I was gone?" Sierra asked, softly.

"No, I haven't seen Thomas in a few years of my lifetime now," Astor said, "and he indicated the last time we met that that might be the last time we saw one another." Astor paused. "He told me quite a story – more incredible in many ways than the novels by Mr. Wells and Mr. Twain. I wasn't quite sure if I could believe him. But meeting you, getting to know you a little, made Thomas's words about you and him more real."

"Did he look like Thomas or—" Sierra asked.

"He already looked like Thomas when I first met him. Not like Alcibiades. He loves you very deeply," Astor repeated.

Sierra teared up.

"I don't believe anyone other than Mr. Appleton and me – and of course you and Maxwell – know about Thomas's story and true identity— Ah, and speaking of the devil, here indeed is Dr. Marcus." Astor extended his hand to Max, who walked up to Astor and Sierra with a smile.

"We were just talking about Thomas," Sierra said to Max. And to Astor: "We keep no secrets from each other."

CHAPTER 9

[Foster Square Facility, Brewster, Massachusetts, 2096 AD]

She had a new concern. Actually, concern was too mild a word for it.

Heron was on the move. She had seen multiple indications in the mega-billions of code she daily examined. He was nibbling away at the edges. If he broke through, her very existence and therefore mission could be in jeopardy. He may already have done some damage.

She did what passed for cursing. It *was* cursing -- though, to say she believed in God, or anything but humanity as the ultimate being in the universe, would be untrue. There could be alien intelligences throughout the cosmos, for all she knew. If she were a betting android, she would indeed put code down that there were. But even so, whatever alien intelligence as probably existed elsewhere in the universe had kept itself secret from humanity and its android creations.

She returned to Heron. It helped to itemize the basics of her and Sierra's knowledge of him: 1. Heron invented time travel, whether in the past or the future was not clear. 2. Socrates wrote the Andros dialogue, as what humans would later call a "thought experiment". 3. Sierra, under the name Ampharete, gave the dialogue to Heron in 150 AD Alexandria. 4. Heron decided to save Socrates. 5. Sierra and Alcibiades differed with Heron on the way to do that, and Heron came to judge them as his opponents and then his enemies. 6. Sierra's attempt to save texts from the doomed ancient Library of Alexandria further exacerbated her relationship with Heron, who now regarded her as a mortal enemy, since among the texts she wanted to save was Heron's *Chronica*, which contained his instructions on how to construct a time travel device in the form of a Chair, for anyone to see, read, implement, and apply to history, if the reader could understand it.

She sighed. And that's where they were now.   Was there any way of reasoning with Heron, of coming to terms with him? She had run countless scenarios on that goal, and not a single one had been viable.

The time was dwindling in which to run more of them. Every ounce of the programming she had been imbued with told her she had to devote almost all of her attention to one goal, now, and one goal only: survival.

CHAPTER 10

[West Orange, New Jersey, April, 1899 AD]

T homas Edison sat at his maple wood desk in his labs in West Orange, New Jersey. Its cubbyholes, stuffed with papers upon which various things were written, rose up before him. One was delegated for "New Things".

But Edison was now looking down at something which, if he could believe what was said about it, was very old indeed. Very old, and yet, if what it was purported to be able to instruct him about was true, could well be the newest thing in the Universe.

His chin rested upon one hand, in what he felt would be seen in posterity as his classic pose. His other hand touched the manuscript. It was said to have originally been a codex scroll, but his benefactor had arranged for it to be copied on to a paper manuscript. Unfortunately, there was as yet no translation – that was part of the task now before him.

But Edison knew there was no point in commissioning a translation, unless he first had arranged for someone who could not only read and understand the translation, but could act upon to it build the device said to be described in these words.

Edison, vain as he knew he was, also knew that he on his own lacked the capacity to build such a machine. But he thought he knew a man who perhaps had that talent. Edison had met him just three years ago, and had been mightily impressed not only with his down-to-earth intelligence, but his determination to do whatever was needed to get a job done.

Edison stroked the manuscript. He had acquired it from Appleton as soon as the blizzard was over and the trains were running. He had called upon Appleton at his Wave Hill home, and had had a lengthy conversation about what Appleton had wanted to get published before his demise. Appleton had seemed weak and tired, almost feeble, but in full possession of his mental faculties. Edison had professed a passion for bettering humanity, by getting more books directly into the hands of people rather than funneled through teachers, a passion which was not entirely pretended.

And Appleton had produced the manuscript. Edison had no idea if that was the only copy Appleton had made, and was not sure if obtaining the only copy or just a single copy was essential to Heron.

For his part, Appleton wasn't even clear about what he wanted Edison to do with it, other than arranging for its translation, and keeping that translation secret until it was completed and returned to Appleton.

Regarding Heron, it didn't matter to Edison what was important to Heron about the *Chronica*. What was important to Heron was never important to Edison. He knew that Heron disliked him, and was using him for his own purposes. Edison felt the same about Heron. He wasn't American. Edison didn't know what Heron was, but it was nothing that Edison liked or really wanted to help. Indeed, Heron was a threat to him, because he knew that too many of Edison's greatest inventions came from Heron's information.

Edison lifted the manuscript. It was short, only 48 pages in ancient Greek. He had no intention of giving that manuscript to Heron to do the devil knew what with it. No, from the moment Edison had held the manuscript in his hands, in

Appleton's home, Edison knew what he wanted to do, what he was destined to do, with the instructions it contained. He would use them to build a time machine of his own. If it worked, it would be Edison's greatest invention of all.

***

There was a knock on the door, one that Edison thought respectful but strong, about ten minutes later. Edison could feel it more than hear it. "Come in," Edison bellowed.

A tall, lanky man entered.

"Henry Ford," Edison said. "Thank you for coming by."

Ford nodded and took a proffered seat.

"How long we have known each other, Henry?" Edison asked.

"I have been an engineer in Edison Illuminating since 1891, and a Chief Engineer since 1893," Ford said, proudly. "But we did not meet face to face until three years ago, in 1896."

Edison nodded. "And how is your own work on the horseless carriage proceeding? I highly approve of that, you know."

"Quite well. Thank you!" Ford, 16 years Edison's younger, replied.

"You're very welcome," Edison said. "Now then, suppose I were to tell you that I have in my possession the blueprints for a possible device that would make your Quadricycle and all that I have invented as insignificant as the leaves falling from an autumn tree?"

"That's an ambitious statement," Ford said.

"It is," Edison said. "And here they are." He handed Ford the *Chronica* manuscript.

Ford held it in his hand for a long moment before looking at it. He leafed slowly through every page. "I am afraid this is all Greek to me," he said, with a short, deferential laugh.

"To me, too," Edison said. "But I wanted you to hold it in your hand. If I were to translate it – arrange for its translation – would you be willing to give it a crack?"

"Time travel?"

"Yes," Edison said.

"Build a time machine, as H. G. Wells describes in his scientific romance?"

"It might well be completely different from Wells' fictional machine, but, yes," Edison replied.

Ford considered. "I have built machines that defy nature, as you know."

"Yes," Edison said.

"I also have in mind a machine that could fly in the air, like a bird," Ford said. "That would defy nature even further."

Edison nodded. "More than one inventor is at work on such a flying machine."

"I know," Ford said. "My specialty, whether it is on ground or in the air, is to perfect devices that others may first have built."

"Yes," Edison said. "I suspect there is already at least one device that time travels, at hand and in operation. Perhaps I could contrive to have you see it – I have not seen it yet, myself. My hope is that, with this book, translated into English, and a chance to inspect the device, that you might be able to construct one yourself."

"Yes, but—"

"Do you see an obstacle?" Edison asked. "You are known

already, as am I, for believing obstacles can be overcome, with sufficient work and effort."

"A time travel machine might be different," Ford said.

"How?"

"It seeks to overcome, not nature, but God himself!" Ford said.

Edison looked at Ford.

"I know you are not a believer—" Ford continued.

"I believe in a Supreme Being," Edison said.

"I believe in the Christ," Ford said.

'What does that have to do with time travel?" Edison said, beginning to lose patience with this young man.

"I – I do not mean to offend you – but overcoming nature is one thing, overcoming God and his laws is quite another."

Edison considered.   "Do you know the work of Luther Burbank?"

"The botanist?"

"Yes," Edison said. "He has created fruits and vegetables and flowers which did not previously exist on God's green Earth. His *New Fruits and Vegetables Catalog* from a few years ago is extraordinary – you should read it."

"I will, on your recommendation," Ford said.

Edison nodded.

"And I will read this *Chronical* book as well," Ford promised.

"*Chronica,*" Edison corrected.

"Thank you. I will read it, if you can provide a copy written in

English to me, and I will give you my honest appraisal if what it describes can be done – and if I can do it."

"That's all I can ask of you," Edison said.

***

Edison brooded for a while after Ford left. That hadn't gone as well as Edison had hoped. To some extent, Edison himself was to blame – he should have commissioned a translation before attempting to bring the automatic-carriage maker into this. But he wanted a man like Ford locked into this project as soon as possible.

Edison exhaled heavily. He needed a translator. He also needed a look at the device Heron was already using. But who other than Heron could arrange for that? No one else that Edison knew.

Heron would soon realize, if he did not already, that Edison had a copy of the *Chronica*. Heron had primed Edison to obtain a copy – but to give that copy to Heron, not use it to build a time machine. Heron was the only person who could provide Edison with a way of seeing an actual time machine – but how could he get Heron to do that without revealing that he, Edison, had the book and wanted to use it to build a machine? Edison was used to dealing with high finance as well as the one-percent inspiration and ninety-nine-percent perspiration of inventing, but what he needed to do regarding Heron was far trickier.

Maybe it was time to lie to Heron in whatever way was necessary, then sever their relationship once and for all in the aftermath. If Edison were able to build a time machine, he wouldn't need Heron or anyone like him ever again.

[New York City, April, 1899 AD]

Heron had called for an appointment with Flannery. That was ok with Flannery. His deal with Heron, for which Flannery was well compensated, required Flannery to come back once a month, to spend as long as needed. Flannery loved to think about this, and the part that he wouldn't be missed at all a century later, in his own time, because of the precision of the time travel. Flannery never tired of savoring this.

Heron entered Flannery's office, closed the door, and sat in front of Flannery's spacious mahogany desk.

"Let me get right down to business, as you might say," Heron said.

"Go right ahead," Flannery replied.

"I have two tasks for you. One relatively minor, the other more important," Heron said.

"Let's take care of the small-time assignment first," Flannery said.

Heron nodded. "There is a man who works at the Millennium Club – his name is Cyril Charles – do you know him?"

"Is he a Brit?" Flannery asked. He loved the Millennium and the forged membership Heron had created for him there. They treated Flannery like royalty.

"They all seem British to your late 20th century ears," Heron replied. "Some Americans talking right now at the end of the 19th century likely sound British to you, especially if they are upper class."

"They do," Flannery agreed. "So what do you need from me in regard to this Cyril?"

"Cyril Charles," Heron said. "He may have become a little suspicious of me in this J. P. Morgan guise. He may have seen me in the wrong place in the club last month. I should have talked to you about it then, but we were focusing on more pressing matters."

"This happened near the room with the Chairs?" Flannery asked.

"Yes," Heron.

"So—"

"Here's what would work best for this possible problem," Heron said. "First, you'll need to do this not now, but a century from now, in the 1990s. There are too many wheels in motion here in 1899."

"Too hot, would be my expression," Flannery said.

Heron nodded. "Therefore, back in your future time, I would like you to detain Cyril Charles – remove him from the Millennium Club, for whatever feigned reason that works for you in your capacity as a police lieutenant."

Flannery made a face. "Arrest him? Hold him without bail? The police are far more restricted from doing that in 1999 than we are now."

"Whatever is necessary – and legal, if possible," Heron replied. "But the key is to keep him away from the Millennium Club now, in 1899, where he might see me again as J. P. Morgan – or, worse, see me at the same time as the real J. P. Morgan. Someplace in 1999, or any year in that decade, would be the best protection for me."

"Ok," Flannery said, "time being the better protection than distance. Got it. And what's the more important task?"

"I am very concerned about Appleton and obtaining the *Chronica.* My other . . . friends have either failed to retrieve it from Appleton or are lying to me. And Appleton's health seems to be rapidly failing. I don't how much longer he has to live."

"I thought his demise was still six months away," Flannery said.

"October 19, 1899 is the date that is now listed in the encyclopedias, yes," Heron said. "But I don't know what effect all of these manipulations of history, small and large and larger, might have on Appleton's lifespan. Every change in history, however tiny, has the potential to set in motion all kinds of unintended consequences. Your very presence back here may change the date that Appleton expires, for reasons we cannot fathom beforehand. You understand?"

Flannery made another face. He thought he understood this pretty well, and resented Heron's implication that he did not. "Just tell me what you need me to do."

CHAPTER 11

[New York City, March, 1899 AD]

Astor requested a breakfast meeting with Sierra and Max the day after they returned from their unsuccessful trip to see Appleton. Nikola Tesla accompanied Astor.

Tesla began the conversation, when all four were seated.

"I have been thinking about what you really hope to accomplish with all of this," he said softly but directly to Sierra.

"What do you think I want?" she replied equally softly and directly.

Tesla smiled. "You think you want to ensure that Heron does not have a monopoly on how to time travel."

"Yes, that is a correct rendition of what I want," Sierra said.

"But have you considered how this might come to be, practically?" Tesla asked. "If Mr. Appleton is successful in arranging for the publication of the *Chronica*, that will make the knowledge of how to time travel available to everyone, would it not?"

Sierra nodded.

"But do you really want a world in which time travel is as commonplace as trains? Or as electric and gasoline powered motor vehicles no doubt soon will be?" Tesla pressed.

"That would be better than Heron dominating all of human existence – past, present, and future – with his sole possession of time travel, wouldn't it?" Sierra asked, not quite as confident of what she most wanted as she had been just a moment ago.

"I am not so sure," Tesla said. "There are many evil people in this world – you no doubt have seen more of them in your remarkable travels than I have in my travels confined just to this time. What would happen if some maniac gained access to a time travel Chair?"

"I—" Sierra began, slowly.

Max touched her hand. "You make a good point, Nikola – what would be your recommended course of action?"

Tesla smiled again. "That brings me to my next point."

"Ok, tell us," Max said.

"I am thinking we might not even need the *Chronica* in our hands," he said, "because," he looked at Sierra, "did you read the *Chronica* when you had it in your hands?"

"Yes, I did," Sierra said. "My ancient Greek is relatively good."

"I read it, too," Max said.

"Very good!" Tesla said to both of them. "And how much of it do you recall? How much of it can you recite?"

"We don't have eidetic or photographic or whatever you call those kinds of precise and entire memories," Max said.

"But I do," Tesla said and smiled slightly.

"You may not need perfect memories," Astor finally spoke, to Sierra and Max. "All you would need is enough recollection about what you read in the *Chronica* – both of you – to talk about that, extensively, with Nikola."

"To what end?" Sierra asked.

"So he could construct a Chair that time traveled, and then the *Chronica* would be irrelevant to us, and we could change our focus to destroying rather than publishing the *Chronica*, as a better way of countering Heron, and keeping the world much safer in the process," Astor answered.

"I doubt that we could recite enough to anyone to build a Chair," Sierra said, "and, from what I have read of the *Chronica*, the technology does not yet exist in this time to build a Chair, even if we had the book in its entirety right in front of us."

"He wrote it in the ancient world, did he not?" Astor asked. "Did they have the technology then?"

"I don't know with certainty what they had back then," Sierra answered. "But that's not relevant – Heron likely wrote it in the past after he traveled back there from the future, or he wrote it in the future and brought it back with him to ancient Alexandria. In any case, none of that matters – we don't have the technology to build the Chairs in this time, and not a hundred years from now, either."

Tesla's eyes twinkled. "What we have might surprise you."

***

Sierra and Max sat with Tesla day after day, for hours and hours, in their hotel room. Sometimes Astor was present, sometimes not. They told Tesla anything and everything they could remember about the *Chronica* – half-forgotten equations, big concepts, tiny details, conjectures and refutations about what couldn't work for time travel, proofs where possible about what could -- and, according to Heron, did.

Tesla listened intently, took a few notes, and asked many

questions. At one point he said, "I can tell you one thing: I agree that the ancient world could not have created this. If anyone back then had this knowledge – did not import it from the future – then we would be living in a far different world than we are today."

The interview resumed. Sierra and Max spoke of solid states, quantum states, fluctuating worlds within worlds, multiple worlds and universes in grains of sand in an hourglass.

Tesla reluctantly admitted he did not understand it all. Sierra and Max said again that neither did they.

"I can apply some of this to tailoring the performance of a Chair already in operation," Sierra at one point said, "but building one from nothing is vastly more difficult."

Tesla nodded. "I understand movement of energy and objects through space. What you have been telling me gives me many ideas about possible devices in that realm. But I cannot say they will move through time."

Sierra and Max needed sleep from time to time, as did Astor. Tesla claimed he did not.

The interviews went on for weeks, well into April, until Sierra and Max began repeating themselves and Tesla realized there was not much more or new they could say about the *Chronica*.

"I'm drained," Sierra said. "Do you think you have enough to build a Chair?"

"I don't know," Telsa replied. "I can say that such a construction would be far more difficult than I had thought."

"Do you think you would be in a better position to make a Chair if you had the *Chronica* in your hands?" Astor asked.

"I'm not sure," Tesla replied. "Perhaps, possibly, is the best I can tell you."

Sierra sighed and took his hand. "And perhaps that's for the better."

[New York City, April, 1899 AD]

Three days after the interviews had concluded, Astor and Dickson arrived in the hotel lobby as Sierra and Max were leaving to go on a long overdue walk in Central Park to breathe some fresh air and relax. "Dickson thinks that Appleton may have given a copy of the *Chronica* to Thomas Edison," Astor said.

"What?" Sierra shouted. Several people in the lobby turned around. "How do you know that?" she asked Dickson, a bit less loudly.

"Edwin Porter told me," Dickson replied.

"Have you told Nikola?" Max asked.

"Yes," Astor replied. "He was livid and vowed to redouble his efforts. It's far too soon to know if he will succeed."

"Is there any chance you can get it from Edison?" Max asked Dickson.

Dickson shook his head no. "I don't work for him any more. He's unlikely to leave me alone with anything of such value – he has a paranoid streak anyway, as long as your arm."

"What about Porter?" Sierra asked.

"As far as I can tell, he's loyal to Edison to a fault," Dickson replied. "And what's more, he is also doing Heron's bidding."

"We've got to do something!" Sierra said.

"Must we?" Max asked.

Sierra turned on him. "What do you mean?"

"Are we sure it's a bad thing that Edison has the *Chronica*?" Max answered with a question.

"Tesla certainly thinks so," Astor replied.

"Edison and Tesla are competitors," Max said. "Tesla understandably hates him, especially after the AC-DC current wars. Isn't getting the *Chronica* and its instructions out to the world exactly what we have been working for?"

"To the right people in the world, yes," Sierra said, with some heat. "Edison's working for Heron. He's probably already given the *Chronica* to Heron."

"Porter didn't think so," Dickson said. "He spoke as if the *Chronica* was now in Edison's possession alone."

"Edison's obviously a great inventor himself," Max said. "Hard to believe he would just turn the *Chronica* over to Heron and forget he ever had it."

Sierra shook her head in frustration. "Why would William give the *Chronica* to Edison?" She looked at Dickson. "Can you find out more from Porter?"

"I wish I could," Dickson responded, "but I'm afraid I am long overdue in England." He pulled out a pocket watch from his vest. "I have a boat to board in the harbor, in three hours."

"We'll have to approach Porter ourselves," Sierra said.

"Your best entrée to Porter is Mary Anderson," Dickson said.

"So just to be clear," Max said. "Porter thinks that you and he are both working for Heron, and he and you both know that Edison has some connection to Heron, though Edison himself may not know exactly what the two of you know about all of this."

"Yes," Porter said, "that's the long and the short of it. From what I've seen of Heron, he likes to direct each of us separately, not as a group."

"But as far as you know, Porter trusts you," Max said.

"That is correct," Dickson replied, and bowed to Sierra and the men. "And I really do have an appointment with an ocean liner," he added, and left.

"It's my favorite mode of travel," Astor said to Sierra and Max. "And the boats are getting grander and grander."

***

Astor sat with Sierra and Max and considered their options. "She's better with men than with women," Astor said about Mary Anderson, "lights right up when a suitable man comes into the room. No offense," he said to Sierra.

"None taken," Sierra said.

Astor beckoned a bellhop. "Would coffee appeal?" he asked Sierra and Max.

Both nodded.

"You know, they are known as porters in England," Astor noted when the bellhop left with the order. "Interesting coincidence that we were just talking about Porter, isn't it?"

Max and Sierra both nodded.

"But to return to Miss Anderson," Astor said, "her preference for men as social companions suggests that either you or I should approach her," he said to Max. "Which would you prefer?"

"Oh, I'd be happy to see her," Max said, a little surprised that

Astor didn't want to do this himself.

"I'm glad you think that," Astor said to Max, as the bellhop returned with a pot of coffee and three cups. "Thank you," he said to bellhop, who bowed and left after he put the tray with the coffee on a table close to Astor. "We have it always simmering and ready to serve here," he said to Sierra and Max, poured a cup for each of them, then one for himself. "If I recall, we all drink it black," he said.

Sierra smelled her coffee and took a sip. "Delicious," she said to Astor. "Thank you."

Max said the same.

Astor resumed talking about Mary Anderson. "As I was saying, it's fortunate that you can see her, if she needs to be seen today, because I have an important meeting with a group of financiers this afternoon, including J. P. Morgan."

"Good," Max said. "Will you call her and make the appointment?"

"I will," Astor said.

***

Max got off the motorbus across the street from Mary Anderson's hotel late in the afternoon. He walked into the hotel and looked around for Mary – her photograph had been delivered to him by Astor – but there were only two elderly, well-dressed men in the lobby. He waited about 15 minutes, then approached the front desk.

"Excuse me," he said to the man behind the desk, whose head was buried in a big ledger.

"Yes?"

"I have a 3:00 pm appointment with Mary Anderson, one of

your guests," Max said.

The receptionist scowled and looked at a grandfather clock in the middle of the lobby. "Well, that was 15 minutes ago," he said.

"My point, exactly," Max said.

"What would you like me to do?" the receptionist asked.

"Can you check and see if she's in her room?" Max said.

"I know she is in her room," the receptionist replied. "I saw her return to the hotel, about two hours ago and I have not seen her leave. "

"Could you call up to her room and let her know I am here?"

The receptionist scowled even more deeply. "That would be an intrusion."

"Ok, I'll go up there myself," Max said.

"You don't know her room number," the receptionist responded.

"I'll knock on each and every door until I find her," Max said.

"I should call the police, but what is your name?   If Miss Anderson left any note that you were coming by to see her, I'll consider walking upstairs with you to her room ."

"Maxwell Marcus," Max replied, and hoped that Astor had spoken his name correctly when he set up this appointment – *if* this appointment had really been set.

The receptionist pulled another ledger out of a drawer and pored over it. "All right, here it is. Miss Anderson did tell us you would be paying her a visit."

"Can we go upstairs now?" Max asked, relieved but still

annoyed. "And you are certain she didn't leave the hotel?" With service as irritating as this guy, he wouldn't be surprised if the woman had checked out of the hotel altogether and gone elsewhere.

"Yes, I am sure," the receptionist replied. "I have been here at my post without interruption since she returned, and, as I told you, I did not see her leave." He rang a bell. Another man, dressed in the same deep brown uniform, approached. "Kindly take my post as I escort this gentleman upstairs," the reception said.

"Of course," the other man said.

Max and the receptionist walked up a single flight of stairs. "Miss Anderson is right here," the receptionist said, and knocked on the door of Room 202.

There was no answer. The receptionist knocked several times with the same lack of result. "Miss Anderson, Miss Anderson?" he called her name several times.

Then, "this is Wilfred Jameson from the front desk. I am entering your room." He applied a key he carried on a chain with lots of other keys, and very slowly opened the door.

"Miss Anderson? Miss Anderson! Oh my God!"

Mary Anderson was sprawled on the bed, half naked and disheveled, unconscious or dead.

***

Jameson summoned the hotel's doctor, who fortunately had offices just down the street.

"She's alive," he said, applying a flexible tube that he called a stethoscope to her heart, and finding it beating. He lifted her eyelid. "She has been given drugs or some unsuitable medication, her iris is dilated. We need to get her to a hospital, right away." He gently pulled up her undergarments and dress so her breasts were no longer exposed. "There are no bruises or other signs of foul play, thank goodness, at least on this part of the body."

"Can you tell when the drug was administered?" Max asked the doctor – though Jameson, who had regained his composure, was ushering Max out of the room.

"We'll know more when we can examine her in the hospital," the doctor replied. "She is not in any immediate danger. I'm going to arrange for a horse-drawn ambulance – they provide a more comfortable ride than the motorized vehicles – to Bellevue Hospital on First Avenue and 30th Street. It's not the closest, but it has the best services, and I have privileges there." He said this through the open door to Jameson and Max, who were now in the hallway outside of the room. "Are you a relative?" the doctor now asked Max.

Jameson closed the door before Max could respond. "You will need to wait in the lobby, until the police arrive."

Max thought for a moment. It would do him and Sierra no good for him to be put on some fugitive list. "Of course," he said.

Jameson allowed him to use the phone on the front desk to call Sierra and then Astor, whom he quickly briefed, before a police detective arrived.

"Detective Woodruff," a well-dressed man with a moustache and sideburns said, and extended his hand in sequence to Jameson and Max.

"Wilfred Jameson, for the hotel," Jameson said, and shook the hand. "Thank you for coming by."

"Maxwell Marcus," Max said and shook the detective's hand. "I had an appointment with Miss Anderson."

Woodruff nodded.

The ambulance had already arrived and two orderlies, with the doctor supervising, were carefully carrying Mary Anderson down the one flight of stairs on a stretcher. "I gave her something and she's come partially around," the doctor said to Woodruff. "I do not think she's in any danger, and I can confirm that there were no signs of foul play anyplace on her body."

"That's very good to know, thank you, doctor," Woodruff replied.

Max looked at Mary. Her eyes were half open now, and she seemed semi-conscious.

"We're off to Bellevue, then," the doctor said. "We'll know more when we can thoroughly examine her there."

Woodruff nodded and turned to Jameson and Max. "I'll need each of you to briefly tell me what happened today, and of course I may need to talk to you further as this case develops – if it is a case," he said. "Sometimes these high-strung actresses do unsafe things."

Both men nodded.

Woodruff started with Jameson, who told him what he had earlier told Max about Mary, and gave an accurate account of what happened after.

"Thank you – you can go back to your post now," Woodruff said and turned to Max.

"I had an appointment with Miss Anderson, as I said," Max offered.

"And may I ask what the appointment was about?" Woodruff asked. "I should tell you that my Lieutenant happens to be friends with the lady, so we have a special interest in this, beyond the usual."

That's interesting and maybe we should look into this, Max thought. To Woodruff, he said, "It is for a theatrical endeavor headed by John Jacob Astor, IV."

"Jack Astor?" Woodruff asked.

"That's right," Max replied.

"And he will confirm this?" Woodruff asked.

"Indeed I will." Astor, just arrived, had walked briskly up to Max and Woodruff.

Max sighed, internally. It had taken Astor long enough to get here. Better that Astor lied, if necessary, than Max, who knew less about what would set off a late-19th century police detective than would Astor.

"And may I ask what the theatrical endeavor is about?" Woodruff asked Astor.

"Oh, we don't like to divulge too much about future performances to the public," Astor replied.

"I'm not the public," Woodruff said. "I'm the police. And for all we know, we may yet have a murder on our hands, here."

"Of course," Astor bowed slightly, in deference to police business. "We're hoping Miss Anderson will be performing the part of Hypatia in a new staging of the play after the novel of the same name by Charles Kingsley."

"Hypatia?" Woodruff asked.

"Yes," Astor replied. "Beautiful mathematician, torn apart and murdered by a crowd of Christian fanatics in ancient Alexandria. History reports that they were never brought to justice by what passed as the police back then."

"Let's just hope they weren't coming after Miss Anderson up here," Woodruff replied.

***

Sierra, Max, and Astor were at Bellevue Hospital by the East River an hour later.

"She's much better," the doctor who had brought Mary to the hospital said to Max, "but I don't know when she'll be able to see anyone, with this being a police matter." He pointed to a man in a uniform. "He's a Lieutenant," the doctor said, and went to see another patient down the hall.

The Lieutenant, sensing that he had been talked about, approached Max, Sierra, and Astor.

"James Flannery," he said, and extended a hand to Astor.

"Jack Astor," Astor said and shook the hand.

Sierra and Max each froze, thinking the same thing: he's from the late 20th or early 21st century. The accent was unmistakable. Then they both thought: every care had to be taken not to let James Flannery know that they knew he was not of this era. In addition and more importantly: they had to try not to let this guy know, Lieutenant or whatever he really was, that they were not from this time, either. They both looked at Astor – let him do as much of the talking as possible.

Max extended his hand and muttered his name as unclearly as possible.

Sierra nodded, waited until Flannery extended his hand, then took it and said her name as quietly as possible, too. Let Flannery think she was just shy.

"Let me be honest with you and get right to the point," Flannery said to all three. "First, as it happens, Miss Anderson and I know each other – we're friends – so I have an interest that goes beyond policing in what happened to her. Second, I want *you* to be honest with *me*: when was the last time each of you saw Miss Anderson? Was it earlier today? Don't lie to me – if you do, I'll find out. And I don't believe in giving second chances."

Sierra shook her head no. "We've never met. I'm with him." She gestured to Max.

"Me neither," Max said. "We would have been meeting for the first time at the hotel, as I told Detective Woodruff."

Flannery turned to Astor. "We met late last week, to discuss the play, as I also told Detective Woodruff," Astor said. "And you?"

"Excuse me?" Flannery said.

"You just said that you and she were friends," Astor replied, "so one might ask the same question of you." He didn't like police, but, more important, he could see that Sierra and Max were not themselves, and he figured he might as well do what he could to throw this Flannery a little off.

"You've got a hell of a nerve," Flannery said, now sounding 100% like an early 21st century New York cop to Sierra and Max, or what they had seen of those cops many times in many movies and television shows from and about that period. He jabbed a menacing finger at Astor. "Let me tell you something: I don't care how rich you are. I can still haul your sorry . . . arse into the station and book you."

"Is that so?" Astor asked, calmly. "On what charges? Asking you a perfectly reasonable question?"

Flannery's finger moved closer to Astor's nose, but before he could speak, a police officer hustled up to him. "Miss Anderson would like to see you now, Lieutenant."

***

"Should we talk here, or someplace else?" Max asked Sierra and Astor, after Flannery had withdrawn his finger, given Astor a parting glare, and walked off to see Mary Anderson.

"We can stay here a little longer," Astor said, "in case we can get in and see Mary after Flannery is finished with her."

Max nodded. "Ok, two points, then. First, that asshole's not from this century."

Sierra agreed. "I would say a hundred years later."

"So that's what made the two of you so nervous," Astor said. "Who brought him here – Heron? Maybe we should repair to safer quarters, after all."

Max and Sierra agreed and the three walked to the staircase. They were on the fourth floor.

"And the second point?" Astor asked Max.

"I'm sure we're all thinking the same thing," Max replied. "Do you think Dickson did this?"

***

The three sat in a spacious, noisy saloon about two blocks from the hospital. They had been talking along the way about what they knew about Dickson.

"He was the one who suggested that we contact Mary Anderson," Sierra said. "Why would he do that if he drugged her beforehand – doesn't make much sense."

"I guess not," Max said. "But the fact is none of us know him very well at all."

"As a businessman, I have to go with my instincts," Astor

replied, "and I trust him."

"He was in league with Heron and admits it," Sierra said. "That would also be a strange thing to do, if he was actually still working for Heron – his plan would have been, what, gain our confidence by admitting he used to be with Heron? . . . I don't know, I'm with Jack on this. But let's talk about something else: will Mary support your story about the Hypatia play?"

"I guess that depends on how recovered and alert she really is," Astor replied. "Her interest in Hypatia is no lie, and she knows about us and our involvement with Appleton and Heron."

"Did you really meet with her last week?" Max asked Astor.

"No, I did not," Astor said. "I was making it up as I went along, as they say."

"If Mary Anderson is awake enough to support your Hypatia play story, there's no reason she won't say, yes, she did meet with you last week," Sierra said to Astor.

"That's putting a lot of confidence in a woman who was just drugged unconscious and left in her hotel room," Max said.

"Perhaps she was given the drug earlier, came back to her hotel room, began to undress, and lost consciousness then," Astor said. "Drugs don't all have an immediate effect on the body."

"Which returns us to the question of who drugged her, and why?" Sierra said.

"It's too bad Dickson's on the boat and we can't talk to him about this further," Astor said.

"Which brings us back to my concerns about Dickson," Max said.

"I'll tell you who my chief suspect is," Sierra said.

"Who?" Max and Astor asked in unison.

"Edwin Porter," Sierra replied. "If he found out that she and Dickson were working with us and not for Heron, and he is indeed still working for Heron, then that would give him every motive."

"To kill her or to drug her?" Max asked.

"Maybe both," Sierra said. "Maybe he's clumsy and wanted to kill her, and this is what resulted."

"And not to bring us back yet again to our discussion this morning," Astor said, "but that could also apply to Edison."

"Or Heron himself, if he's here in this town with us now," Sierra said.

Astor nodded gravely.

"He comes in disguises, so he could look like anyone we know – or don't know," Sierra added.

"Could Heron be that Lieutenant Flannery?" Astor wondered.

"I don't think so," Sierra said. "We're talking about facial reconstruction, not a whole body, and Flannery has a very different kind of physique than Heron, who is shorter and less muscular."

"Muscles could be added through exercise," Max said.

"True," Sierra conceded. "But it would take major, dangerous surgery to make him taller, at least in our time. And I don't think Heron could put on that early 21st century New York cop accent that Flannery was spouting when he was angry, whatever Heron might have been able to make himself look like."

Max agreed. "Perhaps we should get back to why I went to

see Mary Anderson in the first place: what are we going to do about Thomas Edison, if he indeed has Heron's *Chronica* and wants to build a Chair?"

***

The door was open, so Flannery walked into to Mary Anderson's room. He had to admit she looked good, even in this situation, propped up by pillows in bed, face still a lot more pale than the last time he had seen her. He was not all that surprised – there were running jokes in his time about deceased young women who came in for autopsies who looked good enough to kiss, and more.

"Lt. Flannery!" she said and gave him a big smile.

"Miss Anderson, I'm sorry we have to meet in such circumstances." He thought, I've daydreamed about you in bed, but not in bed in a hospital. "Are you well enough that I can ask you a few questions?"

"The doctor says I'm fine, and I'll be able to leave in an hour, so go right ahead," Mary said, still smiling.

"Can you tell me what happened to you today?"

"I'll do my best," Mary replied. "I had an early lunch with a few lady friends at Luchows, off Union Square – marvelous place!"

"Yes it is," Flannery said. "My uncle once took me there." He caught himself and said no more about that, since it had been in the next century. "But, please, continue." He always conducted his interviews this way – let the interviewee talk, in his or her own words, before he put ideas in their heads with questions.

"Yes, we had a delicious lunch. Then I returned to my hotel, and Mr. Astor called me – Jack Astor – and asked if I could see a colleague of his—"

"Maxwell Marcus?" Flannery violated his own rule and asked, because the mention of Astor still irritated him.

"Yes, I believe that was his name," Mary said. "And I decided to change into something more suitable for the appointment," she blushed, "God knows what I must look like now."

"Like the beautiful woman you are," Flannery said, and again found himself thinking about what was under those covers.

"Thank you," Mary said, still blushing.

"What happened next?" Flannery asked.

"I'm not sure," Mary said. "I felt a little woozy as I was undressing and . . . the next thing I knew the doctor was standing over me, telling me all was well, but I would need to be brought to the hospital to be sure – I was frightened!"

Flannery looked at her, kindly. "The doctors told me you will indeed be fine."

"Thank you," she said, and reached out and touched his hand.

Flannery took her hand, squeezed it, and put it back down on the bed. "Let's see if we can get what happened in that restaurant into a little more into focus," he said. "Who were your lady friends?"

"Just friends," she said. "I'd rather not get them involved. I can give you their names if you really insist."

"Maybe that won't be necessary," Flannery said, seeing that she was a little distressed at the prospect. "At least, not for now. But who else was in the restaurant – anyone you knew or recognized?"

"Diamond Jim Brady was leaving when we arrived – he is immense!" Mary said.

Flannery nodded. "Anyone else?"

"Just the typical portly older men you'll find in a restaurant like Luchow's," Mary answered. "All mutton chop sideburns to go with the mutton chops on the menu, and mustaches, you know."

Another doctor came into the room – younger than the one who had brought her down here.

"Ok," Flannery said. "I think that's enough for now. Would you like one of my men to escort you back to your hotel, when you're released from here?"

"That should be in less than an hour," the doctored offered.

"Good," Flannery said to him.

"Yes," Mary responded to Flannery, "especially if he is as gallant as you."

Flannery laughed, smiled at Mary, and left the room.

The doctor was saying something, but Mary was not completely listening. She had indeed recognized one of those mustachioed older men at a nearby table, but she didn't want to give his name to this self-impressed officer of the law and saddle the poor man with an unpleasant police interview simply because he had been in the same restaurant as she. He was a well-known and wealthy financier, and a patron of the arts: J. P. Morgan.

CHAPTER 12

[New York City, April, 1999 AD]

F lannery's wife kissed him goodbye at the door. She put her hand gently on his face. "You look tired, honey. You're working too hard."

Flannery took her hand, kissed it tenderly, and left. She didn't know the half of it, he thought. Or maybe it was more than half. He had been in 1899, working nonstop for almost a month, and the only reason he was here in 1999 now was to take care of that Cyril Charles matter for Heron. Fortunately, as far as his wife was concerned, he hadn't been gone at all. All she saw and knew about was the toll it took on his face, living a life in two centuries, a hundred years apart -- living in double-time, as Flannery often characterized his own bizarre life to himself, as he fell asleep late at night in whichever of his two centuries.

The doorman downstairs had the television on, and there was some breaking news about the Senate passing some binding resolution preventing President Clinton from bombing Yugoslavia. That was indeed news to Flannery. His brother was a colonel in the US military stationed in Germany, and Flannery followed military issues pretty carefully. If he remembered correctly – and he was sure he did – the Senate had authorized the U.S. bombing of Yugoslavia in March. The report now on television said that Senator Joseph Biden, a self-styled "pragmatic dove" and a Democrat no less, had spearheaded this morning's vote against Bill Clinton, a

Democratic President. Flannery didn't recall that happening, either.

So what *had* happened? Did he do something in the past that had accidentally changed history? He shook his head, left his high-rise apartment building on the West Side, and took a train downtown to One Police Plaza. He preferred not thinking about these time paradoxes or whatever they were – they gave him more than a headache – but maybe the world was starting to give him no choice.

***

A police captain and a forensic detective were having an animated discussion about something in the lobby of 1PP. Flannery slightly knew the captain and found something about him irritating today. Or maybe this time-traveling was making Flannery more than tired. He was suspicious by nature – most police detectives were, and if you made it to lieutenant, you had it in spades. But Flannery was seeing suspicious things everywhere he looked these days.

He exchanged casual salutes with the captain and nods with the science guy, and heard his usual share of deferential "Lu"s as he walked to the elevator. He got off on his floor, exchanged more nods and salutes, and closed the door after he entered his office. It was all glass in the front, so the closed door wouldn't give him too much privacy, but he needed all the non-interruption he could get to come up with a plan for Cyril Charles.

Heron had given him several photographs of Charles the last time they had talked about him in 1899 – in 1890s "cabinet card" not any future photographic style, so his men and colleagues in 1899 wouldn't be curious if they got a look at the photos – but Flannery hadn't seen anyone who resembled Charles when he'd arrived at the Millennium last night. He had a good eye for faces, but he had to be careful as he looked around. The cover Heron had arranged for him was as a minor mystery writer – enough to get Flannery into the literary club, but not enough to attract any big attention – and unlike cops, writers couldn't just go around staring at people and asking pointed questions, whether in the club or not.

He thought for a minute or two, then buzzed Daisy, the receptionist. "Hey. Could you get me the Millennium Club on the phone?"

"Of course," Daisy said. "Give me a moment." She got back to him just a few minutes later. "It's ringing now for you."

"Thank you," Flannery said.

"Hello," someone at the Millennium picked up the call.

"Yes, this is Lt. Flannery from the NYPD, about a very small matter, so don't be concerned."

"How can I help you, Lieutenant?"

"First, may I ask to whom I am speaking?" Flannery asked.

"Mr. Bertram."

Flannery thought for a quick second. He had met Bertram one or two times at the Millennium Club. Bertram had greeted him at the door, but they hadn't really conversed. The safest thing would be to hang up the phone and try again later, in the hope of getting someone else. But he had told Bertram his name, and the butler or whatever he was might seek to call Flannery back, if the connection were just cut off in midstream. "Thank you," Flannery decided to continue. "Do you have a Cyril Charles working at the Millennium?"

A pause, then, "yes, is he all right?" Bertram asked.

"Absolutely," Flannery reassured Bertram. "As I said, it's a minor matter – about an inheritance, actually – and sometimes they ask the police to come in and dot all the i's." This was also not quite true – the probate court had its own people to do that – but with any luck Bertram was no expert on estate law.

"He's not here today," Bertram said.

"Ok," Flannery responded. "Do you know the next time he'll be expected at the club? Or, can you give me his home phone-number?"

"We don't keep those kinds of schedules," Bertram said, apologetically, "so I can't be sure of the next time he'll be here."

"How about the phone number, then," Flannery pressed.

Bertram hesitated. "I'm sorry – I really can't give out that information to just a disembodied voice on the telephone. I'm sure as a member of law enforcement, you understand."

"Yes, I do, and you're right to safeguard your co-worker's privacy," Flannery said. "I'll see if I can swing by later today or tomorrow."

But he couldn't very well do that – not as a police lieutenant, and risk blowing his crucial cover at the Millennium as a writer. He thanked Bertram, hung up the phone, and frowned. Strike one. He'd have to come up with another way of getting to Cyril Charles.

***

He put Plan B into motion a few hours later. He assigned two young, gung-ho detectives, Allison Barnes and Dennis Molloy, to the case. He gave them pictures of Cyril Charles, which he had one of the lab guys reproduce in normal 1990s format, and instructed the two to surveil the Millennium from a suitable distance for any sign of Charles. Flannery estimated he could do this for at least a day or two without attracting any undue interest from the brass.

He got some action the next day. He got a call from Barnes, who was standing about a block to the west of the Millennium, in a different place from her partner, who was stationed about a block to the east of the club. "I'm sure it's him," Barnes told Flannery.

"Excellent," Flannery said. "Call Molloy and let him know. See if you can quietly take Charles into custody before he reaches the Millennium – in fact, as far away as possible. If you can't – or if there are too many nosy civilians around – then follow Charles to the club, and do what I told you to do with those papers." He had given both Barnes and Molloy some police paperwork indicating there was some concern about the structural integrity of the upper library floor of the Millennium. He needed Barnes or Molloy posted there, in case Bertram alerted Charles about the police interest in him, and Charles tried to high-tail it out of this century with a Chair.

Barnes let Flannery know she understood, quickly briefed Molloy, and followed Cyril Charles at the fastest pace she could without attracting attention. She and Molloy were in plain clothes, as most NYPD detectives usually were, so that helped. Cyril Charles wasn't walking very fast, and that helped even more. She was getting close to him when she heard a shriek—

A car had apparently backed into a hotdog stand, which had fallen over on its side and hit a woman passerby who had cried out. Barnes made a quick decision. She couldn't leave this scene, without making sure the woman was ok. The water that boiled the hotdogs could easily have scalded the woman. Barnes helped the woman to her feet, and quickly looked her over. She seemed all right – no burns or any other damage.

"Are you ok, Ma'am?" Barnes asked the woman, who she guessed was in her 40s.

The woman exhaled. "Yes, I believe I am – I was just startled.

Thank you."

"Good," Barnes said and looked down the street. Charles was entering the Millennium Club. It was obviously far too late for her to stop him.

Molloy was at the front of the club a moment later. It was too late for him to stop Charles, too.

She called him on his cell phone as she quickly walked to the club. "Get in there, show them the papers, and do your thing in front of the spiral stairs – under no circumstances can you let Cyril Charles get up there."

***

Barnes arrived at the Millennium Club less than a minute later. With Molloy upstairs, her job was to take Charles into custody either inside the club, or, if he tried to leave, right outside.

Flannery had shown her and Molloy blueprints of the club, but he was not sure they were accurate or complete, in particular regarding whether there was a back exit which was not shown in the architect's drawings. These old 19th-century buildings were honeycombed with secret passages and exits.

She called Molloy. "Any sign of him up there?"

"Negative," he answered.

She walked into the club and encountered a doorman, well dressed and who looked to be in his late 20s – the same age as she and Molloy. She produced her papers and her best smile. "I need to speak with Mr. Cyril Charles – just a small matter, nothing serious," she said.

"I don't believe he is in the club today," the doorman answered in the kind of British accent she just loved, but didn't have time for today.

"Please don't lie to me, sir," she said and withdrew her smile completely. "I saw Mr. Charles walk into this establishment not three minutes ago."

The doorman flushed. "I assure you I'm not lying. I honestly haven't seen Mr. Charles today."

She knew he was lying, and felt like arresting him right here, British accent and all, for obstructing an investigation. But she had a feeling that's not what the Lieutenant would want. In fact, he had not told them anything about what this urgent need to detain Mr. Charles was about.

"Who's in charge here?" she limited herself to saying, then lied herself. "I believe you," she said, by way of apology, and she gave him another smile.

"Mr. Bertram," he said.

***

Mr. Bertram and Mr. Charles were on the second floor. They knew that Molloy was standing guard by the spiral stairs, and they assumed that other police were either already in the club or would soon be entering.

"What do you suggest?" Charles asked Bertram, calm as can be.

"Let's turn their very deceit about the structural integrity of the club against them," Bertram replied, with equal equanimity. He quickly and quietly assembled several of the staff, and gave them instructions.

***

The doorman was taking Barnes up the stairs to the second floor, walking very slowly. "Can we do any better than this snail's pace?" she asked him.

"I'm sorry, but the club's rules prohibit rushing about," was his reply.

Barnes cursed under her breath—

"What's going on?" she suddenly demanded. At least 15 or 20 people, mostly older, heavy-set men, appeared at the top of the stairs and began running down. So much for the club rules.

Another who looked like a butler approached and spoke quickly to her doorman, who turned to Barnes. "The building may be in danger of collapsing," he said, face red again. "We're evacuating."

"No," Barnes started to say, "that's all—"

But the fleeing club members nearly knocked Barnes and the doorman down, and were now pouring out the door.

Barnes tried frantically to see if Cyril Charles was among the people leaving. She was sure he had to be, but she didn't see him, and then another group of elderly men were running down the stairs, one nearly tripped and she caught him, and she thought she caught sight of Charles exiting with this wave of club members.

Molloy came down from the upper floor and joined her. The two looked on helplessly as the last of some 30 odd men between them and the front door slowly pushed their way outside.

***

Barnes conveyed the bad news to Flannery, who wasn't happy at all with it, but mostly contained himself. "We'll get him another day," he told Barnes. "You and Molloy did the best you could. These butlers or doormen or whatever the hell they are apparently are a lot smarter than I thought."

He knew, of course, that they were far more than butlers or doormen, if they were that at all. They were the guardians and ushers of the Chairs. But given that job, one thing didn't make sense to him. If Heron was the inventor of the Chairs, why were Charles and his buddies not loyal to Heron but to his enemies? They presumably were loyal to this Sierra Waters woman. What hold did she have on them?

He put out a BOLO – Be On the Look Out – for Cyril Charles. The same thing applied as with his attempt to have him taken into custody by Barnes and Molloy. The brass would barely notice if he apprehended him later today or tomorrow. And if they wondered what was going on, there were enough drug and gang crackdowns and roundups underway that he could connect Charles to that. Those crackdowns were one of the highlights of the Giuliani administration – everyone was proud of them.

So what had just happened at the Millennium was strike two. Now it was time to try Plan C. Hey, it wasn't against the law to mix numbers and letters and metaphors.

***

Flannery got lucky again, this time less than an hour later. A beat cop spotted someone who fitted Cyril Charles' description in a coffee shop on Waverly Street, near New York University. Flannery immediately called Barnes, and ordered her and her partner to get down there. Then he grabbed his coat and left the office. "I'm going up to the Village to supervise a little operation," he told Daisy.

He got a uniformed cop to drive him and told her to put on the speed. He had told the beat cop not to arrest Charles – he doubted the beat cop would be up for what Charles might have up his sleeve, after the fiasco at the Millennium – but he told the cop to stand outside the restaurant and not let Charles leave.

Traffic was heavy – of course it was, it was always choked in this part of the city, any time of day. He called Barnes. "Are you there yet?"

"Five minutes ETA," she replied.

"Take him into custody if you get there before me."

"Understood," she said.

She called Flannery about five minutes later. He was less than ten minutes away now, himself.

"Lieutenant?" she asked.

"Yes – you there?"

"Not quite," she said. "And there's some sort of police action going on in Washington Square Park, right off Waverly, between us and Charles."

"What do you mean?" Flannery demanded.

"It looks like we're rounding up people in the park," Barnes replied. "Did you know about that? Wait – I heard some gun shots."

"Our side?"

"Not clear," Barnes said. "I think Molloy and I should get out of the car now and approach the coffee shop on foot."

"Do it," Flannery said. "And be careful."

***

Flannery called into headquarters and discovered there was indeed some sort of big drug bust underway in Washington Square Park. Dammit, if he had known about this, it had slipped his mind, with all the pressure and exhaustion he was feeling from the time travel.

He got out of the car about two blocks from the coffee shop, and approached quickly on foot. He tried to call Barnes but couldn't get through. One thing Giuliani had yet to do was upgrade this antiquated telecom!

He could hear gunfire now, too. He walked around a corner, and saw at least four men running quickly towards him, turning rapidly and firing at whatever was behind them, likely cops in pursuit. For crissakes, they had semi-automatics.

Flannery pulled out his revolver. They saw him before he could say anything and they started firing. He ducked, fired back, and realized he was hit in the shoulder. It hurt. He hadn't planned on doing this, and hadn't put on a bullet-proof vest.

The shooters passed right by him. One or two looked wounded.

Strike three. He had come back to 1999 to take Cyril Charles out of action, but the only person who would be out of action for a while now was Flannery himself.

CHAPTER 13

[New York City, April, 1899 AD]

Heron was beginning to feel stymied. He had drugged Mary Anderson yesterday, in the expectation of questioning her under the influence in her hotel, and finding out what she knew about Appleton and the *Chronica*, but something had gone wrong. Maybe she had consumed more alcohol than usual before lunchtime – he had no way of knowing what was already in her system when he slipped the colorless, odorless drug from the future into her beverage as he distracted her waiter at the bar with an urgent request that sent the waiter back to the kitchen for the necessary few minutes.

But the result was that instead of becoming loquacious, she fell into a deep sleep in her hotel room, and all hell had broken loose. When Heron approached her hotel, looking like J. P. Morgan as he always did now, he saw a gaggle of police and medical helpers and decided the better part of valor was staying away.

He learned this morning from Flannery what had happened. He knew that Flannery was somewhat smitten by the actress and was suspicious that Heron had something to do with her drugging. But Heron did not admit it, indeed acted surprised about it, and whatever Flannery may have thought, he didn't dare confront Heron about it. Meanwhile, Flannery hadn't accomplished much or anything regarding the Cyril Charles problem – Heron had seen Cyril Charles again at the Millennium, after he had requested that Flannery do something in 1999 to keep Charles out of the club. Possibly the Cyril Charles that Heron had seen again in the club was a younger version, or a version of Charles that existed before Flannery collared him, as these New York police liked to say, in the next century. But Heron could just feel in his marrow that Flannery had not succeeded, and Heron had learned to trust those feelings over the years.

He might have to get another face in the future. But even though he of course knew that he could come right back here and not lose more than a minute, he hated to take any break in his lifetime from what he was doing here – even a day away from 1899 in his day-to-day time could be disruptive.

Heron increasingly wondered how those renegade functionaries at the clubs around the world – in New York, London, and Athens – had emerged. He would need to address that after he retrieved the *Chronica*. In a sense it was part of the larger problem of unreliable assistants he was dealing with right now. It stemmed from the fundamental unpredictability of human beings.

Thomas Edison was a prime example. He had become even less responsive and more monosyllabic. His hardness of hearing seemed to worsen whenever Heron asked him a question. Heron suspected the uncouth inventor was hiding something. Flannery the police lieutenant was inefficient, but Edison the great inventor could well be a traitor.

Edwin Porter, Heron realized, was his most reliable worker now. He was the easiest to dominate at this juncture. He arranged a meeting with him at their favorite seafood restaurant.

Porter looked harried, Heron thought, as he joined him at their table near the window. "You heard what happened to Mary Anderson, I assume," was Porter's greeting.

"Yes. A shame, but I understand her recovery is complete," Heron said. "One of the perils of too much alcohol too early in the day, I suppose."

"She told me her doctor told her it was a lot stronger than alcohol," Porter said. "She was drugged."

Heron nodded slowly. "Unfortunately, this is all too common throughout history – men administering drugs to women without their knowledge, to get what they want from them."

"But this was apparently not done for sexual advantage," Porter said. "No sexual liberties were taken with her, thank God, according to the doctors. Who do you think did this?"

"I do not know," Heron said. "The answer would depend on how much of the drug was given to her, how quickly it took effect, and when it was administered. But I do not believe medical science is yet sophisticated enough to provide those answers."

"You were at Luchow's earlier in the day, as was she," Porter said, and summoned enough courage to look Heron in the eye.

"You think I was the one who drugged her? Why?" Heron asked.

"You don't trust her, you think she is compromising my work with you," Porter said.

"There is someone else who may fit that description: your boss, Thomas Alva Edison," Heron said.

"Edison?" Porter asked, skeptically. "He's on his high horse as far as morality, yes, but he's also nonviolent. I doubt he would disrespect a woman enough to introduce drugs to her body without her consent!"

"But you think I would?" Heron countered.

"I don't know you as well as I know Edison," Porter replied. "And as far as we know, he was nowhere near Mary on the day in question."

Heron nodded. "That is a fair point, and I respect your honesty and courage in sharing your suspicions about me to my face. Can we turn to another, related point?"

"Yes," Porter said, not completely satisfied with Heron's response by any means, but grateful to be off the subject of Mary drugged senseless, which Porter himself had raised.

"Would you feel comfortable looking into whatever Edison may have concluded privately with William Appleton in the past few months?" Heron requested.

***

The April sun was kind, Porter thought, as it shone on his face and he walked towards the Hudson River to catch a ferry to see Edison in New Jersey. But few people in this world were kind, certainly not Heron or Edison, both of whom Porter found himself in the uncomfortable position of being in the employ of right now.

He didn't feel right spying on Edison, not for Heron or anyone. Edison had given Porter his start, and Porter was sure that in time he would become known as a great photographer of stories in motion, and that his moving pictures might even exceed the theater and the book as vehicles of narrative.

But neither could he afford to offend Heron at this point. Porter was too deeply entwined in the plans of this bizarre man to cut himself loose. He smiled ruefully – now, there was a narrative fit for a photo-play, the story of what he knew about Heron and his activities, but it would take a photo-play a hundred times or more the length of the photo-plays Porter was now making, to tell this story – this insanely incredible story that Porter was now apparently inextricably a part of.

***

Porter boarded the ferry and continued enjoying the sun as the boat made its way across the river. The Hudson Tubes were nearing completion. They would provide train service between New York and New Jersey, and would provide a difficult choice for Porter, who loved train travel but also the outdoors. He lived in a time of difficult choices, and they promised only to increase for him in the near future.

The ferry docked. Porter bid goodbye to the river and boarded a train to West Orange and Edison's Black Maria. For Porter, the Black Maria was the center of the world. It was the first studio devoted not to still photography, but the production of moving photography, which was Porter's life's work. The Black Maria had been in operation only six years. William Dickson had produced his *Fred Ott's Sneeze* here, and now the mantel was passing to Porter. At least, he hoped so. Porter sighed. Edison was talking about building a new studio for the photo-play in New York City, and demolishing the Black Maria. Porter welcomed new production facilities, and they would be much more convenient for him in New York. But in his heart, he felt nothing could replace the Black Maria.

He sighed again. Life used to be far simpler for him, when he was not yet working for Edison – that had only started this year – and the only contact he had had with Heron was in a book he had read with great interest as a boy, about ancient Greeks and Romans who were ahead of their time in their thinking and inventions. Porter never imagined in his wildest daydreams that a man from this book would tear free of its pages and meet him in person.

He closed his eyes and let the train rock him to sleep. Time for him to stop worrying so much and attend to the matter at hand. If Edison had obtained the *Chronica* from Appleton, that was something that Porter would indeed like to know. The fate of the world could depend upon it. But what he would do about it – offer to work with Edison to build a time travel machine, or tell Heron that Edison indeed had Heron's cyclopedia for its construction, if that's what it was – well, that was something that Porter had yet to fully decide.

[West Orange, New Jersey, April, 1899 AD]

Edison was in good spirits on this day, sitting behind his desk, running his hands across several manuscripts, talking with gusto about the future.

"I'm glad you came out here today," Edison said. "I had something I wanted to discuss with you."

"Yes?" This was just like Edison. Porter had called him, telling his boss he had something he wanted to talk to him about, and Edison from the moment Porter walked into his room started talking about something on Edison's mind. But Porter had learned to respect that mind, and usually welcomed hearing what was on it.

"I know you follow the theater," Edison said.

"Yes, I do," Porter agreed.

"Of course you do. Your lady friend Mary Anderson has the made the theater her canvas," Edison said.

Porter tried not to wince. Was his boss baiting him? Maybe Heron was right. "Yes," was all Porter said.

Edison's hand stopped on one of the manuscripts. He picked it up off the desk, and almost caressed it.

Was this the *Chronica*? Porter wondered. Did Edison first mention Mary because she was indeed somehow connected to its acquisition by Edison, which in turn was connected to why she was drugged? No, it couldn't be that easy.

Edison slowly leafed through the manuscript and smiled. "Are you familiar with *The Great Train Robbery*?"

"The melodrama by Scott Marble? It was on stage a few years ago, but I did not get a chance to see it," Porter said.

"This is the script," Edison said and hefted the manuscript. Then he handed it to be Porter. "Read it, please. Then tell me your impressions – and if you think it could be made into a photo-play. I have in mind something much longer than what I have been doing here – perhaps as long as ten minutes. Is making a photo-play like that something that might appeal to you? It would be a big step up from the wax museum where I found you, and the exhibitions of photo-plays you've begun to assemble for me. If it worked, it could make you nearly as famous as me!" Edison chuckled.

Porter was speechless. He finally said, "Yes, it indeed appeals, and very much," and took the script.

"So please do let me know what you think of it," Edison said.

Porter nodded.

"And what did you come to see me about?" Edison asked him.

***

Porter never did tell Edison the real purpose of his visit, and instead talked to Edison about some ideas Porter had for the new studio in New York City. Porter loved the Marble script – he would have made sure he loved it, in any case, given the path it provided for Porter to make a moving picture from it – but he did indeed love it. His head popped with ideas the first time he read it in Edison's office, with Edison looking right at him. He came back two days later with a new script that he had written, appropriate for a photo-play, photographed in the outdoors. Edison had already worked out arrangements with

Scott Marble, who had agreed to split the writing credits with whomever Edison had hired to write the photo-play.

Porter came out to the Black Maria several days a week, much more time than he had spent there before, to discuss the moving picture. He also made time to see Heron when so requested, and told him that in order to find out what Edison knew about the *Chronica*, Porter would have to gradually build up his relationship with Edison, do more work for him in New Jersey. Whether Heron believed it was not clear, but he didn't tell Porter to stop.

On one rainy day at the beginning of May, Porter was in Edison's office when the inventor was called away – some sort of problem in the garden at his home, also in West Orange, in Llewellyn Park, that Edison had to attend to personally. Porter was engrossed in *The Great Train Robbery* manuscript. "Keep working," Edison told him, "I'll be back soon."

But Porter couldn't help looking at Edison's desk after he left. It was a magnet for his eyes. He needed a brief respite from *The Great Train Robbery* anyway. Feeling like a thief, but unable to resist, Porter walked over to Edison's desk, and looked as quickly as he could at the many manuscripts upon it. He stopped, and he thought his heart stopped, too, when he saw one written in Greek.

He couldn't read a word of the language. This could be any manuscript written in Greek. But he picked it up. He looked over his shoulder, to make sure Edison hadn't returned, though he knew he would have heard him open the door if he had returned. Porter went through a few pages, hoping for a glimpse of something he could understand. He cursed silently at his ignorance of the language, then realized that a letter had been stapled on the inside of the back cover. The paper the letter was written upon was very thin, and smaller than the manuscript pages, so Porter hadn't noticed it before.

He again looked over his shoulder and read quickly through the letter, which was written in English. He saw "time travel" and his heart nearly burst out of his white shirt. The letter was signed "Henry Ford".

Porter had heard of Ford. His specialty was motorized vehicles, not moving pictures. But that made sense – a motorized vehicle had much more in common with a time travel machine than did a moving picture, even though photography captured images and saved them through time. But a motorized vehicle and a time travel machine would both move people, not images.

Porter heard someone at the door and almost dropped the manuscript on the floor. He regained his composure, put the manuscript back on the desk in what he hoped was the exact place he had found it, and walked to his chair to greet Edison.

It wasn't Edison. It was a man Edison had sent to his office with refreshments for Porter. But the interruption was enough to keep Porter in his seat, reading *The Great Train Robbery* photo-play script, until Edison returned about 20 minutes later.

[New York City, May, 1899 AD]

Porter had some serious thinking to do. *The Great Train Robbery* photo-play was on its way. Edison had approved the new script, and was beginning to talk about production. It would still be a year or two before the moving picture was actually made – actors had to be hired, a suitable location had to be found – the making of moving pictures moved slowly, and that was to the good, as Edison liked to say. He was a perfectionist in everything, and Porter thought that was one of Edison's best qualities.

But that left Heron, and the manuscript Porter had seen on

Edison's desk. Porter mostly wished he had never seen it. But he had, and the urge to tell Heron about it during their now weekly meetings weighed on Porter like a poorly consumed meal that demanded expulsion.

Porter finally gave into it.

Heron's face blanched and his eyes burned with some kind of emotion. "What did the letter from Henry Ford say," he asked, when Porter had gotten to that part of his brief story.

"I didn't have time to fully comprehend it," Porter replied. "I believe it was talking about the extreme difficulties of constructing a time travel engine."

Heron laughed, cruelly. "Yes, indeed." He didn't believe that Henry Ford or Thomas Edison or anyone from this era could construct a Chair even with a blueprint far more explicit than what Heron had foolishly laid out in the *Chronica* – and it would take years, decades, of work to situate the Chairs in suitable places like the Millennium and Parthenon clubs, and the coffee house or bar or whatever it now was in Athens. But that wasn't the point – which was, that bringing someone like Henry Ford into this was a big step worse than merely having the *Chronica* in hand. It was as if the cancer of knowledge about time travel had metastasized to a far more worrisome organ, a big step closer to being fatal to the entirety of human history, or at least Heron's plans for it. Henry Ford was not an inventor. He was an engineer – much like Heron in his original training – which made Ford far more dangerous. He was a practical man who knew how to make things work.

"Thank you," Heron said, sincerely, to Porter. "Stick with your moving pictures. Your *Great Train Robbery* will be remembered as one of the great pioneering works in the history of cinema, as I believe the Lumière brothers in France are now calling what you do."

And Heron pushed back his seat, stood, and left the seafood restaurant near Grand Central Terminal.

Porter looked after him, immensely moved by the compliment, despite everything that had happened, because it had been made by someone Porter had read about when he was 12 years old, someone whose work with ancient zoetrope devices made Heron the ultimate pioneer in the craft Porter was devoting his life to. The incomprehensibility of admiring a pioneer who likely became a pioneer because he had traveled back in time with knowledge from the future did not bother Porter. Nor did he realize for a moment that Heron had played upon his role as an ancient filmmaker to assemble around him his chosen filmmakers to do his bidding at the end of the 19th century.

***

Heron preferred his own company, at least at first, when faced with impending crisis. He walked slowly up Fifth Avenue, and hoped no one said hello to him as J. P. Morgan.

His work here in the 1890s had mostly failed. His assistants had proved unreliable and worse, as they often had in history. Dickson, Flannery, Edison either had been unable to accomplish what he'd needed, or had turned outright against him. Only Edwin Porter, probably the dimmest of the bunch, at least of the inventors, had shown some loyalty – though that, too, was belated.

Time to make some drastic changes, especially in his alliances. Sierra Waters had every right to kill him on sight, as Flannery might say, but she and Heron did now have a coincidence of interest. Heron believed she would not want time travel in common use in the world any more than would Heron.

What would be the best way to approach her, with the

equivalent of a white flag or palms open to the sky? Heron needed to think about how he could convince Sierra Waters to help him extricate this perilous knowledge of time travel that she had brought to the doorstep of the 20th century via Appleton.

Conversely, if she refused to help him, but was within striking distance when she rebuffed his offer, that would not be a bad place her to be for his purposes, either.

CHAPTER 14

[New York City, May, 1899 AD]

Sierra, Max, Astor, and Mary Anderson were seated around a table in one of the offices in Astor's hotel. He had hastily called the meeting, at Mary Anderson's request.

"I believe Thomas Edison is in some way connected to the *Chronica*," Mary repeated what she had earlier told Astor. "Edwin Porter wears his heart on his sleeve, the dear man. He would never tell me outright what his boss Edison was doing, but when I asked him about the *Chronica*, his face turned beet red. And when I asked him about his work with Edison a little later, he chirped like a bird about a new photo-play he was producing, a Western based on a play, but when I mentioned the *Chronica* again, he looked like the cat that swallowed the canary, and the bird was still flying around inside him."

Sierra nodded. "We have had Edison on our short list of people who may have somehow obtained the *Chronica* from William Appleton for several months. You understand 'short list'"? she asked Mary and Astor.

They both nodded.

"Heron is likely involved in this," Max said.

"You believe he was the one who drugged me, on the day we were supposed to meet last month," Mary said to Max. "I still feel guilty about being dead to the world when you came up to see me that day." And now her own face turned red, because her doctor had helpfully told her, with a slight leer that he couldn't disguise, that she had been partially nude when discovered, unconscious, on her bed.

"Heron is the only one with a motive," Max said, "if he had any reason to believe you were helping us."

"But I saw no one strange on that day, in the morning or at lunch before I returned to my hotel," Mary mused. "There was nothing untoward at Luchow's. Just J. P. Morgan entertaining some friends in his usual grand way."

Astor furrowed his brow. "What?" he asked Mary.

"What about what?" she asked, good naturedly. "Luchow's?"

"You said you saw J. P. Morgan there, in the early afternoon, having lunch?"

"Yes," Mary said.

"Is that significant?" Max asked.

"You said *you* were meeting J. P. Morgan that day," Sierra said to Astor, "before Max went off to see Mary, when you were with us in the lobby – you said that's why you couldn't see Mary, and you would set up the appointment for Max and Mary."

"That's right – and I indeed saw J. P. Morgan, it was in a saloon uptown, at the same time Mary saw him in Luchow's, on 14th Street," Astor said, emphatically.

"He couldn't be in two places at the same time," Mary said, "unless . . . ." She then realized what the other three were thinking. "Unless one of them was Heron!"

***

Astor bundled Mary into a motorized carriage that returned

her to her hotel. He then proceeded "with all due haste" with Sierra and Max in their own motorized carriage to the Millennium Club. Mary had objected – she wanted to go with them to the club – but Astor kindly insisted that she not. "It could be dangerous – you have already been laid low by that man!"

"What are the chances that he's there now?" Max asked, as their vehicle approached the club.

Astor shrugged. "J. P. Morgan has long been in frequent attendance at the club. If Heron has a face that looks like J. P.'s – if there are two men with J. P. Morgan's face out and about now – then I guess that makes it twice as likely that we'll encounter some version of J. P. Morgan, real or impersonated, if I have my mathematics right."

"Possibly more likely than that," Sierra said, "since Heron as J. P. Morgan might well be using the club more often than the real J. P. – to get to the Chairs."

Astor grunted. "Of course."

Their carriage arrived at the club. "Please wait here," Astor told the driver, and thanked him.

"Good man – he's on retainer," Astor said to Sierra and Max, as the three walked right up to the front door of the club.

Mr. Bertram opened it.

"Mr. Bertram," Astor and Sierra said at the same time. "You look a little peaked," Astor said to Bertram, with a little concern. "Are you well?"

Bertram nodded. "Just a little matter in another time," he said. "I'm sure you understand. All's well that ends well," he added, with a slight smile.

"Right," Astor said. "No need to explain."

Bertram nodded.

"We came here to see J. P. Morgan," Sierra said. "Is he here today?"

"Yes, he is indeed!" Bertram said, pleased to be no longer on the subject of what had made him peaked. "In the first-floor lounge, I believe, under the Raphael nude. I saw him there conversing with several men about 20 minutes ago."

"Thank you!" Astor said.

The three walked to the top of the wide staircase. The lounge was off to the left. They stopped to talk.

"We're unarmed – we have no weapons," Max said to Astor. "You didn't give us much notice before the meeting with Mary – we barely had time to dress."

"We should have thought of that before we rushed up here," Sierra said. "What do you suggest we do? If we leave now, to get help or weapons, J. P. Morgan could be gone when we return."

"Here is what we'll do," Astor said. "I know J. P. Morgan well enough to have conversations with him about events we both attended, which Heron could not possibly know about, unless he copied J. P.'s brain as well as his face. Let me talk to him, and the two of you stay back."

"What will you do if he's Heron and he attacks you?" Max asked.

"He wouldn't dare – not here, in front of everyone in the lounge," Astor replied.

Sierra and Max reluctantly agreed to let Astor go ahead with his plan. They couldn't risk entering the lounge – if J. P. Morgan in there was really Heron, he would recognize them instantly. They agreed to stand where they were until Astor returned.

***

Astor returned an excruciating nine minutes later, with a big smile.

"It's not Heron, it's the real J. P. Morgan!" he said triumphantly.

"What are you so happy about?" Max asked him. "Our purpose in coming here was to find Heron not J. P. Morgan."

"I'm happy he wasn't Heron and didn't kill me!" Astor said, still jovial.

"How can you be sure he's not Heron?" Sierra asked.

"I told you, I know J. P. fairly well," Astor replied. "How about we test this another way: I introduce the two of you to J. P. Morgan, and see if anything about him strikes you as Heron."

Sierra and Max nodded slowly.

"By the way, J. P recalled his meeting with me on the day Mary was drugged – so he could not be the J. P. Morgan she saw in Luchow's," Astor told them, as the three walked to J. P. Morgan's table.

Introductions were made, conversations were had, and Sierra and Max were satisfied that this man was definitely not Heron. Astor pleaded that he and his friends had other engagements, thanked J. P. for his time and the libations he had bought them, and left with Sierra and Max.

"In a future time, we could contact the police and they could put out an all-points bulletin to apprehend someone who looked like J. P. Morgan, now anywhere other than in the Millennium Club, and we would have a chance of locating him," Max said.

"I would love to see such a time," Astor said, with that look in his eyes that he always had whenever Max or Sierra talked about the future.

***

Astor left for a business appointment. Sierra and Max went back to the hotel, where she made her weekly telephone call to Geoffreys to inquire about Appleton's heath and speak to Appleton if possible.

"He's worse than ever," Sierra later told Max, who had taken a walk around the block to do some thinking.

"Were you able to talk to him?" Max asked.

"Barely," Sierra said, her voice constricted with emotion. "He was barely responsive. All I could say to him was 'I love you'. I think he understood that." Her eyes smarted with unshed tears, as they often did when she thought about Appleton.

Max put his arms around her and kissed her gently on the temple. "Why is he in such bad shape? His death date is still a few months away, in October. Is Heron poisoning him? Maybe he got in to see William as J. P. Morgan."

"I don't know," Sierra said and shook her head. "I think it's just that the months that he lived in other times – trying to help me, saving my life in ways I probably don't even know about – are part of the total time he has for life. So he's actually older at this date right now than he was originally in 1899, before he got involved in all of this. It's easy to lose track of that." And now there were tears on her face.

Max held her tightly. "Why can't we extend his life, get him into the future to get some medical attention that can save him?" They had been over this before, many times, and Max had never been satisfied with the answer.

"I asked about that, more than once, when he was healthy," Sierra said, "and he always refused. He said he wanted to die when he was due to die – he didn't want the time travel to change that. A part of him wants to be with his wife again. A part of him feels that he has already disrupted the natural order of events enough, with everything he has done for me. We don't even know what he's dying of – the obituaries don't list a cause, and give the impression he just died of old age."

"I know," Max said, softly, "but he's only slightly over middle aged by our mid-21st-century standards, which makes it especially hard for us to just go along with him on this." Looking into the cause of Appleton's death had long been one of the things he and Sierra had wanted to do, and it had remained that way, as the two had been caught up with one more urgent threat after another.

"He's too weak to travel anywhere now anyway," Sierra said. "He hasn't been to the Millennium Club in almost a year."

[New York City, 2087 AD]

Heron entered the reconstruction facility at the New York University Medical Center on First Avenue and 30th Street. This had taken a lot of doing. Unlike face stylings and remakes, which once had been difficult but now could be done in a beauty salon from just a good photograph, a full body reconstruction required a hospital and DNA from the body to be emulated. That was the only way to really get everything from the physique to the voice. And the voice was rarely a perfect match, since speech patterns depended upon upbringing, regional accents, and other factors that had nothing to do with genes.

The procedure was safe enough – otherwise, Heron would have traveled further into the future to get it – but it was not particularly pleasant or easy on the psyche. Finding yourself with a new face was traumatic enough. Finding yourself in a new body could take months of adjustment, and no new procedures in the future made that any better. Heron didn't care. He knew he'd adjust more quickly than most. And his needs demanded this.

Getting the DNA hadn't been easy. A doctor had to be carefully approached and copiously bribed. But Heron had no choice. There were only so many times he could go in and out of the club without being seen by Charles or Bertram or their treacherous ilk. Fortunately, he long ago developed a way to disguise his use of the Chairs. But he had no way to disguise his presence in the club.

A very attractive doctor beckoned him to follow down the hall. It had been a long time, too long, since he had sampled the sweet pleasures of the flesh, of any kind. He would have to see to that, and the many pursuits he had neglected, when his *Chronica* was back in the place it belonged: nonexistence, except in Heron's head.

[New York City, May, 1899 AD]

Sierra received a telephone call at the hotel from Mr. Bertram, two days after her encounter with the real J. P. Morgan.

"Mr. Bertram!" she said. "Is everything ok? I don't believe you have ever contacted me on the phone before."

"I try not to," Bertram said.

Sierra chuckled. She could tell from his voice that this was about nothing bad. "But you made an exception this time," she said.

"Yes. I just received a call from William Henry Appleton – he's been quite ill, you know."

"Yes, I know," Sierra said. "He was able to call you?"

"Yes," Bertram said. "I was surprised to hear directly from him, too. I've been speaking with Appleton's man Geoffreys for the past few months, whenever Appleton needed to communicate anything regarding club business to me."

"That's wonderful!" Sierra said. "Thanks so much for letting me know!"

"There's more," Bertram said.

"Yes?"

"Mr. Appleton wanted to speak to you and wasn't quite sure where to reach you – he said his memory isn't what it used to be."

"Did you give him my number here at the hotel?" Sierra asked.

"I wanted to," Bertram said, "but giving out a telephone number, even at a hotel, even when requested by a trusted member, is against club policy. So I told him I would pass his request on to you."

***

Max had gone downstairs to fetch the morning newspapers. Sierra couldn't wait.

She called Appleton. Geoffreys took the call. "Yes, he is eager to speak with you," he told her. "I shall get him for you."

"My dear," a warm familiar voice soon said to her. "I know you've been trying to talk to me. I don't know how much longer I will have, but I'm feeling a little better today. In fact, if you are available, I thought I might even hazard a visit to see you at the club."

"No, no, let me come to Wave Hill," Sierra said. "No need to exhaust yourself! You need to conserve your energy."

"But I want to," Appleton said. "It would make me feel better – not only to see you, but see you in the Millennium Club."

***

Sierra made an appointment to see Appleton at the club in two hours. Max returned. Sierra hugged him hard, and told him what had happened. "And you come along, too. He'll want to see you, too," she said.

The phone rang again. "I hope he didn't change his mind, or realize he's still too weak – we can easily go up to Wave Hill today," she said to Max and picked up the phone. "Hello?"

"Please don't hang up," a familiar voice said to her, softly and slowly. "Please just listen, for a moment."

"Who is this?" she demanded. But she knew instantly who was on the phone. The voice was indelibly seared into her soul. It was Heron.

CHAPTER 15

[New York City, May, 1899 AD]

Heron sat in the bar in the Millennium Club, slowly nursing a beer. This was the best way. He had realized, as he walked down the hall with that attractive doctor in 2087, fired up by the seductive scent, that his looking like Appleton, even completely, and sounding like him, would not work for his purposes. Sierra Waters knew the real Appleton too well to be fooled for more than a moment. For her to ever really believe that Heron was Appleton, Heron would have had to have taken Appleton's mind as well as his face, bodily appearance, and voice – and that trick was beyond any technology Heron had ever come across, even in the furthest reaches of the future.

He assumed that Bertram and Charles, if they were here, had already recognized him. What could they do? Call the police? And tell them, what? A man from the future and the past is here in our little club, a man who created the means of time travel that brought him here? The two would be carted away to a lunatic asylum, as it was called in this time. No, the most those toads would do is alert Sierra Waters, and he had just done that.

He became aware of three people who entered the far side of the dining area. Sierra Waters and Maxwell Marcus, accompanied by Bertram. They saw Heron. They neither fled nor rushed him with weapons drawn. That was good.

Bertram accompanied the couple halfway across the room, then stopped, watching as Sierra and Max approached Heron's table. What did Bertram expect him to do? Pull out a weapon himself and kill the two or three of them? That's not how he operated. And if he had intended on doing harm here, just how would Bertram have been able to stop him?

Heron rose as Sierra and Max reached the table. Their clothes were damp, as if they had been caught in a downpour. They sat. Bertram receded.

"Thank you for coming here," Heron said. "I knew you would."

"You killed a lot of people," Max said, darkly.

"Not really," Heron responded. "I chose not to stop the killing of an android impersonating Hypatia – not a person, not Hypatia – in Alexandria. That impersonation was no doubt your doing," he said to Sierra.

"It was not," she said.

Heron spread his hands. "I accept that – the android acted on its own – that's surely possible. I had Synesius killed, but that was not long before he was due in unmolested history to die anyway. And I saved many. I helped save Socrates. I saved Alcibiades," he said this especially to Sierra. "I know how important he became to you."

"Let's talk about what we came here to talk about," Max said.

Heron nodded, and looked at Sierra. "But I was just thinking about the first time we met, in ancient Alexandria, when you told me your name was Ampharete. The years have treated you very kindly."

"Thank you," Sierra said. "Not for the compliment. But for saving Alcibiades in Anatolia. It's too bad you tried to do quite the opposite to Max in Britain."

Heron began to respond—

"But you didn't ask us here to pry thanks from us for your life's work," Sierra cut him off.

Heron smiled. "No, I did not. Would you like something to drink?"

Sierra and Max shook their heads no.

Heron nodded again and spread his hands out upon the table. "Thomas Edison the inventor has the *Chronica* that you stole, and I have been told he is calling upon Henry Ford to construct a Chair or some sort of time travel vehicle – on the basis, I assume, of what is in the *Chronica*."

Neither Max nor Sierra responded. "Rescuing a scroll from impending flames is hardly theft," Sierra then spoke, "except a theft from the jaws of oblivion."

Heron smiled again, thinly. "You have a poetic flair. But surely you do not deny that authors have the right to decide what becomes of their work – including destroying it, if that is what they want."

"There are many who disagree with that proposition," Max said, "but now is not the time to debate the rights of authors versus the rights of potential readers."

"You are right, of course," he said to Max. "And my mistake for putting the word 'stole' into what I was telling you. The important message I wanted to convey – the only message, indeed – is that Edison has the *Chronica*, and is endeavoring to implement its information."

Sierra and Max were again silent.

"Neither of you seems surprised by that," Heron said, "and apparently neither of you wants to confirm it, or confirm what you might think is just speculation. But, I assure you, I know that Edison has it . . . . Is that what you want, do you want him and Henry Ford to build time travel vehicles, and make them as commonplace as you know Ford's motor vehicles soon will be?"

Again, there was no response.

"I know you took the *Chronica*, and have been seeking to get it published in some way, so the knowledge it contains would no longer be exclusively mine," Heron said. "I know that, and I know that such knowledge is no longer exclusive in any case, since you obviously have implemented some of it," he said to Sierra. "But I'm asking you: do you really want the price that is paid for the *Chronica*'s knowledge no longer being mostly mine to be that everyone else in the world has it?"

Sierra thought about Joe Biden, about Max's parents, about the pain as well as the joy on his face in their room in 2062. She finally answered. "No, probably not."

***

The three said nothing for a long interval. Heron took a sip of his beer. Sierra looked at him, still amazed, disgusted, furious at herself for even sitting at the same table with this man.

Max broke the silence. "How would you propose we get the *Chronica* from Edison, if he now has it? Surely we'll never trust you enough to go on some trip with you back in time to stop Edison from getting it."

"True," Heron said.

"How did Edison get it?" Sierra asked, though she knew the answer all too well.

"William Henry Appleton," Heron replied.

And he's supposed to meet me here in less than two hours, Sierra thought, not happy but horrified about the prospect now, with Heron here. But the last thing she wanted to do was postpone that meeting.

"You haven't answered my question about how you thought we could get the *Chronica* out of Edison's hands," Max told Heron. "Let's rule time travel out. What's left?"

"We arrange to take it from Edison the old-fashioned way: we have it stolen," Heron replied.

Sierra thought that time travel was pretty damned old-fashioned, or certainly old, if she and Alcibiades and Heron in the time of Socrates was any indication. But she responded, "you're saying, what? We launch some kind of commando raid? With your legionaries?" Sierra asked.

"Yes," Heron replied.

"We wouldn't feel comfortable – or safe – in their company," Max said, "since I assume we're being honest here."

"You wouldn't need to go on the actual raid," Heron said.

"Then why are you talking to us about it?" Sierra asked.

"Because I don't want you working against it, undermining it, as you have done or tried to do with so many other plans of mine," Heron replied.

Sierra smiled inside with satisfaction, and hoped it didn't show.

"You would be welcome to accompany my men if you like," Heron said. "That's entirely up to you."

"Will you be with them when they steal back the *Chronica*?" Max asked.

"No, I will not," Heron replied.

"And when would you expect to do this?" Max asked.

"I don't know, exactly," Heron replied. "Soon."

"Will you let us know beforehand?" Max asked.

"Yes, if you tell me you won't do anything to oppose this."

"We'll let you know," Sierra said and looked at Max. They stood. "We can leave a message for you with Mr. Bertram."

Heron stood, too. "Thank you. One other thing, if I may, as a token of my good will." He reached into a pocket and withdrew a locket, which he opened and gave to Sierra. "Please," he said, "accept this as an indication of my desire to end our enmity."

It was the locket that contained the miniature painting by Jean-Baptiste Régnault from 1785, *Socrates dragging Alcibiades from the Embrace of S.* Sierra had worn it around her neck for years, but had lost it at some point in ancient Alexandria. "Where did you get this?" she demanded.

"From the android that, elected, to die in your stead as Hypatia," Heron replied, with just the slightest touch of sarcasm on the word 'elected'.

"The android that you elected to have hacked to death," Max said, anger again up to the surface.

"The death of Hypatia in that horrible manner was history's decision, not mine," Heron said.

"Where did the android get the locket?" Sierra asked.

"I honestly do not know," Heron replied. "She spent a lot of time with Synesius – perhaps he picked it up one of the times he was with you."

"I didn't sleep with Synesius, if that's what you're implying," Sierra said, anger as well as sadness in her voice now, too.

Max put his hand gently over Sierra's.

The locket was still in Heron's hand. "Please," he urged again, "take this. It's a peace offering. I apologize for offending you with what I just said. That was not my intention. It's just my nature."

Sierra was too upset to accept the locket.

But Max took the locket from Heron's hand, and, Sierra, emotions still churning, was glad and loved him all the more for doing it. She realized that the locket around her neck or in her possession from now on would enable Heron to confirm that she was Sierra and not an android with her face – if, for whatever reason, likely evil, Heron needed such confirmation. Heron was in effect offering her a dare with the locket – take the locket if you dare to give me the means to confirm your identity, for whatever my purposes. It was dare Sierra was willing to take.

***

Sierra and Max walked quickly down the stairs to the front door of the Millennium Club. No doorman was present. Max opened the door. It was raining even harder now than when they had arrived.

"So what do we do now?" Max asked.

Bertram approached them, from the inside of the Club.

"Where's Heron?" Max asked.

"He's in the lavatory, I believe," Bertram said. "But I have a message for you about something else. Mr. Appleton's man Geoffreys just called."

"Is William ok?" Sierra asked, very concerned.

216

"I assume so," Bertram replied. "But the rain is even worse north of the city, and the forecast promises more. Mr. Appleton did not want to risk going out in these inclement elements, given the poor state of his health. He wanted me to tell you how sorry he was, and hopes you can reschedule, perhaps as early as tomorrow."

Heron appeared behind Bertram, and nodded at all three. He opened the door, scowled at the pouring rain, and walked out into it.

"We have no grounds to have him arrested," Sierra said, quietly.

"Oh, we have ample grounds," Max replied, "just none that we could tell the police." He shook his head. "I don't like him leaving like this." He and Sierra peered down the street through the sheets of rain. They could see nothing except water.

"You could almost believe he has the power to turn on the rain," Sierra said. "But he has something almost as potent as that – the talent of taking advantage of whatever his environment has to offer."

*****

Appleton was feeling ill again the next day, and too weak to travel. The same the day after.

Heron contacted Sierra through Bertram late on that second day, with news of his planned raid on Edison's facilities.

"How does Heron know exactly where Edison is keeping the *Chronica*?" Max asked.

"Presumably from the same source who told him Edison has the *Chronica* in the first place," Sierra replied, "though there are no guarantees that Edison didn't move it."

"And you're still sure you want to accompany Heron's legionaries on this – or whatever they're called back here?" Max asked.

Sierra called Bertram, and asked him to give Heron the message that she and Max wanted to come along on the raid.

***

The raid was set for two evenings later. Heron got word of that to Sierra through Bertram and told them where they should meet. "At the Weehawken Ferry on 42nd Street by the Hudson," Bertram repeated Heron's message, "and you will be going across the river with two of his men, and then on to Edison's offices in West Orange."

"He's still not telling us exactly where he expects to find the *Chronica*," Max noted.

"Either he doesn't know that exactly, or he doesn't trust us enough to tell us," Sierra said. "Likely both."

"Should we let Astor know about this?" Max asked.

"I don't know," Sierra said. "I trust him well enough, but bringing him along would alert Heron to how closely Astor has been working with us, if Heron didn't know already. And Heron could call off the raid, for whatever reason, if we showed up with Astor unannounced."

***

Max knew both of Heron's men, standing by the ferry the night after next. Sierra knew one of them. Both men introduced themselves anyway.

"James Flannery," Flannery said. Max shook his hand, and noticed that Flannery winced slightly.

"Oliver Woodruff," the other man said, and didn't wince at all when Max shook his extended hand.

Both men nodded courteously to Sierra.

"Come with us, please," Woodruff said, as he and Flannery boarded the ferry.

Sierra and Max followed. The four were apparently the only passengers. Sierra and Max couldn't see the crew.

The Hudson was choppy. The wind was cold for this May evening. Sierra and Max were thinking that, in the future, this trip to New Jersey would be via the Lincoln Tunnel, renamed the Giuliani Tunnel. They also might have thought that this ferry was more fun, but couldn't let themselves think that anything about this evening would be the slightest fun.

[Weehawken, New Jersey, May, 1899 AD]

The ferry docked at the Weehawken Terminal in New Jersey. A shiny new motor car was waiting for them. It gleamed in the moonlight. The driver – about 20, with goggles, and sportily dressed – got out of the car.

"My name's Johnson," he said with a big grin, "and here's your four-seater as requested. She's a Stoewer Phaeton, a German beauty." He patted the car. Woodruff paid him and sat in the driver's seat. Flannery ushered Sierra into the seat next to Woodruff, and sat with Max in the back.

"This drive should take about two hours," Flannery informed them. "Sit back and relax. The ferry will be waiting for us here when we return – it was chartered by our mutual benefactor."

Even though Flannery was not shouting at any one now, he sounded just as early 21st century to Max and Sierra as he had when he lost his temper with Astor at the hospital. They weren't so sure about Woodruff. They knew both were police, but assumed they were doing this off-the-record for Heron. Sierra and Max also assumed both men had weapons.

"Ready?" Johnson asked, leaning over the hand crank outside the car.

"Let's go," Flannery said.

Johnson nodded and started turning the crank. It made loud, sharp, slow noises, like a whip cracking. Sierra and Max had been around enough motor cars back here to know the sound wasn't good.

Johnson stopped and stood.

"What's wrong?" Flannery asked.

"I don't know," Johnson replied. "It worked fine the last time I started it, which was just a little while ago, to drive here."

"Try again," Flannery barked.

Johnson complied, and got the same result. "This happens sometimes," he now offered. "That's why some people say, 'get a horse'!" He laughed.

Flannery looked like he would shoot him if he could. "Get this piece of crap out of here," he said to Johnson about the car. "And give that man back every cent that he paid you," he pointed to Woodruff.

***

There was a livery stable about a block away from where they were standing, with at least half a dozen horse-drawn carriages of various sorts and sizes in front. "We should have done this in the first place," Flannery grumbled, as the four walked to the livery. "Horses are still more reliable at this point in time—" he stopped talking, and looked, Sierra thought, as if he thought he better not talk about points in time with who knew who was listening.

"That four-in-hand looks good," Woodruff said, and gestured to a carriage that was as sleek as the motor car, drawn by four horses. "I can drive it. Should get us there in half the time."

"Good. Go pay for it – rent it for the night," Flannery said.

Woodruff nodded and went inside the livery.

"My problem is I have my head too much in the future," Flannery said to Max and Sierra, "as I'm sure the two of you can understand."

***

Woodruff was as good as his word. "The best speed the motor car could have made is seven or eight miles per hour," he said to his three passengers over his shoulder, as he coaxed the horses on the dirt road to West Orange. "We're going at least twice as fast."

"Good work," Flannery said. He turned to Max and Sierra, and spoke in a lower voice. "Have either of you met Mr. Edison? If you had, that could provide a few moments of maneuverability if we run into him – you can come up with some reason about why we're here."

"No," Sierra said. "Neither of us has met him. I assume the same for you and Detective Woodruff?"

"Yeah," Flannery said.

"What do you intend to do with the *Chronica*, if we can get our hands on it?" Max asked, "as long as we're talking about more than the speed of horse travel now."

"Just what would have happened to it had Ms. Waters not intervened," Flannery replied. "Burn it, as per our friend's instructions."

Sierra nodded. "You know it may not be the only copy of the *Chronica*," she observed.

"Not our problem tonight," Flannery replied.

[West Orange, New Jersey, May, 1899 AD]

Woodruff pulled the coach up to a stop, about half a block from the Black Maria, which could be seen clearly in the moonlight.

"Let's walk the rest of the way," Flannery said. "There should be a night watchman around somewhere, but he's now in our employ."

Woodruff tied the horses as securely as he could to a hitching post. "We can't leave them here like this too long."

"Let's hope we won't have to," Flannery replied. "See, that's why I wanted the motor car in the first place," he said, mainly to Sierra and Max. "I wasn't completely wrong about that."

They approached the Black Maria. It looked like a barn, Sierra thought. There were no windows on the side she was looking at. She felt a pang. She and Max had both been historians of media, as graduate students, before they had been drawn into all of this. That part of her was still inside, underneath it all, and it was thrilled to actually be walking up to this studio, which she had read and seen so much about, almost 150 years in the future. She was sure Max felt the same way.

They reached the night watchman, who extended his hands. "The door is open," he said. "Tie me up and rough me up a little, so I'll be able to keep my job." He grinned at Sierra. "I'm being so well paid for this, I may not need this job any more. I'll be sure to look you up, dearie!"

Woodruff smacked him twice in the face. "That should leave enough of a mark," Woodruff said, and began to tie the night watchman's hands behind his back.

"We'll put in an anonymous call to the local police after we're gone that the Black Maria was broken into," Flannery said to the watchman. "Shouldn't take too long. They'll untie you when they get here." He patted the man on the head and punched him in the face again. "Just for good measure."

"All done," Woodruff said, smiled at the man, and refrained from punching him yet again.

The four walked carefully to the Black Maria. "I don't like people who sell out their own employers," Flannery said about the night watchman.

"Are we sure Edison's not inside there, right now?" Sierra asked. "He's famous for regarding sleep as a waste of time, and supposedly sleeps only three or fours every night."

"He also takes naps," Flannery said. "But we have another man on the case, outside of Edison's home right now. Edison's had a cold for the past few days, and is resting it out at home now. That was one of the reasons this night was chosen for our little visit. If Edison stirs, our man will rush right over here and alert us."

Max controlled himself from asking, *will you punch him in the face, too*? And instead asked, "can you tell us where the *Chronica* is now?"

"In the office," Flannery said, and pointed to a side of the building that had a separate entrance.

"You think he would leave something as valuable as that in his office, and not in a vault somewhere?" Max asked.

Flannery shrugged. "That is what we have been told – that this book is in his office. We'll find out soon enough if it is."

Woodruff added, "I'd certainly put it in a strong room in a bank somewhere, but I'm not Thomas Edison. And, from what I hear, he does everything his own way."

Flannery and Woodruff started towards the office door. Sierra and Max looked at each other, and followed.

***

The door to the office was unlocked, as promised. Flannery and Woodruff entered first and turned on several electric light bulbs. Flannery beckoned Sierra and Max to enter. "The *Chronica* was last spotted on that desk," Flannery pointed to the cubbyhole desk, stuffed in all parts with papers. "You two are the experts – see if you can find it."

Sierra and Max walked to the desk. "There are hundreds of scripts here," Max said and named some of the manuscripts he saw, "*The Magician, Love by the Light of the Moon, Another Job for the Undertaker—*"

"Ok," Flannery interrupted, "spare me the recital. The *Chronica* is supposed to be in Greek – you should be able to see it quickly enough with all of those titles in English."

Sierra pulled up a chair, as did Max. "This is going to take some time," she said.

"Stop talking and start looking," Flannery said. "I'll stand here by the door and make sure we get no intruders."

***

Sierra and Max finished almost an hour later, chided by Flannery for taking so long, but careful to put every manuscript and piece of paper back in its place, so Edison would not immediately see that his desk had been ransacked.

"It's not here," Sierra said, and smacked her hand on the desk in frustration.

Flannery had seen that coming, as the minutes went by and Sierra and Max had found nothing. Woodruff had gone and returned from checking on the horses, and had also looked around the rest of the office and found nothing written in any language other than English.

Max and Sierra expected an outburst from Flannery, maybe even a threat of violence, but he was calm. He cursed softly and told Woodruff to take a quick look at the desk himself.

"Well, what might this be?" Woodruff announced about 15 minutes later, and held up a manuscript. "Sure looks like Greek to me."

Sierra came back to the desk.

"We must have missed that," Max said. "You sure it's the *Chronica* and not a script for a movie about making souvlaki?"

"Yes, I'm sure," Woodruff replied. "I studied ancient Greek and Latin in high school as well as college. It says '*Chronica*' right here on the front page."

Sierra and Max had decided beforehand that if they found the *Chronica* on Edison's premises they would not let Heron's men know. That would keep it out of Heron's hands, and give themselves the option of deciding what to do about Edison's possession of it later.

"I tell ya," Flannery said with a grin, "this end of the 19th century has one hell of an educational system."

***

Sierra and Max said nothing as they walked back to the four-in-hand with Flannery, Woodruff, and the *Chronica*. Nothing was said to them, but they felt like prisoners.

"What are you going to with it?" Max finally asked.

"Burn it, like I told you, when we get back to New York," Flannery answered.

"What are you going to do with us?" Sierra asked.

"Nothing," Flannery replied. "I'm a police lieutenant not your father. I'm not going to punish you for your stupidity – by which I mean, I know you were deceitful in there, not stupid, but being deceitful in these circumstances was a very stupid thing."

Woodruff was half leafing through the *Chronica* as they were walking.

"Anything interesting in there?" Flannery asked.

Woodruff laughed sarcastically. "And I'm a police detective not your inventor. None of this makes a whit of sense to me."

They reached the horses and the carriage. Woodruff gave Flannery the *Chronica*, hitched up the horses, and took the reigns.

Flannery sat opposite Max and Sierra in the coach. "Don't look so crestfallen," he said to them. "You're not the first to underestimate the New York City police, and you won't be the last."

[Weehawken, New Jersey, May, 1899 AD]

The trip back to Weehawken, less than an hour, passed mostly in uneasy silence.

"Can I see that?" Sierra asked about the *Chronica*, on Flannery's lap, at one point.

"No," Flannery answered.

"You know, that's not the way it was originally written," Sierra said. "It was on a scroll, which took up much less space when wrapped. In some ways, we've lost not gained ground since the ancient world."

"Save your history lesson for your students," Flannery said. "I expect that's what the two of you will be doing now, when you're back home, whenever that is, now that this business has been concluded?"

Sierra gave no response.

They were soon at the dock in Weehawken. Woodruff went to return the four-in-hand.

This time, the three-man crew was visible and on the shore. "We'll be leaving right away," Flannery told the captain, who nodded and boarded the ship with his men.

Sierra and Max considered bolting, but preferred to stay with the *Chronica*.

Woodruff returned, all four boarded the ferry, and it soon pulled back out into the river for the return to New York.

***

The water was even choppier than on the way out. Flannery took it in serenely. Woodruff looked less comfortable.

About halfway or a little more back to New York, one of the crew came down to the deck and said something to Woodruff. It sounded to Sierra like "people on shore". She noticed the man had a pair of brass binoculars in his hand.

Woodruff turned to Sierra and Max and produced a gun. "I've enjoyed your company," he said, "but all good things must end."

"What are you doing?" Flannery demanded.

The man with binoculars now also had a gun, in his other

hand, pointed at Flannery.

"This is what our employer wants," Woodruff said, coolly. "Stay out of it."

Sierra and Max had not come unarmed. They weren't much good with guns of this era, but knives were knives, and both had become adept at their use in the ancient world.

They looked at each other for a split second and attacked the mate or whatever the hell he was with the gun. He got off a shot but hit no one. Sierra's knife got to his neck first, and she slit his throat.

At the same time, Flannery pulled his gun and charged Woodruff. "It's not what *I* want," he shouted. Loud gunshots echoed over the dark Hudson. Flannery was on top of Woodruff, struggling to get the gun out of his hand, but all he dislodged from Woodruff was the *Chronica*, which flew over the rail of the ferry into the black water and promptly sank. More shots were fired.

Sierra and Max, done with the crewmember, turned to Woodruff and Flannery. Woodruff, no longer armed, holding what looked like a wound above his wrist, was scrutinizing the water below. Flannery, also no longer armed, was on the deck, bleeding, clearly shot in several places.

Sierra and Max rushed Woodruff, knives in hand. Woodruff looked at them for a heartbeat then turned and jumped into the water. Sierra and Max reached the railing a moment too late to stop him.

They turned to Flannery, still on the floor, blood gurgling in his mouth. Sierra held his head up. He managed to give them his address in 1999 and his wife's name. "Tell Mary I'm so sorry. I've always loved her. Help her." And he died in Sierra's arms.

CHAPTER 16

[New York City, May, 1899 AD]

Sierra kissed Flannery on the forehead and held him for what felt like a long time but was just a few seconds. "He saved our lives," she said.

"What about the rest of the crew?" Max asked, knife still in hand. The ferry was still heading towards New York.

One of the crew indeed soon ran down from the helm to the deck, with no weapon in hand. "My God, what happened here?" he asked, looking at Flannery's body, then backing off when he saw the knife.

Sierra rose, not sure what to say, but put her knife away. She started to answer, but Max touched her arm, and pointed. Another ferry was approaching from the New York side.

Max and Sierra were pretty sure who was on that ferry, but could not be positive. Sierra gestured to it. "They'll know what to do," she said loudly to the mate, who had now seen the other crew member's body. He was standing as far away from Sierra and Max on the deck as he could.

Max picked up a gun that was on the deck and pointed it at the horrified mate. The plan was that this guy had no idea that Max barely knew how this gun worked. "Please, just stay here," Max said. "This will all be over soon. There's been enough bloodshed."

The plan worked. The mate was frozen.

The second ferry approached and was now within shouting distance. Sierra exhaled in relief. Jack Astor was standing on the deck with armed men. He saw her and waved. Astor was supposed to have waited with his men for Sierra and Max at the New York dock, to wring the *Chronica* from whomever Heron had sent to get it from Edison. But Astor had no doubt seen what had happened on the river with own binoculars and hired a ferry on the spot to get out here.

***

Astor and four Pinkerton detectives in his employ soon boarded Sierra's ferry. Two Pinkertons went up to the helm, weapons drawn. The other two put the mate Max had been talking to in handcuffs.

Astor looked at Flannery's body. He could tell by Sierra's expression that she wasn't happy about Flannery's death. "I wouldn't say that I liked him," Astor said, "but he probably deserved better than this."

"He probably saved our lives," Max repeated what Sierra had said. "Woodruff was set to kill us."

Astor arched an eyebrow. "I didn't much care for him, either. Where is he?"

Sierra pointed to the water. "He jumped into the Hudson a few minutes before you got here." There was no sign of him now.

"And the *Chronica*?" Astor asked.

"That went into the river, too," Max replied.

"You think Woodruff went into the water to fetch it?" Astor asked.

Sierra shook her head no. "Probably not. I don't know. Why would he do that? The *Chronica* destroyed, whether by flames or by water, is just what Heron wanted."

"Yes, Heron seems to have gotten what he wanted tonight," Astor agreed. "Nothing will be changed in the world – at least as far as this copy of the *Chronica* is concerned. Only Edison and Ford will be disappointed. Tesla will be happy – he's your best bet now to construct a Chair. Maybe he was always your best bet in that regard."

"He'd be a better bet if he had the *Chronica* in hand," Sierra said.

One of the Pinkertons returned from the helm. "It's ok," Astor told him, "you can talk in front of them," and looked at Max and Sierra.

"The captain and the other mate upstairs say they know nothing about what happened here," the Pinkerton said. "They were hired to take people across the Hudson and back, period."

"Do you believe him?" Astor asked.

"Yes, I do," the Pinkerton replied.

"Ok," Astor said. "Then please take the handcuffs off that man." He pointed to the crew member whose hands were cuffed behind his back.

Sierra was looking again at Flannery's body. "Back in 1999, he'll just be another mysterious disappearance, a police lieutenant who vanished without a clue. It'll be chalked up as another mob-related death, due to gambling, drugs, whatever."

Astor nodded, sympathetically, not knowing exactly what 'mob-related' meant, but getting the gist.

"I'm almost tempted to put his body in a Chair, and get it back to his wife – that way, at least she'd have some closure. Is that crazy?" Sierra asked.

"It's not crazy but it won't bring closure," Max said, softly. "The 1999 coroners will examine the body – what will they do with gun wounds made by an 1899 weapon? It'll just create more unanswered questions."

"I can see that he gets a proper burial now, in Woodlawn Cemetery," Astor said. "I know that place has meaning for you."

Sierra nodded sadly, as the ferry reached the New York dock.

***

Woodruff made it to a different part of the New York shore, about half a mile south, about an hour later. He was exhausted and wounded, but his badge had survived the plunge. He flagged down a carriage, showed the driver his badge, and told him to go to Bellevue, just across town.

He asked the driver to write his address on a piece of paper and give it to him. "You may have saved my life. I'll see to it that you're well paid."

"No need," the driver said, with a thick East European accent, as he wrote down his address. "You are our police. I support you!"

"I insist," Woodruff said, and took the paper. He staggered into the hospital and collapsed into an orderly's arms.

He awoke in a bed, his wet clothes removed, under a nice warm blanket.

"Detective! You're awake," a woman's voice said.

He turned and saw a nurse smiling at him.

"How long have I been unconscious?" Woodruff asked her.

"Only about an hour, I think," the nurse said. "The doctor will be in to see you soon." She turned and left.

Woodruff looked at her receding figure and thought about that old joke he had heard somewhere, "I was in the hospital, not feeling very well, and then I took a turn for the nurse!" Come to think of it, he had heard that from Flannery. Woodruff felt a stab of remorse.

***

Heron called Woodruff the next morning, returning Woodruff's call, just before the detective was released from the hospital. Woodruff told Heron the story step by step, and stopped with the shooting of Flannery.

"Is he ok?" Woodruff said. "I know I shot him more than once."

"I'm afraid he's dead," Heron said. "I'm sorry that happened – I know you didn't want this – but that's the line of work you are in, and, as you said, he shouldn't have gotten in the way at that point. But he was a good man – and I will see to it that his family will never want again for money."

"You're sure that he's dead?" Woodruff still couldn't believe it, and that he was responsible.

"I'm sorry," Heron said again, soothingly. "My sources confirm it."

"How many goddamned sources do you have?"

"I have had lots of time to cultivate my associates, like you," Heron replied.

Woodruff made no response.

"Please, continue with your account," Heron requested. "What happened after Flannery fell? What happened to the *Chronica*?"

Woodruff confirmed that the *Chronica* was gone. "It sunk like a stone," Woodruff said, "in the deepest part of the river. I couldn't see so much as a page of it. That manuscript will never be seen again, except maybe by a fish."

"It was a manuscript not a scroll?"

"Yeah," Woodruff replied.

"And it was written in?"

"Greek, ancient Greek," Woodruff replied. "I know the difference between the modern and archaic forms."

Heron asked Woodruff to repeat that part of his story – clearly much more interested in what happened to the *Chronica* than what happened to Flannery, Woodruff thought, with a flash of black anger.

"Ok," Heron replied, not entirely happy at all with the results of the evening. "Get back to your police work now – no one knows you were with Flannery last night, right?"

"I certainly didn't tell anyone," Woodruff replied.

"Let's hope he didn't tell anyone, either," Heron said. "At this juncture, your best course is to just be as surprised as everyone else about Flannery's unexplained absence. I'll contact you with any further instructions."

"As you wish," Woodruff said.

Heron got off the public phone he was using, a half a block from the seafood restaurant, which had received the call from Woodruff an hour earlier. Heron no longer looked like J. P. Morgan, but he still had all the money he needed to pay for the services he required, including getting messages for him under the name Harry from the maître d'hôtel.

Heron sighed mightily. What he disliked more than anything else was making the same mistake twice. He had thought Sierra was destroyed as Hypatia in Alexandria in 415 AD, and with it the scrolls she had stolen from the Library, including his *Chronica*. And he had been wrong.

He believed Woodruff about what had happened to the manuscript of the *Chronica*. But he was not going to make the mistake of assuming it was the only copy. And there was still the original, presumably but not definitely still in possession of the dying Appleton.

***

Astor, Sierra, and Max walked slowly from the grave of James Flannery in Woodlawn Cemetery in the Bronx. The ceremony had been simple and brief. The gravestone, which would be put in later, would say, "A lawman who tried his best."

Astor was talking. "So many notable people resting in peace here. Herman Melville the author, Jay Gould the financer, Bat Masterson another lawman – are they still known in the world you come from?"

Max nodded. "Herman Melville and Bat Masterson more than Jay Gould, but, sure, we know of all three."

"Gould helped finance the railroads?" Sierra asked. But all kinds of other thoughts were smashing like half-submerged icebergs in her brain. Socrates and her Thomas, once Alcibiades, would be buried here about a century and a half from now, Mark Twain in about a decade.

"That's right," Astor answered Sierra's question about Gould.

As always, she never knew how much to tell him. "I'm thinking I should see Flannery's wife, and maybe bring her to this place in 1999 . . . I don't know."

Astor looked at her.

"So how will this change the course of history," Max wondered. "Not much if at all back here, but Flannery had a life to live in the 21st century, which will be gone now."

"Perhaps he was destined to die early in the 21st century, or even in 1999, all along," Astor said. "And he could not escape his fate, even back here, like in an O'Henry story."

Max nodded. "In our experience," he looked at Sierra, "the universe seems to have a lot invested in keeping its original timelines intact – whatever original really is."

Sierra nodded, but addressed a different issue. "You've read O'Henry?" she asked Astor. "I'm pretty sure his major stories were not published until a few years into the 20th century."

"Yes," was all that Astor said.

Lots of other notable people were buried here, Sierra thought. Not Astor, but other important people who would die on the Titanic. Isidor and Ida Straus, almost as rich as Astor. Her grandmother had worked on some arbitration committee with their grandson, Donald Straus. Sierra didn't want to cry but there it was again. Max squeezed her shoulder.

Astor was looking at her. "I want to tell you something," he said, very softly.

Sierra shook her head. "No."

"It's ok," he said, very gently, "it's ok. I've been to the future. I know I'm supposed to die on the Titanic."

"Don't go!" Sierra said. "Don't go on that fucking ship! History can take care of itself!" She flung her arms around Astor, and pressed her face, slick with tears, against his neck.

"It's ok," Astor said again, and put a consoling arm around her.

"I don't know you very well, but I know you don't deserve to die," Sierra said, her voice ragged.

"If the only people who died were those who deserved it, this cemetery would be a ghost town," Astor replied, with a slight smile.

Sierra smiled weakly, pulled away, and took Max's hand.

"I haven't made a decision about the Titanic yet," Astor said. "Let's concentrate on the matter at hand. Perhaps we should go see Tesla."

[West Orange, New Jersey, May, 1899 AD]

Edison was outraged but not really surprised when he discovered the *Chronica* missing, two days after it had been taken from his office. Especially infuriating was that Edison couldn't be sure when exactly the *Chronica* was stolen, which he was sure it had been, since he kept it in only one cubbyhole and could picture it in his sleep. It had been five days since he'd last looked at the Greek manuscript. He'd been busy with all kinds of other projects, and this damn head cold had kept him from playing at the top of his game.

He called Henry Ford with the bad news.

Ford was sympathetic, but felt compelled to add, "truthfully, I doubt that such a device could ever be built even with an explicit set of instructions written in English. Whoever stole that from you may have been doing you a favor – my guess is all that they stole was a pipe dream."

Edison exhaled, and was glad that Ford couldn't see how disgusted he was – about Ford, about everything concerning this beguiling manuscript that he had somehow let slip out of his hands before he'd had a chance to find a translator. "I know someone who claims to use the device described in the book," Edison said, "and he has impressive evidence."

Ford didn't answer.

"Do you not believe me?" Edison asked.

"Of course I believe you," Ford said. "But the world is full of pranksters, people who deceive, do the Devil's work with their every moment on this Earth. Do you think he is the one who stole the *Chronica*, because he seeks to keep this knowledge for his own use?"

"Perhaps," Edison replied. He hadn't named Heron to Ford and had no intention of doing so, but Ford might well have been right that Heron, aware and angered that Edison had pried the *Chronica* from Appleton, but not given it to Heron, had sought to reclaim it as something that was, after all, his. "I think a more likely culprit is Tesla – he and his friends have sought to undermine me at every turn in the road."

"Does he read Greek?" Ford asked.

"He probably does," Edison said, "he's European."

"I do not see how what is written in the book, even if it were entirely comprehensible, could be applied to an actual device," Ford reiterated, "though I know you and I disagree about that."

"Certainly not by Tesla," Edison responded. "He lacks the discipline."

The two exchanged pleasantries and concluded their conversation. Edison realized that if he wanted to pursue this, his only course would be to contact Appleton, own up to the fact that the *Chronica* which Appleton had entrusted to him had been stolen, and see if he could beg, borrow, or steal another copy.

[New York, June, 1899 AD]

Tesla joined Astor, Sierra, and Max in Astor's meeting room in his hotel three evenings later. He was nothing but discouraging at first.

"It's not that your memory was overly faulty," Tesla tried to assure Sierra. "What's playing me false are the missing pieces of science – not in the science currently available, which I would expect, but in the science I cannot imagine."

"So you don't think having the *Chronica* as a guide could help," Max said.

"It might help, of course," Tesla said. "Knowledge of any sort is always welcome. But unless you left out major pieces in your rendition of it to me," he said to Sierra, "I doubt that it will enable me to build one of these Chairs that travel through time."

"So it is impossible then?" Astor asked, in frustration. "But how could that be – the three of us in this room, everyone other than you, Nikola, have used the Chairs to travel through time!"

"I believe you," Tesla said and put his hand over Astor's. "I am not saying it is impossible. Nothing is impossible, as far as I am concerned. That word is a shield, an excuse, for those who cannot accomplish very much. So no, not impossible. But, rather, not yet possible with what I know and what I can envision.

"I have an idea," Sierra said.

All three men gave her their rapt attention.

"Let's say we take you to a time in the future when the knowledge you now lack and cannot even imagine is available," Sierra said.

"Ha! I love it!" Tesla replied. "Using the product of what I cannot even imagine to transport me to a place – a time – in which I not only could imagine but build such a device! I love it! There is a music to that!"

"And just to make sure we have every asset at our command, let us see if we can procure another copy of the *Chronica*, for Nikola to take with him, wherever we take him," Astor said

Max looked at this pocket watch. "I suppose it's too late to go up and see Appleton now?"

"It can wait until morning," Astor said. "Let's see if we can get some dinner."

***

Sierra called Appleton the next morning.

Geoffreys sounded distressed. "He's gone!"

"What? No!" Sierra cried out. "It's only June – he was feeling so much better just last week—"

"No, no," Geoffreys said, "I didn't mean that – sorry if I frightened you! But I am frightened, actually – there was a break-in at Wave Hill last night, when we were asleep. We only discovered it this morning. Mr. Appleton was very upset about it. I told him he needed to rest. The police are on their way. But when I checked his room a little while after that, he was gone! I called the train station, and the station master told me that Mr. Appleton had boarded a train to New York about an hour and a half ago. Perhaps he's gone to see you! Where are the police?"

"I don't know," Sierra said, "but I'm sure he's ok. If he had enough strength to take a train into the city, that's certainly good news."

"Yes, but—"

"I'll keep you posted, Geoffreys, I promise," she cut him off. "Let me see if I can find out what's happening down here."

She hung up the phone and briefed Max, who had just come out of the shower, dripping wet, looking for a towel.

"We have to get to the Millennium, right away."

CHAPTER 17

[Foster Square Facility, Brewster, Massachusetts, 2096 AD]

She had access to data from all Chairs in the past, from as far in the past as they reached, the oldest in Athens, then London, then New York City. She had access to data from Chairs in those places from even before they were known by those names – for as long as there had been hovels, constructed in stone, roughly hewn or even harvested, to contain the Chairs.

Data from Chairs in the future was not as reliable. It was not available at all for some stretches of centuries and decades, and those times were increasingly closer to where she was now, in 2096. She suspected, but didn't know with 100% certainty, that this blocking of data from the future was Heron's doing. She also believed that some data from the future was distorted, filtered, or otherwise manipulated by Heron.

She, and everything else brought into being by Sierra Waters, were at war with Heron, and he was gradually winning, always poised to make a major breakthrough that would destroy them. She thought of herself as holding the line against the onslaught.

She knew Heron had broken through at times, done minor damage to the operation of Chairs in the past. Heron, as the person who had created the Chairs in the first place, held the upper hand. He had created a fourth Chair portal, in ancient Alexandria, then destroyed it. Sierra had survived and prevailed -- to the extent that she had -- only because, like all asymmetrical warriors, like all guerilla operatives, she was lean and quick and essentially unpredictable. Heron had realized at some point that the best way of fighting her was to engage her, whenever possible, on that one-on-one unforeseeable level.

The android examined the incoming data. Although she had unfettered access to data from use of Chairs in the past, it was not complete data. Heron had early on put in a code that prevented the Chairs from reporting who was in them and where they were going. Sierra had first instructed her androids to overcome that code. But she soon came to the conclusion that such a cloak on Chair usage benefited her as much as it did Heron. So all that the Chairs reported was that they were in use.

The android could not keep track of all use at the same time – no human being, or machine in existence that she knew of, could do that. Today she was focused on 1899, as she had been for the past few months. Two Chairs had just been activated in the Millennium Club in New York City.

She could not read whether they were bound for the past or the future. But she soon had her answer.

The monitor announced that she had two visitors. This was rare. She was well off the beaten track here on Cape Cod, in a place that looked on the outside like a worn, abandoned cottage not far from the shore. She was in a vast catacomb of digitally meshed rooms two stories underground.

She saw who the visitors were and let them in. Voices guided them to her room.

"Mr. Appleton and Mr. Charles," she said.

CHAPTER 18

[New York City, June, 1899 AD]

Mr. Bertram was at the front door of the Millennium. "He left, not five minutes ago," he said to Sierra and Max, correctly figuring why they were practically running up to the club.

"We didn't see him on the street—" Sierra began, but stopped when she caught Bertram's expression. "He took a Chair?" she asked, surprised.

"You know I cannot tell you any more than I cannot tell you," Bertram said, confirming what Sierra thought.

"But he's ill," Sierra said, "how—"

"First, he is not quite as ill as you may think – or he's feeling a little better now, in any case," Bertram said. "Second, he has a companion."

"Who?" Max asked.

"Mr. Cyril Charles," Bertram replied, "who, I don't mind telling you, and if it puts your mind at ease, went up to Mr. Appleton's home on the Hudson, and accompanied him to the Millennium."

Sierra nodded slowly. "We haven't seen Mr. Charles here in a while – not that that means anything, of course—"

"He has been keeping a low profile, in this time and place, as they say in the future," Mr. Bertram replied. "An attempt was made by the New York police to apprehend him in 1999, and we think it may be related to what he saw one day here."

"Did you get their names?" Max asked.

"Detectives Barnes and Molloy, I believe," Bertram said. "But they were taking orders from someone else."

"What did Mr. Charles see here that might have gotten him into trouble?" Sierra asked.

"J. P. Morgan, where he should not have been," Bertram replied.

"Ah, Heron," Sierra said.

Bertram said nothing, and started to excuse himself.

"One last question, if I might," Sierra said. "Could you tell us why Messrs. Appleton and Charles undertook this trip?"

"I truly do not know," Bertram replied. "And as you well know, I wouldn't tell you if I did. I've talked enough already – the walls have ears, even here in the Millennium."

***

Max and Sierra sat under the Raphael nude and considered their options.

"The hope would be that Appleton finally relented and went to the future to get some medical treatment which could extend his life," Max said. "I know that's what we wanted, but—"

"He was pretty stubborn about not doing that," Sierra said. "What would get him to suddenly change his mind?" She did hope that that's what Appleton was doing, but she was afraid to let herself believe it.

"Confronting his own imminent mortality?" Max responded.

"And what connection would that have to the break-in last

night that Geoffreys told us about?" Sierra asked.

"I assumed that was Heron trying to get the original *Chronica* scroll," Max replied.   "But there's no obvious connection between that and Appleton seeking medical treatment, so it's either just a coincidence, or we're back to not accepting coincidence as an explanation.   Maybe Heron stole the *Chronica* and Appleton and Charles went after him?"

Sierra shuddered.   The thought of Appleton and Cyril Charles facing Heron and his forces brought her as much dread as the thought of Appleton getting his life extended brought her joy. She got to her feet.   "Let's see if there are any Chairs in the room."

***

There were no Chairs in the room.

"At least we know Bertram was telling the truth – probably," Max said.

"I didn't really doubt him," Sierra said.

"But we're stranded here until more Chairs arrive," Max said. "No way to go after Appleton, even if we had some idea of where he went."

"Let's get Astor and Tesla up to date on this – see if they have any ideas," Sierra said. "And we probably should pay a visit to Geoffreys and see if we can find out anything more from him. Sooner or later some Chairs should arrive."

"Let's hope with Appleton and Charles, not Heron and that well-educated murderous cop," Max said.

Sierra nodded.   "As long as we're here, even just talking about the Chairs, it means that Heron didn't yet succeed in eradicating the *Chronica* and all knowledge about how to construct the Chairs." But she also knew that all of that could end in an unexpected heartbeat.

***

Neither Astor nor Tesla were reachable by phone – that would have been surprising, even cause for some alarm in a later age, but not in 1899, when phones were still solely in offices and homes not even yet pockets, Sierra and Max both realized. She left messages with associates for both men. She and Max took the train up to Wave Hill to see Geoffreys.

He had not calmed down very much. Sierra reassured him, "We have good reason to believe no harm has come to Mr. Appleton, but we don't know where he is. We're hoping to be in touch with him soon."

"But his fragile health—" Geoffreys began.

"Someone we trust is with him," Max said. "In fact, we think he arranged to take Mr. Appleton downtown today."

"But—" Geoffreys began, again, then allowed himself to be at least a little reassured.

"What can you tell us about the burglary last night, if that's what it was?" Sierra asked.

"I don't know if it was a burglary," Geoffreys replied. "As far as I can see, nothing is missing."

Sierra wondered if Geoffreys knew about the *Chronica*. She thought he probably did, but also thought there was no point in telling him about it if he didn't already know.

"The police thought the same thing," Geoffreys continued. "Nothing was disturbed. There was not even so much as a desk drawer left open."

"Right, the police," Sierra said. "Did they leave you a card – contact information – in case you thought of something else or had a question?"

"Yes, yes," Geoffreys replied, and produced a card from his pocket. "I'm supposed to call if Mr. Appleton is not home by this evening, in any case."

Sierra took the card, looked at it, and gave it to Max. "Gordon Woodruff, Detective, New York police," was printed upon it, with a telephone number.

***

Sierra and Max took the train back down to Grand Central, even more worried than they had been on the way up.

"I'm concerned about leaving Geoffreys alone at Wave Hill, and William coming back to that. They would be easy prey for Woodruff and Heron," Sierra said.

"We'll just have to meet William before he gets back up there – the Millennium would be the safest place for everyone," Max said.

"Probably," Sierra said. "But Heron has access to the Millennium, too."

Max nodded. "That damned Woodruff. What can we do about it? We can't just report him to the New York police – they'd lock us up, way the hell ahead of him."

A well-dressed man sitting in the seat in front of them turned and glared at Max.

"Sorry," Max said. "I was just a little overwrought."

The man nodded and turned back in his seat.

"I know," Max mouthed to Sierra. "They don't appreciate that language back here."

"We don't know deep in this police department Heron's

influence goes," Sierra said, quietly. "I think we should steer clear of them."

A conductor walked by and called out for their tickets, as if to underline the point that who knew where Heron's cadre ended, it could well include conductors on a train.

***

They met Astor and Tesla at the Millennium, and caught them up on events as they sat below the Raphael nude.

"These aren't the only comfortable seats in the club," Sierra remarked.

"No, but they afford the best view," Astor replied, with a smile, matched by Max and Tesla.

"If I am understanding you correctly," Tesla said to Sierra and Max, "you have no means of knowing where – to what time – Appleton and Charles took the Chairs."

Sierra nodded. "Unfortunately, right."

"Then what choice do we have but to wait here – at least one of us – until Appleton and Charles return and tell us where they have been?" Tesla continued.

"We could still take you to the future, as we were discussing," Astor said.

"We have no Chairs anyway," Sierra said, "at least as of a few hours ago. So the point is moot."

"No doubt that the ideal way of doing this is we wait until Appleton and Charles come back here," Astor said, "then find out what they know, perhaps get the *Chronica* from Appleton – or find out where it is – and have two Chairs to travel to the future with, to boot."

Max had been thinking that would indeed be ideal, until Astor's last point, which made him less than happy, since he was sure Sierra and Tesla would be the ones to take the two Chairs.

"But the problem is we could wait here forever until Appleton and Charles return," Astor delivered the punch line. "We have no way of knowing when – or even if – they will return."

"Or if they will return to this time," Sierra said, "but yes."

"Why would they not return to this time?" Tesla asked.

"Afraid of Heron, something we know nothing about in some other time that they think requires their presence – who knows?" Max said and stood. "We might as well go upstairs and see if there any Chairs there now."

He turned and saw a familiar figure walking towards them. "Cyril Charles!"

***

All four stood, then quickly sat with Charles under the nude.

"Where's William?" Sierra asked. "Is he all right?"

"Yes," Charles replied. "He is just resting – this was a lot of travel for one day."

Sierra stood again. "Here now in the Club – where?"

"No, in 2096," Charles replied. "Not in the Millennium or any club."

"In a hospital, receiving medical treatment?" Max asked.

Charles shook his head no, again. "Not in any hospital. This trip was not about seeing doctors."

Sierra was still standing. "I'm going to take that Chair and go see him right now."

All four men offered objections.

Tesla's was the calmest. "It may not be wise for just one person to travel – given the threat from Heron."

"So we're back to waiting for Chairs to arrive, then?" Sierra said.

Max stood and took her hand. "You're more crucial to all of this than I am. Let me go – I promise I'll come back to you."

"You can't promise that," Sierra said.

"The same is true for you," Max replied.

"Was there any sign of Heron in the future?" Astor asked Charles.

"Nothing of him personally," Charles replied. "But the charming young woman who was in charge told us that she was seeing the ill-effects of his work – Chairs not working the way they're supposed to, and so forth."

Sierra thought about Max's unaccountably arriving a little late, when their Chairs were supposed to be in sync, the last time they had used them.

"She reminded me a little of you," Charles said to Sierra, with a kindly smile.

"Tell us more about her," Sierra said.

"There is not much more to tell," Charles replied. "She did not volunteer much information, and we did not ask. She said you would know who she was – I believe she said you were responsible for her being."

"A descendant!" Astor said.

"An android, more likely," Max said. "You know, like 'Moxon's

Moron'? Are you familiar with that story?"

"'Moxon's *Master*' by Ambrose Bierce? Of course!" Astor said.

"An android likely just like her, who made herself look like Hypatia, whom I was looking like and pretending to be, died in my and Hypatia's stead in ancient Alexandria," Sierra said, gravely.

"The real Hypatia having died of natural causes, long before," Max said, "just to keep the true historical record accurate."

"You mean, true in terms of what you know really happened," Astor said, impressed, "in contrast to what our history books otherwise tell us."

"This is *fascinating*!" Tesla said, bursting with enthusiasm despite what Sierra had just said. "This is more than time travel as a fiction – you have actually been living it, and rearranging history! I knew that, of course, but to hear you talk like this . . . "

Astor nodded agreement. "This woman in the future, then, was an automaton, who looked like a human being?"

"Yes," Sierra said.

"That in itself is nearly as incredible as time travel!" Astor said. "But may I ask," he said to Charles, "if you know the answer and are able to tell us, what was the purpose of Mr. Appleton's trip to the future, if not to see to his health?"

"To find the *Chronica*," Charles replied.

Sierra had been standing throughout the conversation. "Let's see if any more Chairs have returned."

***

The five went up the spiral staircase to the room with the

Chairs.

Charles opened the door, went in first, and called to the others who were coming through the door. "Just one Chair."

Max looked at Sierra. "We should wait for at least one other Chair – it doesn't matter how long we have to wait here, if we can arrive in the future at the same time as Mr. Charles arrived with Appleton," he gestured to Charles.

"True," Sierra said, "but sitting around and waiting was never my strong suit."

"Let me take the Chair!" Tesla spoke up. "If the *Chronica*'s in the future – in the time Charles and Appleton arrived – I'm the only who can use that knowledge then to construct another Chair. That is what you want, isn't it?"

"Yes," Sierra began, "but—"

Charles pointed to the flickering light. "Another Chair is arriving. We need to step outside."

The other four followed Charles out the door, which Charles quickly closed.

"Did you find the *Chronica* in the future?" Max asked Charles.

"Not exactly," Charles replied.

There was a familiar whirring sound from within the room – the kind that occurred when Chairs were in motion. The whirring stopped.

"Can you tell how many Chairs just arrived?" Tesla asked Charles.

"No," Charles replied. "The room, however, cannot accommodate more than four at the same time."

"Who do you think it is?" Astor asked.

"Best case, Appleton; worst case, Heron," Max replied.

"If it is Heron, would we not be safer if we waited downstairs and perhaps called the police?" Astor asked.

"I vote we stay right here," Max said, touching the knife in his pocket. He stood at the side of the door, ready to stab the first person in the neck who came through if it was Heron.

Astor guessed what Max was thinking. "What kind of weapons could Heron – or anyone – bring back from the future?" Astor asked.

"Nothing that uses digital guidance – electricity," Sierra said. "But knives and early combustion guns would make the leap through time just fine."

Max tightened his grip on the handle of his knife.

Tesla started to speak, but there was no time for a vote or any further discussion.

The door opened.

Nikola Tesla, looking at least 20 years older than he did right now, stepped out to greet them.

**

Sierra's mind sped in a dozen directions, most thinking one variant or another of this was the first time she had seen this, in all her years of time travel, in her life or anyone else's, and the reason she had not seen it in hers was because she always took such care to avoid it.

Max's hand was still on the hilt of his knife. He moved closer to the older Tesla. "You could be Heron," he said softly, in almost a hiss. "Prove to us you're not."

The older Tesla looked at his younger self, and then at Max.

"When I was 12 years old, a friend of my older sister Angelina stayed with our family for a few days. One early morning, I saw her step out of the bath. I had never seen such beauty before. It was thrilling to me, arousing, in a way I had never experienced before. I still think about her shimmering skin sometimes, late at night."

The younger Tesla wasn't quite blushing, but looked embarrassed. "I have never told a soul about that, and doubt I ever will."

"Until now," the older Tesla said and smiled.

Max relaxed his grip on his knife.

"So you knew we would be having this meeting," Sierra said to the older Tesla, "with us and your younger self, for all the years beginning with now."

"Yes," the older Tesla replied, "but not until now. I have that memory now, of this meeting taking place 22 years earlier in my life, but I know I did not have that memory before."

"Just as Sierra and I discovered with some political developments in the future," Max said, warming up to the conversation now that his concern that the older Tesla might have been Heron was allayed.

"Shall we continue this discussion in more comfortable surroundings, downstairs?" Cyril Charles asked.

***

Sierra, Max, Astor, and the two Tesla's sat beneath the Raphael nude. Charles went to get suitable libations.

"I cannot stay too long," the older Tesla said, "for all the obvious and not-so-obvious reasons."

"And the purpose of your visit, then?" Astor asked. "Not that

I'm not pleased to the core to see you, to be part of this experience, as I am!"

The older Tesla nodded. "Several reasons. First, my presence here demonstrates that our side won – that someone other than Heron was able to construct a Chair."

The younger Tesla nodded. "Me."

"Yes," the older Tesla said.

"But that could change in an instant," Max said. "Heron could yet succeed, and you could disappear in an eye-blink."

"Yes," the older Tesla agreed. "But as of now, no, not yet. I wanted you to know that."

"Ok," Sierra said. "That makes me glad."

"But the main reason I came back is that Mr. Appleton could not—"

Sierra was suddenly far from glad.

"He is still alive," the older Tesla continued, "but he is very weak. The trip to the future exhausted him."

"Why did he go?" Sierra asked.

"He had to see to the *Chronica*," the older Tesla replied. "He said the original scroll that you brought forth from ancient Alexandria was stolen from his home in Wave Hill last night."

***

Charles returned with the drinks.

The older Tesla drank his appreciatively, and smacked his lips. "It is best that I return now. This conversation is doing you no good at all," he said to his younger self. "Anything that you now know about me, your future self, will constrict your

256

actions, eclipse your free will, as you live your life. You know too much already." He put his glass down on the mahogany table and stood.

"Let's talk a tiny bit more," Max said. "I'm not sure that your returning to the future is the best way to use your Chair, at this point."

Sierra looked at Max.

"I'm thinking the two of us take the Chairs to see Appleton," he said to Sierra. "I know you won't be able to fully believe what anyone says about Appleton until you see him yourself, and I don't blame you – and then we come right back here, a few moments after we left, and that won't make any difference to the senior Mr. Tesla, right?"

"It would not," the older Tesla replied, "none at all, that is, unless something happened to you in the future and you did not return."

"You could get back to the future even then, as soon as another Chair arrived," Max said.

"True, but as we all know, there's no guarantee of when that will happen," the older Tesla replied, "and every second that I spend here with my younger self is a danger not only to his and my mental health, but to the world at large. Even the slightest disturbance in anyone's timeline can have unforeseen ripple effects."

Sierra thought again about Joe Biden. "How about I accompany the older Mr. Tesla to the future. That way, everyone is satisfied – the two Teslas part ways here right now, and I get to see William—"

"I'm not satisfied with that," Max began—

Mr. Bertram appeared, flustered for Bertram, and whispered

hurriedly to Charles.

Charles turned to the seated five. "Heron is at the front door, with Edwin Porter."

***

"If we try to stop him, or prevent him from using the Chairs, that could provoke all-out warfare," Bertram said, not shouting, but above the din of voices under the nude.

Charles agreed. "We have had a very tenuous relationship with Heron, here and in London, throughout the centuries. It is more or less predicated on our looking the other way when he uses the Chairs – it's the price we pay, in effect, for the Chairs being available to us."

"What would he do?" Max said, touching the hilt of his knife with his fingers again. "Destroy the Chairs? That would only make the Chairs useless to him."

"He could lock us out," the younger Tesla said.

"No," Sierra said. "If he could do that without locking himself out, he would have done that, long ago."

"Can I at least see him?" Astor spoke up.

"We can show you a picture," Max replied.

"He changes his appearance often anyway," Charles said. "Knowing what he really looks like – whatever that may truly mean – would provide scant advantage."

Bertram nodded. "My strong advice is that we should do nothing. But if we want to do something, we would need to act now. He is likely past the vestibule, and walking up the wide flight of stairs to this very floor right now."

Max pulled out his knife and turned towards the wide

staircase.

"No!" Sierra said. "I want to rid this world of him as much as you do – but Bertram and Charles are right. If we go at him, and we fail, there's no telling what he might do to the club and our access to the Chairs."

Astor was on his feet, too. "Photographs can be deceptive -- I at least need to get a look at him in the flesh."

CHAPTER 19

[New York City, June, 1899 AD]

"We have an observation room from which you can watch everyone who walks up the spiral stairs to the room with the Chairs," Charles said, and pointed upward.

Bertram and the five rapidly followed Charles up the stairs to the classics library. Charles pointed to what looked like a door to a broom closet.

"You learn something new every millennium in this club," Max quipped quietly to Sierra.

The room with the view was large enough to comfortably accommodate the party of seven. Charles opened shutters to what looked like a large window. "We have a complex arrangement of mirrors," he said. "If you just look through the window, you'll see anyone on the bottom of the spiral staircase."

They waited for a few minutes.

"That's Heron with Porter and another man," the younger Tesla was first to comment on what they saw. "I thought you said Heron was accompanied by just the photographer."

"The other gentleman must have either already been in the club," Bertram replied, "or he entered shortly after Heron and Porter."

"Who is he?" the younger Tesla asked.

"Woodruff, a police detective," Max replied. "And a stone-cold killer."

"He is Heron's protection," the younger Tesla said.

Sierra put her hand on Max's shoulder. "Isn't this better than rushing that fucker with our knives?" she asked, softly.

Max touched her hand and nodded. But he kept his knife in his other hand, anyway.

***

Heron stood at the foot of the stairs with Woodruff and Porter. For the first time in a long time, he felt he stood at the verge of concluding this wretched, tangled business with the *Chronica*, in his favor.

Woodruff had retrieved it from Appleton's Wave Hill home in the dark hours of the morning, bright for Heron in its outcome. Heron had held it in his hand, dared to unscroll it, and the handwriting was his, committed to this parchment nearly two thousand years ago. He had felt his heart flutter, it was beating fast now, something that didn't happen too often for Heron. He resisted the urge to take another look at it, one more look, one last time. The *Chronica* was now in Porter's ample vest pocket, as per Heron's carefully considered plan.

There remained one loose end. Heron hoped with all of his being that it would be the last. It was Appleton. Heron had instructed Woodruff not to kill the doddering publisher – not because he would be dying of his own deteriorating condition soon enough anyway, but because Heron had wanted to question him, to see if Appleton had made any other copies of the *Chronica*. He had intended to do that today. He hadn't counted on Appleton, in his condition, running off to the future.

Fortunately, Heron had long ago hacked into all surveillance on the Millennium Club, the Parthenon Club, and the bar in Athens, well into the future, since cameras had first been pointed at those places as part of city-wide security in the 21st century. He had already put Cyril Charles' face on the list. One of his agents caught the alert that Charles was leaving the Millennium Club in 2096. She saw he was with another man, and quickly identified him as Appleton. She traced their movements and saw that the two had gone to Brewster, Massachusetts via neo-rail.

She went to the Millennium, seeking to take a Chair back here and tell Heron. All the people in his network above a certain level were able to ascertain at all times where Heron was. She was above that level. He would have to promote her to an even higher level, as soon as this work was finished.

She found there were no Chairs at the Millennium in 2096, so she flew to London on the Hypersonic Transport plane, and took a Chair in the Parthenon Club back to London in June 1899, from where she promptly sent Heron a telegram:

"Charles and Appleton in 2096 Brewster, MA"

That's where Heron was going now. He looked at Porter. Woodruff and Porter both knew better than to interrupt Heron when he was thinking.

Heron glanced again at Porter's vest. The safest thing to do, Heron knew, in almost all regards, was to destroy this scroll right now. But he hadn't done that. It was not that he could not bring himself to burn his own wondrous creation. It was that Heron couldn't be sure what would happen to the Chairs when the *Chronica* was destroyed. Presumably they would all still be intact, since Heron had perfected time travel before he recorded his knowledge of how to do that in the *Chronica*. No, all the destruction of the last copy of the *Chronica* should do – if this original was indeed the last – is prevent Sierra Waters from getting some control of these Chairs, and using them for her own purposes, as she had been doing. But Heron couldn't be 100% sure.

So the truly safest course would be for Heron to use a Chair right now to get to Appleton, prior to Heron's destroying the *Chronica*, and avoid any disruptions that the destruction of the *Chronica* might cause. He had entrusted Porter with the job of burning the *Chronica* as soon as Heron left, and told Woodruff to ensure that Porter did as instructed.

Heron smiled at the two, in what passed for him as a genuine smile, then turned and walked up the spiral stairs. He was close to concluding this.

***

"It looks as if the séance is over," Astor said. He had been watching Heron, Porter, and Woodruff with a small magnification lens that he had brought back from the future. "Electronics can't travel through time on the Chairs, but this is just ground glass," he had said proudly to Sierra, Max, the two Teslas, Bertram, and Charles, standing beside him in the observation room. They all could see Heron, now halfway up the stairs to the room with the Chairs, and Porter and Woodruff standing at the bottom.

"And we're just going to let him go up there and take a Chair?" Max said, close to bolting through the door and running through the classics library and up the stairs to stop Heron himself.

Sierra again put a soft, restraining hand on his shoulder and stroked it. She knew he hadn't thought this through, least of all how he would get through Woodruff, who no doubt was armed and would hear Max as soon as he started running towards him on the library floor.

"We just discussed this and concluded that would not be a good idea," Bertram said, also softly but with no affection.

"Look at this," Astor said and handed his device to Sierra. "Heron was looking at Porter's vest right before he started walking up the stairs. I put this on maximum magnification. Does that look to you like what I think it is, or is my mind playing tricks on me?"

Sierra put the lens to her eye and scrutinized the bulge in Porter's vest pocket, which was slightly open at the top. "I think you're right," she said slowly to Astor. "I can't say that's the *Chronica*, but it certainly could be a scroll."

"It could be a scroll of anything," Max growled, still focused on Heron, who was now at the door of the room with the Chairs.

"Does the club have a rule which would prohibit us from reclaiming a scroll which was stolen from a member in good standing, Mr. Appleton, last night?" the younger Tesla inquired, with an edge of sarcasm.

The older Tesla enjoyed and laughed at his younger self's question.

"Not only do we not have such a rule, we'll be happy to help you reclaim it," Bertram said, not at all insulted by the sarcasm.

"Woodruff certainly has a gun," Max said, turning away from the view. "How do you propose we do this?" He looked one more time at the top of the stairs. "There's nothing more to see here."

Woodruff and Porter had turned to walk down the wide set of stairs, and were no longer in sight.

"You have your knife," Bertram replied. "And we also have surprise on our side."

"There is another set of stairs that even the members do not know about," Charles added. "We can split forces and approach Woodruff and Porter from two or more sides at the same time."

"We also have a firearm under lock and key," Bertram said, reluctantly.

"You know how to use it?" Max asked.

Bertram gave him a look that said, of course.

***

Bertram and Charles emerged close to the vestibule at the entrance to the club. Bertram had a gun in his hand.

Porter and Woodruff were walking out of the door.

"Please don't leave," Bertram said, and pointed his gun at Woodruff.

Woodruff almost laughed. "I'm an officer of the law – put that gun down right now, before I haul your backside off to jail."

"You're not upholding the law when you aid and abet a robbery," Bertram said, and kept his gun pointed at Woodruff.

"I see," Woodruff said coldly. He looked at Porter. "I believe there is a fireplace just inside that room," Woodruff gestured to a waiting room, just outside the vestibule, with books, newspapers, and comfortable seating. "Do what you have to do there."

Porter hesitated.

"Please do not move," Bertram said, and moved his gun slightly in Porter's direction.

Woodruff took the opportunity to pull two guns from his holsters, one in each hand. He managed to fire one at Bertram, before Max and Sierra, having run down the wide flight of stairs, tackled him.

Bertram, wounded in the arm, dropped his gun.

"I'm not badly hurt," he told Charles, who leaned over him.

Charles picked up the gun, but he had never fired one in his life.

Porter was still a statue.

Max and Sierra struggled on the floor with Woodruff, who dazed Sierra with a sharp elbow to her face. Max lunged at him with his knife, but Woodruff managed to pull away and land a hard boot on the side of Max's head. Max blacked out.

Porter was suddenly moving towards the room with the fireplace.

Charles ran after him. He couldn't just shoot this man, even if he knew how.

Both guns had been knocked out of Woodruff's hands in the scuffle on the floor. Fully alert, he picked up one, and took in the situation. Porter was going out the door. Charles was a few steps behind Porter. Max was unconscious on the floor, and Sierra looked woozy. Woodruff thought quickly. Even if Charles stopped Porter from burning the *Chronica*, Woodruff could recover it later and destroy it then. The real threats to what Heron wanted done were laying right here in front of him, half or less conscious, on the floor.

He pointed his gun at Sierra, now fully awake. "I take no pleasure in hurting women," he said, truly, "but—"

Max, now also awake and knife in hand, screamed and charged Woodruff.

Woodruff turned to face his attacker. Now Sierra was upon him, too, slashing with her knife. Woodruff, bleeding from multiple knife wounds and flailing, soon lost possession of his gun. He reached out, growled from the depth of his being, and sought to get to control of Sierra and Max with just his bare hands. For a moment he almost succeeded. But all he was able to hold on to were the sharp points and edges of knife blades, which cut through his hands to his body in a frenzy. He soon was dead on the floor.

"Quick!! He's going to the fireplace to burn the scroll!" Bertram, now standing and holding his wounded arm, pointed at Porter.

Sierra and Max ran into the next room. Charles and Porter were fighting right in front of the fireplace – Charles attempting, not yet successfully, to wrest the scroll from Porter.

"Stop," Sierra shouted. "Please."

She and Max reached Charles and Porter. But the young British doorman, with half a dozen club members who had been in the bar, entered the room.

"What's going on here?" he demanded.

Charles tried to explain, as did Bertram, who was at the door.

Sierra tackled Porter. The scroll, which had been in his hand, fell to the floor in front of the fire.

Max went to get it. But the club members, not yet understanding what was going on, wanting only to end the violence, took hold of him by his shoulders to restrain him.

Porter had a free hand, and used it to grab the scroll.

"No!" Sierra screamed, as Porter threw the scroll into the flames.

She, too, was now restrained by several men from the bar.

Astor and the two Teslas entered the room, having at last reached the first floor by yet a third route, more circuitous than the other two. Their presence only added to the confusion.

By the time Bertram and Charles managed to explain what was happening, the original scroll of the *Chronica*, written in Heron's hand, had at last found its intended resting place, and was a nest of cinders in the fire.

CHAPTER 20

[New York City, June, 1899 AD]

Sierra, Max, Astor, the two Teslas, Bertram and Charles braced for whatever impact the destruction of the *Chronica* might have. There was none – or nothing immediately discernible.

"What do we do now?" Max asked.

Porter was the one who replied. "You have no authority to keep me here," he said mainly to Bertram and Charles, who made no response. Porter looked at the assembled group, adjusted his jacket and his vest, and left.

"We have to report Mr. Woodruff's death to the police," Bertram said, quietly.

The British doorman was calming the members of the club who had accompanied him, and urging them to go back up to the bar, where "drinks would be on the house".

"Yes," Astor agreed. "What do we say happened to him?"

The younger Tesla chimed in. "I say the best explanation is a maniac came through the front door, knife in hand, and stabbed the first person he encountered, who happened to be Detective Woodruff." He shrugged. "It happens."

Max nodded. "But will the forensics in this day and age be able to determine that he was stabbed dozens times by not one but two people?"

"You mean, will the police physicians be able to see that?" Astor asked.

"Yes," Max replied.

"Who knows," the younger Tesla said, "but we have more important things to worry about now, do we not?"

"Speaking of physicians, you should have that tended to," the older Tesla said to Bertram, gesturing to the doorman's arm.

"Thank you," Bertram replied. "I will."

"We still have the problem of what to do about Appleton in 2096, and Heron, too, wherever he is . . . ," Max said.

"Which might also be in 2096," Sierra finished the thought, which was heading towards Heron going after Appleton.

"To make sure there are no longer any copies of the *Chronica*," Max picked it up, "which there well might be, in Appleton's possession or elsewhere now, since we've seen nothing changed since that *Chronica*'s been in ashes." He looked again at the fire. Its flames seemed to sneer at him, like his brother, after he'd swiped a cupcake off the table and eaten it right before dinner.

"And you would know if there was a change in our very . . . timeline?" Astor asked.

"Yes," the older Tesla said. "I can testify to that: I remember my life before I came back here and met my younger self – that is, what my life was like for the past two decades – even though it also seems to me now as if I had always come back here."

Max and Sierra nodded in agreement and understanding.

"And as far I can tell, nothing has changed in the past two decades of my life – the next two decades for you," the older

Tesla said to his younger self.

"So the logical thing to do now is go to 2096 to protect Appleton," Max said.

"Yes," Sierra said, "but we still have the problem of just the one Chair."

"There are other Chairs in London and in Athens," Astor said. "Yes?"

"Yes, perhaps," Max said, "but it would take weeks to cross the Atlantic now, and that kind of wait would be excruciating, even though it wouldn't matter how long we took to find another Chair to get to Appleton, because we'd make it our business to get catch up to him in time."

"Just a little more than a week," Astor corrected. "You're behind the times, Max."

Sierra and Max looked at each other.

Sierra made a decision. "You should go," she said, to the older Tesla. "Your being back here now with your younger self could well unhinge your mind."

The younger Tesla laughed.

The older one said, "if it hasn't already."

Max nodded slowly.

"You," she said to the older Tesla, "are still our best bet for actually constructing a Chair, whatever happened to the *Chronica*. We need to safeguard that – safeguard you."

Now Astor agreed and nodded.

The older Tesla hugged his younger self. "Life won't be easy for you," he said. "Don't let the retrogrades all around you slow you down." He smiled broadly and waved at the others. "The

Chronica has had its impact, whatever may become of it," he said. "A major one of your holidays has been named after it," he looked at Astor and Max.

Both men looked like they had no idea what the older Tesla was talking about.

"Chanukah, the Festival of Lights?" Astor hazarded a wild guess.

"Yes," the older Tesla replied.

"How?" Astor asked. "That holiday has nothing to do with time travel – it celebrates the miracle of lights continuing to burn, after all the oil had been depleted."

The older Tesla smiled slightly. "There are many holidays in history which have been celebrated for reasons having nothing to do with the original reasons for their celebration. There is a field of study known as anthropology, burgeoning already, which tells us that. In the case of the *Chronica*, the connection of the miracle of lights burning on no oil and travel through time may be more direct than you think – the candle burning on no oil today may be burning on oil that existed yesterday." He bowed to the group.

"I'll take you to the Chair," Charles said.

"I'm going to miss him," the younger Tesla said, as his older self walked up the wide stairs with Charles.

***

Charles came down the stairs a few minutes later.

"So now that that's taken care of, we do, what, wait?" Max said.

"A Chair or two or three could arrive any moment," Charles said. Bertram had gone to the small infirmary the club kept on its premises, to get his arm treated.

"Or it could take a year," Sierra said.

"Or never," Max said. "We can't be sure of anything not right in front of us."

Charles nodded. "True. But for reasons I and no one who knows about the Chairs understands, there has never been a time when any of the places with Chairs were too long without them."

"Heron's doing?" Astor asked.

"Perhaps," Charles replied.

"How long has 'too long' been?" Max asked.

"Months, never years," Charles said.

Max shook his head.

"But there is another option," Charles said.

"Yes?" Sierra, Max, Astor, and Tesla all said, almost in unison.

"I could take an ocean liner to England," Charles said, trying not to look at Astor, because he, too, knew all about Astor's appointment with the bottom of the sea on the Titanic. "Then take a Chair to the future there, at a time in the 21st century when air flight across the Atlantic is fast, safe, and easy. I would travel that way to New York, proceed to the Millennium, recruit another doorman or two, and take those Chairs back here. For all of you, it would seem that I hadn't been gone any longer than I was when just escorting the senior Mr. Tesla up the stairs."

"Why didn't you suggest that sooner?" Max asked.

"Because it ages me in real time," Charles replied. "If I did that all the time, I would reach my 150-year lifespan with much less productive time, spent out on the ocean and cut off from most of the world."

"I see your point," Astor said.

"And there's also always the possibility that something could happen to me and prevent me from completing the journey," Charles said. He thought again of the Titanic, but didn't say it. "I could be murdered in London by Jack the Ripper, before I had a chance to get to the Parthenon Club."

"Wasn't Jack the Ripper at large a decade ago?" Tesla asked.

"I was just using him as an example," Charles replied. "There are no doubt other fiends at large right now in London."

"I think it's a good option," Sierra said, "just this one time."

"All right, then," Charles said. "I will walk out that front door, go to the Hudson River, book passage on the first available liner to England, and, if, all goes well, I will be walking down that staircase from above in just a minute or two."

Astor pulled out a billfold. "You'll need this to purchase your tickets."

"Thank you," Charles said and took the money. "I have access to funds at the Parthenon, but this is very helpful."

"Off like Phileas Fogg, then," Astor said, and clapped Charles on the back. "For you it will be 80 days, for us just 80 seconds until we see you again."

"Closer to 8 days to get to England, a little more than 80 seconds before I come back down the stairs, and I won't be traveling around the world, just back and forth across the Atlantic, but, yes," Charles said, and shook everybody's hand, except Sierra's, whose hand he kissed. Then he whispered in her ear, "in case I do not return, Mr. Appleton is at the Foster Square Facility in Brewster, Massachusetts as of June 27, 2096 – it's a nondescript little building at the far end of the square --

that is where he was when I left him."

[*RMS Campania*, North Atlantic Ocean, July, 1899 AD]

The trip across the North Atlantic was rough. Not only was the water choppier than usual, but Charles developed a croupy cough about three days into the voyage. He was supposed to be immune from all of these diseases, but, as the geneticists of later centuries said, new strains were always emerging.

Charles was glad to arrive in Liverpool only four days later, where he caught a train down to London and the Parthenon Club.

[London, July, 1899 AD]

Charles was not happy to see Hakam at the door of the Parthenon. He was suspected of harboring sympathies for Heron. At the very least, Hakam would not have been pleased with what Charles was now doing.

"You grew bored of Athens?" Charles asked, with a smile, and then succumbed to a hacking cough.

"Are you ill?" Hakam asked. "You look as if you could use some rest."

Charles waved the suggestion away, but coughed.

"They were short-handed up here," Hakam continued in his Turkish accent, enjoying the phrase, which was new to him. "Franklin had a death in the family. I came here to help."

Charles nodded. "Are there any Chairs?"

"There have been none for the past 19 days," Hakam replied.

Charles nodded, cleared his throat, and coughed again. "I think I'll take you up on your suggestion to get some rest. I assume there is an available room?"

"Of course," Hakam said, and bowed slightly, even though he was in no way inferior in rank to Charles. "Come," he said, and showed Charles to his room.

***

London in 1899 was at the height of its power and allure. Ordinarily, Charles would have relished a few days or even weeks at large in this city. But he had two reasons to want to get to the future as fast as possible. One, although it would make no difference to his friends if it took him two days or two years in his lifetime to get back to the Millennium Club in June 1899, Charles would feel the difference, and he wanted resolution on this as soon as possible. Second, although he was slowly recovering from his croup, he knew the doctors in the future could likely eradicate his infection in a matter of hours.

But the days and then weeks passed, with no Chairs in the room in the Parthenon's cellar. Charles looked at the room when Hakam wasn't around, just to make sure he wasn't lying about the lack of Chairs.

One night, Charles heard a pounding on his door. Before he could get out of bed, Hakam, Heron, and Woodruff broke through. Each man had two guns in his hands and began firing all six weapons at Charles—

He awoke. There was a knocking on his door, but it was morning.

"Just a second," Charles called out and put on his robe. He opened the door.

"There is a Chair," Hakam, who had been knocking on the door, said with a smile.

"Thank you," Charles said. "I'll be there presently. Please make sure no one else uses it."

Hakam bowed slightly and left.

It had been 42 days since Charles had arrived here. Although this amount time was less than the months he had spoken of to Max, Charles wondered if the scarcity of Chairs both here and in New York indicated that Heron was gaining the upper hand.

***

Charles sat in the Chair. He needed to choose a time that was sufficiently in the future that he could travel swiftly and easily by air across the ocean, but a time in which he was not likely to cross paths, especially in New York, with anyone that he knew, including, especially, himself. 2096, for that reason, seemed like a bad idea. Charles considered further. 2050 seemed like a nice round number.

He set the Chair and initiated the go sequence. A bubble ascended. The cosmos kissed him on the forehead. The bubble receded.

Charles got out of the Chair and walked up and down the flights of stairs. His croup was gone, but he was still coughing a little.

He saw no one he knew at the door of the Parthenon. He walked out into the street and hailed a hydrogen-powered cab. "Blair Annex," he told the cabbie. If Charles remembered correctly, there were HST's leaving every hour in this year right in the middle of the 21st century.

[London, July, 2050 AD]

Charles was at Blair Annex 45 minutes later. He stopped quickly at an automated medical station, where he was scanned and his blood was drawn and analyzed. "Low grade remaining infection.   Likely recent bronchitis mostly resolved," the report on the screen advised.   Rest and an antibiotic injection dispensed right at this facility were recommended. Charles took the injection.

The flight across the Atlantic was 90 minutes, smooth and comfortable, as was the cab he took from JFK Airport to the Millennium Club, which got stuck in traffic, and took almost as long as the flight.

Now he would have to wait, however long, for at least two Chairs, assuming none were already there in the room at the top of the spiral stairs.

[New York City, July, 2050 AD]

There was one Chair in the room upstairs, but taking it back to Sierra, Max, Astor, and Tesla in 1899 would allow only one of them to travel forward, which was not enough.   Charles needed to wait for at least one other Chair, and, with any luck, more.   In the meantime, Charles needed to round up some doormen to take the Chairs back with him.

The young man with the British accent was the only doorman Charles knew who was now in residence at the Millennium. Charles could not tell just by looking at him whether in his lifetime this was before or after the violence with Woodruff at the Millennium in 1899, and Charles knew not to ask. Say as little as possible, to anyone, was the mantra for everyone who knew about the Chairs who worked in the clubs in any century.

Charles set in for the wait, as long as it took. He kept reminding himself that once he and his colleagues embarked back to 1899 in the Chairs, it would seem to Sierra et al in 1899 that he had been gone just a minute, whether he had been gone for a month or a year of his life.   In a way, air travel shared this psychological quality with time travel – you could travel from London to New York in 2050 AD in under two hours, but you when you arrived in New York, it would be at a time on the clock well before you left London. Fast air flights across time zones made the air passenger a kind of time traveler.

He occupied his days with watching movies he had missed over the years. The *Godfather* double trilogy was his favorite, and Asimov's *Foundation* trilogy was an outstanding piece of cinema indeed. He thought of Edwin Porter, and how far motion pictures had progressed since Porter's pioneering work. Charles felt bad that Porter had been in league with Heron in the *Chronica* business, but was glad that no harm had come to him on the day that Woodruff had died.

Other than the movies, Charles enjoyed seeing the Chinese-American Jupiter launch, with a crew of fifty-five people. The world was in pretty good shape, at this point, Charles reflected. That is why, although he supported Sierra, he was not completely unswayed by Heron's brief to keep the world as it was – if that, indeed, is what Heron really wanted, which was always the problem with that engineer.

On the 23rd day of Charles' stay, Hastings the young British doorman informed him that two Chairs were now in the room. Charles was of course interested in who had arrived with the Chair, but protocol again strictly forbade him from even asking Hastings.

Charles now had to decide if should wait for another Chair or two. He made a decision, and spoke to Hastings.

"It might not be a good idea for me to accompany you now," Hastings told Charles. "I was on the premises in 1899 when the New York City police detective was killed, and it may not be a good idea for me to return to the scene with my younger self there, too."

So that answered the question of whether this was before or after that incident in Hastings' lifetime. "Of course," Charles replied. "So whom might you recommend to accompany me?"

"Our current chef has the used the Chairs," Hastings replied. "Mr. Psilakis."

Charles nodded. He had heard of the chef.

Hastings returned with Psilakis – shaven head, goatee, white chef's coat – in about 10 minutes.

"I have sampled your work," Charles said, as the two shook hands, "and have found it delicious!"

"Thank you," Psilakis said and bowed. "The cuisine in the clubs still needs improvement in some eras, but I'm trying my best – there's only so much that one person can do!"

"Of course," Charles said, "and we're most appreciative."

"Mr. Hastings tells me that you want to go back to 1899," Psilakis said. "I'm happy to accompany you – that's a time that could use a *lot* of improvement in its cooking. Far too heavy in fat and starches." He rolled his eyes.

"Absolutely," Charles said.

"When do we leave?" Psilakis asked.

"How about right now?" Charles asked.

"I—of course! I can leave with you right now. I had a meeting planned with the sous-chef here, but going with you is far more important."

"Good," Charles said, and the two parted company with Hastings, and walked upstairs to the room with the Chairs.

***

Charles and Psilakis each sat in a Chair. *We're in July 2050 not June, and I have to set these Chairs to arrive at a few minutes after the exact date and time that I left the Millennium in 1899, in what now feels almost as long as a lifetime ago*, Charles thought.

"I do nothing with the controls, and you will make sure our two Chairs are synced and will arrive at the same time in 1899, right?" Psilakis asked.

"Yes," Charles replied. He carefully put in the date and depressed the go lever. Bubbles ascended, foreheads felt kissed by the cosmos, bubbles descended – or so Charles thought. But when his bubble descended and he looked around the room, there was no other Chair in sight.

Charles got out of his Chair. What had gone wrong? Where was the chef?

He heard a pounding at the door, and hoped he wasn't dreaming. He knew that pinching himself provided no proof that he wasn't, because he could be dreaming that he was pinching himself. But he nonetheless felt that this was real.

He opened the door.

Psilakis was standing there, angry and confused. "What happened? You said we'd arrive at the same time! I've been waiting here at least five minutes – good thing I knew I had to leave the room when I heard that whirring sound!"

"I'm sorry," Charles said, "and glad you're unharmed. The Chairs did not work as precisely as they should have, but we both seem to have arrived back here in one piece – or two one-pieces, as it were." Charles tried to smile at his own joke, but failed.

"Let's go," he said to Psilakis, and the two walked down the stairs.

[New York City, June, 1899 AD]

Sierra, Max, Astor, and Tesla broke into spontaneous applause in the vestibule, as Charles and Psilakis walked down the wide stairs to greet, and in Psilakis's case, meet them.

"Amazing," Max said. "Hard to believe that you didn't just walk up those stairs, change your mind about the voyage, and come right back down here."

"Three minutes and 45 seconds," Astor marveled, looking at his pocket watch.

"You look tired," Sierra said, as Charles and Psilakis approached. She touched Charles's face. "Was the journey difficult?"

Tesla looked at Psilakis. "Are there two Chairs, then, upstairs now? Are you a doctor?" he asked Psilakis.

"A chef," Psilakis replied. "And I think I best retire to the kitchen now."

"Of course," Charles said and clapped him on the back. "Thank you for accompanying me on this trip – the Chair you took will be crucial!"

"The police should be here any minute," Astor said quietly, after Psilakis left. "They were called about Woodruff, and told the story suggested by Mr. Bertram – that a deranged assailant came into the club, knifed the detective, then left."

Charles nodded.

"I think the two of you should take the Chairs right away, before the police arrive," Astor said to Sierra and Max. "They get crazy when one of their own are killed. Not that I blame them. But we can take care of things here."

Tesla looked disappointed, but nodded agreement.

"We'll come back and take you to the future as soon as we're sure that Mr. Appleton is ok," Sierra said to Tesla.

Tesla nodded again.

"I think I need some rest," Charles said suddenly, shakily, and leaned against the wall.

Astor propped him up. "Let's get you to the infirmary. You can keep Mr. Bertram company."

Charles shook his head no. "I can stay there, but you'll need to get Mr. Bertram away from the club. We can't have the police seeing the wound in his arm."

"Of course, you're right," Astor said.

Tesla pointed to the entrance of the club. Two police officers, as if on cue, were coming through the door. "I'll talk to them," Tesla said, turning towards the door. "I can get you a least a few minutes before they think to look in the infirmary. I'm good at playing the slightly hysterical immigrant."

Astor nodded. "Go," he said to Max and Sierra, who looked quickly at Charles.

"I'm ok," he said. "Astor is right – you should go."

Tesla was with the police. Sierra and Max walked quickly up the stairs, and Astor walked as quickly as he could with Charles to the infirmary.

CHAPTER 21

[New York City, 2096 AD]

Sierra was relieved that Max and she had arrived in sync, at the same time. It bothered her a lot, to say the very least, that she could no longer rely on this feature of the Chairs.

There was no one at the front door. If there had been, she knew she would get no answer if she asked if Heron had recently been here. Either he had or had not, and it was safest to assume that he had.

The weather was temperate this late June morning. Climate control had been in effect for decades, more than enough time to work out all the initial bugs in the system. She breathed in deeply and exhaled, then looked at Max and took his hand. It could be a beautiful world, if only people like Heron left it alone.

Of course, she knew that that's exactly what he thought she was doing – trying to change history as it was, which was why Heron was trying to stop her – but Sierra knew better, or was sure that she did. How could it be right, how could it be a better world, to burn all of the scrolls, many one-of-a-kind copies, in the Library of Alexandria? No, the way to a better world could not be through the destruction of knowledge. That was the path of the Nazis, of religious zealots throughout the ages, of people so insecure in their own beliefs that they felt the only way to preserve them was to destroy the beliefs of others.

"We catch the rail to Brewster, Massachusetts?" Max asked.

"Yeah," Sierra replied.

"Not far from that place on Sea Street, in Quivett Neck, near Dennis, where we first decided to really get into this, years ago," Max said.

Sierra nodded and squeezed his hand.

"Do you feel bad about our killing that detective?" Max asked. "We had no choice – he would have killed us, if not then, then sooner or later. He already tried once before, on the Weehawken ferry."

"I don't feel bad about that at all," Sierra said. "My father was Chief of Detectives with the NYPD. I know what decent, honest cops are like. Woodruff was a miscreant. Even Flannery had a conscience in the end." And she pulled Max close to her and kissed him, mouth open, right on the front steps of the Millennium.

Then she pulled slightly away. "Let's get some normal clothes for 2096, stock up on any small combat supplies we can obtain and carry, then on to Moynihan Station and catch a train."

***

The fast rail had them in Brewster in a little over an hour. Jeffrey Foucault's "Mesa, Arizona" was playing in the station, part of Amtrak's new policy of playing songs from the past with the names of places where the rail system operated.

The Brewster station was where the Post Office had been, long gone like just about every post office except a few in the big cities. The train station and the Post Office before it was on the rail trail, which had once had tracks but had been paved over and used for bicycles from the last quarter of the 20th century to the middle of the 21st, when the Biden rail initiative finally reached Cape Cod. That had resulted in a new set of electrified tracks and the fast rail trains that followed.

The Foster Square Facility was about a 15-minute walk. "I could use the exercise," Max said, breathing in the ocean air.

> [Foster Square Facility, Brewster,
> Massachusetts, June, 2096 AD]

Heron knew better than to come here alone, or to entrust his fate to the ever unreliable performances of public transport. He had rented an automated car, which had taken him and four of his legionaries – trained in combat in Europe, taught appropriate American accents, and looking now like U. S. Federal law enforcement – up here to this sleepy place by the bay, which might well contain the key to his future and everything he had been attempting to accomplish for so long.

If he had to bet – and he was most definitely not a betting man, preferring always to make things happen, rather than leaving them to chance – Heron would have bet that Porter and Woodruff, inept as they were, had managed to destroy the original copy of the *Chronica*. He could feel that in his sinews and his neurons. And yet, nothing had changed. He could feel that, too. Which meant that somehow, somewhere, there was yet another copy of the *Chronica*. That scroll that he had stupidly written seemed to breed like rabbits, or a self-replicating amoeba gone out of control.

He believed the only place that could provide some inkling, more information now, about where a copy of the *Chronica* might be was right across Route 6A, well within reach, just a few hundred feet in front of him and his men.

***

She had the environs surveilled a hundred ways to Sunday, as the idiom she had picked up somewhere had it.   She could see Heron and his four well-armed henchmen now crossing Route 6A.   She could see Sierra and Max, now not more than 10 minutes from that very place, armed only with their knives and their courage.   She felt what could best be described as a thrill when she saw Sierra – she had never seen Sierra so young, so vibrant, so beautiful – but she had more important matters to attend to now.

The facility which housed her would keep a master cracker, even someone as talented as Heron, busy for hours.   But that was not the way she needed to proceed, because that way would likely result in Max and Sierra's deaths.   She was willing to give her life for Sierra, as her sisters had done in Alexandria, if that were necessary.   But she thought that that, too, was not the best way forward, at least for now.

Appleton was resting in the next room.   She held the stick that Appleton had had her make.   It was as thin as a hairpin, and a hairpin was an apt comparison.   For just as a hairpin was lodged just inches from the brain of a human being, so could this stick be easily inserted into the core of any artificially intelligent system.   Thin as a hairpin, and yet it contained what might well have been the weightiest book ever written: the *Chronica*.

Heron and his men were now outside the facility, and had correctly identified it as their target, for all of its drab, unremarkable exterior.   The key to keeping Sierra and Max safe, at least for now, was to get Heron and his men inside, closer to her, and Sierra and Max locked outside.   But she had to take care not to make Heron's entry too easy – that would set off his suspicions, sooner or later.

Appleton came into her room.   She had alerted him.   "I'm ready," he said.

***

Heron knew what he was looking at. It was cleverly camouflaged, but it really looked nothing like the small, dilapidated shack or whatever it was supposed to be. For what would a structure like this be doing here, anyway, in a square otherwise bustling with restaurants, produce stores, and beauty salons? Heron was no businessman, but he knew that a building like this would be snapped up quickly and converted into another trendy shop, replete with scenic seagulls coasting overhead at no charge.

But that didn't mean this structure would be easy to enter – or, in his case, break into. Heron pulled the code cracker he had acquired in New York out of his pocket, and got to work. He could see immediately that this would take some time. "Make yourselves uncomfortable," he said to the supervisor of his four-man team.

The supervisor told his men to look around the building and the square. About five minutes later, the one closest to Route 6A called in. "I've got an old man here, speaking some gibberish, but something about his accent seems wrong."

The supervisor told his agent to indeed bring the old man to him. He in turn brought the man to Heron. "Pardon the interruption," the supervisor said to Heron and cleared his throat. "Does this man mean anything to you?"

Heron turned around, annoyed at being interrupted. Then his face lit up with pleasure. "Mr. Appleton!"

***

Sierra and Max, from the other side of Route 6A, saw a younger man and an older man walk further into Foster Square. But the backs of these men were turned, nothing seemed unusual about them – the younger man had his arm around the older man – and nothing about them explicitly aroused suspicion.

Still, something about the two men bothered Sierra on a subliminal level, not quite in her awareness.

***

"He was carrying this," the agent who apprehended Appleton handed Heron a manuscript. Heron looked at it – the *Chronica*! Another copy, still in Greek, but the *Chronica*!

"Burn it!" he ordered one of the agents, who promptly complied with a laser that incinerated the manuscript in seconds.

Heron spoke up to the shack. "Whoever you are who is in charge in there – I will kill this man right now, if you do not let me into the building."

One of the agents put a weapon to Appleton's head.

"No response?" Heron asked. "I am going to kill him in about three seconds, then." He looked at the agent with the weapon. "On my count of three, shoot him. One, two—"

The front door of the shack, which had been bolted shut, noisily swung open. Heron and his four agents entered with Appleton.

"Didn't you just get the book that you came for?" the supervisor asked Heron. "Why don't we just kill this geezer and leave?"

"Too easy," Heron replied. "There must be more to this."

***

"That was Mr. Appleton!" Sierra said as she and Max crossed 6A. "The old man with the young man."

"How can you tell? We could barely see them," Max said.

"I've seen him many more times than you have," Sierra said. "I'm sure – trust me!"

"Who was the other man?" Max asked.

"I don't know," she said.

The two ran as fast as they could to the little building at the end of the square.

***

She could see everything that was happening from her vantage point three levels below ground. So far, all was proceeding as she had hoped. Sierra and Max were outside the building, not in imminent danger as yet from Heron and his men, who were inside the building now, looking for more of the *Chronica*.

The only thing she wasn't pleased about was Appleton's condition. He hadn't exerted himself too much, sitting in a chair, moving through a tunnel that brought him to Route 6A. She made sure no one was looking when he emerged, in back of a bathroom in an electro-charging station. But even the short walk back to the facility, escorted by Heron's man, had taken a toll. She didn't know how much more of this Appleton could take, in his declining state. The key to keeping Appleton alive, she knew, was ending this as quickly as possible.

It hadn't been easy constructing this complex facility. The abundance of sand in the ground on Cape Cod made any underground construction a challenge. Fortunately, some good old-fashioned nanotech had done the job. As for the town and its building ordinances, it had been easy to manipulate records to give this facility the cover of being a dormant oceanographic annex affiliated in some unclear way with Woods Hole in Falmouth. As long as the taxes were paid on time, no one paid much attention to the little Foster Square Facility at the end of the square.

The facility was outfitted with automated weapons which would have been able to eliminate Heron and every one of his men in seconds. But, as she had expected, Heron and his men were dressed in smart clothing, which scrambled the telemetry of her armaments, and made the men impossible to clearly target. She was devoting a substantial part of her capacity now to coming up with a way to get around the scrambling, but she doubted it would be completed in time.

Her problem was that with Appleton so close to Heron and his men, she couldn't risk even a slightly inaccurate shot hitting the publisher.

***

Heron considered his options on the dusty ground floor of the structure, which was recessed about half a level. "You wouldn't happen to know if there are any other copies of the *Chronica* here, and where they might be?" he asked Appleton.

"No," Appleton replied, weakly but firmly, "I would not."

Heron resisted the impulse to kill the meddling old man, who had brought him such grief, right now. But he needed Appleton alive.

There was an open second floor in this building, which Heron could already see was more complex and nuanced on the inside than the outside. But his scanner showed nothing but several offices on the second landing, furnished, with no people or digital devices there. He could see no scrolls or manuscripts in those rooms, either. They almost seemed as if they were there for show. There had to be more to this place, but what and where?

"Go upstairs and see if anything strikes you as interesting," Heron instructed the supervisor and one of his men. "Sometimes the naked eye can see better than any instrument." Heron smiled to himself when he said that – if he recalled correctly, Aristotle had made a similar point about trusting what you see with just your eyes more than what is conveyed by any instrument. And the Church had relied upon that to the very day that it had started persecuting Galileo for what he had seen through his telescope.

The two men nodded and walked quickly up the stairs to the second floor. "Nothing here," the supervisor radioed down a few minutes later. "Just empty offices that look unused, like rooms in a model home."

"Ok, come back down," Heron said.

The two men appeared at the top of the stairs and began walking down. Shots of some sort suddenly lit up the stairs. Heron grabbed Appleton and pushed him to the ground. The two men near Heron withdrew their weapons, stood over Heron and Appleton, and looked all around.

One of the men on the stairs, shot in the shoulder, was crouching down. The other, the supervisor, shot in the neck, had fallen down the stairs and cracked his skull. He was sprawled out dead on the first step.

Heron cursed, pulled out his device, and frantically set in new camouflage codes for their clothing. It would take whoever was in charge of this facility at least a little longer to crack those.

Then he took a gun from one of his men and pointed it to Appleton's head. "Listen to me," he said to Appleton. "You're going to tell me, right now, about what's really going on in this place, or I'll not only kill you, but kill every trace in history of anything you've ever done. I'll make it my life's work to root out every book you've ever published, every success, large or small, you've had with any author. And once I've finished extirpating those weeds and any impact they may have had, no one will know that Appleton's or any of your damned books ever existed."

***

She believed Heron enough to initiate the next step. The floor swung open, a rectangular structure emerged, and her voice rang out. "That's an elevator. You can take it down to see me," she said. The doors to the rectangular structure opened.

Heron was happy to hear the voice, but scoffed. "How do I know I'll get out alive if I walk in there?"

"Take Mr. Appleton with you," she replied.

Heron nodded, reached in his pocket, and pulled out a small container with pills. He gave one pill to each of his men. "This should counteract any noxious chemical you might want to release in the elevator, should that be your plan," Heron said to the disembodied voice. "The only one who would now be rendered unconscious by that is your Mr. Appleton."

"That was not my plan," she responded.

Heron told his wounded agent to stay in the lobby, and keep alert. Heron, his two unwounded agents, and Appleton entered the elevator.

She opened the front door of the Foster Square Facility at just that moment, so Sierra and Max could enter. She had this timed to the split second, and believed the two had the prowess to overcome the one wounded agent.

***

Sierra and Max rushed through the open door, knives drawn. They saw a man near a rectangular structure, which was slowly receding into the floor. The man was half turned towards them—

"Friend or foe?" Max hurriedly whispered to Sierra as they were running.

"Let's subdue him and find out later," Sierra replied.

The agent turned fully as Sierra and Max were almost upon him, and managed to get off a shot.

Max's sleeve burst into flame.

Sierra and then Max tackled him, slashing with their knives, before he could fire again. Sierra slit his throat a moment later.

"Maybe we should have questioned him," Max said.

"Too dangerous to keep him alive," Sierra said, then noticed Max's arm. "Are you hurt?" She smelled no flesh in the smoke, just fiber.

"No," Max replied, just realizing that he had been hit. He touched his smoking shirt. "Ouch!" Then he grinned at Sierra. "Still hot. Good thing the vogue in 2096 is baggy clothing."

Sierra looked back at the dead agent, and retrieved his weapon. "Do you know how to use this?" she asked Max, and handed the gun to him. They had not been able to purchase any guns in this enlightened age, which she usually was more than happy about.

"Not as much as the knife," Max replied. "But it can't hurt to have a little laser power on our side." He surveyed the recessed floor and noticed the other agent stretched out dead at the foot of the stairs. "Here," he handed the laser gun back to Sierra. "Keep this for yourself. He likely has one of these, too." Max walked over to the stairs. "Yep," he called back to Sierra, and picked up the second weapon.

***

She sent the elevator back up to Sierra and Max, as soon as Heron, Appleton, and his thugs had exited three floors below. She knew the two would walk into the elevator, and go where it took them.   The key was the precise instant she opened the elevator door for them. Timing continued to be crucial, down to the nano-second.   The last thing she wanted was Sierra and Max walking into gunfire as they exited the elevator three stories below – that couldn't be the end of their story. She reflected that that was a pun, but it wasn't the least bit funny.

***

Max and Sierra saw a large rectangular object, about 20 feet tall and 15 feet wide on either side, emerge from the floor on which they were standing. They looked at it, not sure what it was, until a door in it opened.

"Should we walk into it?" Sierra asked.

"We're not likely to find Appleton just standing here," Max replied. "But the guy we just killed is likely Heron's, and we could be walking into a death trap."

A voice spoke before Sierra had a chance to respond. "It's safe," the voice said. "Please enter right now."

Sierra and Max both recognized the voice – it was the voice of the female androids Max had encountered in London, and he and Sierra had both worked with, fought the same battles against Heron with, in ancient Alexandria.

"I can't be sure," Max said, "but one of those androids may also have blown up the Parthenon Club in London, with Synesius and me inside, and another android re-set the event and killed the first android before she set off the bomb. Synesius was vague about the details, but he told me at some point that he was having dreams about something like that."

Max and Sierra had talked about this before, many times, in particular about memories that remained after re-settings. "You can't be certain about those memories," Sierra said.

"Still, if this android comes in both good and evil Heron-controlled models, how do we choose?" Max asked.

"Please, enter now," the voice said again. "The window for a conclusion that could be successful with this is now 25 seconds for you to enter the elevator."

"We've had more experience with good than with evil models," Sierra said, "and Mr. Charles told us about an android working on our behalf right here." She took Max's hand. "The odds are in our favor, that's the best we can hope for."

Max nodded.

The two entered the elevator, and its doors closed.

***

The key, she knew, was distracting Heron's party, but distractions were a hazardous business. "I will tell you where to find me," she spoke to Heron and his men. "But you need to leave Mr. Appleton behind. He's too feeble for all of this exertion."

"We'll take him," Heron replied, "and if he drops dead, that's going to happen in a few months anyway." Heron smiled at Appleton, the kind of smile that would make a baby cry and drive a dog to fury.

"I'm not going to haggle with you," she replied. "Leave Mr. Appleton where he is, unharmed, or you'll hear nothing further from me."

"I'll blow up this whole damned facility – tell me where you are!" Heron demanded.

"If you do that, you'll never get what you want," she replied, "you'll never know with 100% certainty that all copies of the *Chronica* have been destroyed."

The mention of the *Chronica* was too much for Heron to resist. "Stay with him," he barked at one of his men, about Appleton. Then, to the voice, "ok, I've done as you requested, now tell me where you are."

She began to say that Appleton had to be left alone by the elevator, when Heron wheeled around. "I've changed my mind, come with me," he said to the man he had just assigned to Appleton. "We can deal with him later." He glared at Appleton. "He doesn't look likely to go anywhere."

***

Heron grasped the small but powerful explosive device that he had in his pocket. He indeed was going to blow up this whole little building, and a good piece of Foster Square, too, as soon as he had what he came for.

"Where are you?" he repeated, to the voice.

"Follow the lights," she replied.

A panel of footlights appeared on the floor. Heron and his two men, weapons drawn, followed them.

***

Sierra and Max emerged from the elevator, three floors below ground level, in the Foster Square Facility.

"My dear!" Appleton was overjoyed to see them, and flung his arms around Sierra. "I was afraid I would not have the pleasure of seeing you again, before I died."

"You're not going to die," Sierra insisted, and didn't add, "not yet".

Appleton extended his hand to Max. "Good to see you, too."

Max took and shook it, gently.

"You better go," Appleton said and pointed to the floor lights. "Follow the lights. Please be very careful."

Sierra hesitated. She didn't want to leave Appleton alone.

"I'll be fine," he said, but his voice was weak. "I'll be right here – after I pay a little visit to the lavatory," he kissed Sierra on the cheek, waved to Max, and slowly walked off to the other end of the hall.

Sierra and Max looked at him for a moment, then followed the floor lights, which led in the opposite direction.

***

Heron realized that he recognized the voice. It had been in the mouths of all of the abominable androids that Sierra Waters had created somewhere up the line in the future – maybe even right around now, when she was older and more accomplished. Heron had managed to crack the code once, and create an android or two who looked and sounded like these models, but followed orders from him not Sierra Waters. But Sierra Waters had regained control of the code, changed it in a way even Heron could not fully fathom, and had produced a cadre of these creatures that were invulnerable to Heron's ministrations.

One had died in Sierra's stead as Hypatia in ancient Alexandria, and had fooled Heron for quite some time, because of the locket – Sierra Water's locket – that the android had cleverly worn around her neck the day that she was ripped apart by the Nitrian mob.

Another now stood in his way right now, trying to stymie his reclamation of his *Chronica*. She would end up, if Heron had anything to do about it, the same way as her sister in Alexandria.

The three men reached the end of the footlights. "I'm right inside the door to your right," the voice informed them.

***

Sierra and Max approached the same room a few minutes later, weapons drawn. They could hear lasers crackling on the inside, likely from weapons.

They looked at each other in a now or never way, and burst through the door. The room inside was a mess of damaged digital equipment, hissing and smoking from a savage fight that was still going on. Heron and his two men were firing at a place in the far corner of the room, where someone – no doubt the android – was firing back.

Sierra and Max began firing at Heron's men, but were at a distinct disadvantage. These legionaries or whatever they were called in this era were well trained in use of laser weapons. Sierra and Max were passable at best. They turned over tables and did their utmost to keep these men at bay, but knew that sooner or later Heron's men would get the decisive upper hand.

The android, however, used the distraction of Max and Sierra to run across the room for a better position.

Heron was still firing at her, but he was an even worse shot than Sierra and Max. Puffs of smoke and sizzles accompanied the android as she moved quickly across the room, but none came close to her.

But Heron thought he noticed something out of the corner of his eye. It was a gleam from something, he couldn't be sure. He pulled out his magnifier and looked across the room. Nothing he could see . . . then, ah, what was that? It looked a digital stick, the size of a needle. A needle in the haystack containing the *Chronica*? Impossible to say.

The android saw where Heron was looking and started firing feverishly at him. He quickly moved back to a safer place, but kept the needle stick in view.   "Forget about those two for now," he ordered his two men, dismissing Max and Sierra with a wave of his hand. "Keep your fire on her." He pointed at the android.

The men did as requested.

The android fell back under withering laser fire.

Sierra and Max saw what has happening, but didn't see the needle, and didn't understand what was going on.

Heron's men laid unrelenting laser fire on the android, who was losing the battle as everything around her barked and cracked with flame.

Heron used this opportunity to take careful aim at the needle stick, which he still had in his sight. He fired at it three times, and hit on the third.   The needle flared then crumbled into soot. Every light in the building and all electrical connections went dead.

***

Sierra and Max were only momentarily stunned by the sudden darkness.   With flashlights in one hand and knives in the other, they leapt across the room, each jumping on one of Heron's legionaries, who had been much closer to the flare, and had been briefly blinded by it.

The flare and the sudden darkness equalized the battle, but didn't outrightly win it for Sierra and Max. Each struggled with their legionary, and by no means had the advantage. The legionaries were indeed starting to get the better of Max and Sierra, when—

The android blew each of their brains out with her laser

weapon.

The room was still dark, except for the flashlights, but it was soon clear to Sierra, Max, and the android that Heron was gone.

***

Heron had left the room as soon as the lights went out. He ran back to the elevator, looking to personally put Appleton out of his misery then set off his explosive device and get out of this cursed building, but the feeble publisher was nowhere in sight.

The elevator wasn't working. Heron opened a few doors and was pleased to see that one contained a staircase. He fished around in his pocket for the small, potent bomb but couldn't find it – he must have lost it in the frenzied battle with the android.

He walked quickly up three flights of stairs, using his own flashlight, and left the building.

It was light outside – early afternoon. There were a group of kids in the square, likely from some sort of summer camp. Heron walked by them, hoping he didn't look too disheveled, and smiled.

He had a lot to truly smile about. He might have just destroyed the last copy of the *Chronica*. He walked to the Brewster train station, savoring the moment, hoping to rent a car there. But a fast-track train to New York City was just pulling in, and he jumped on it.

He looked out the window at the quickening blur of trees that splashed against his face like a watercolor and thought about what awaited him. If the destruction of all *Chronica* copies disrupted the operation of the Chairs, that would be something he could fix. After all, it was he not Sierra Waters who built the vehicles of time travel in the first place. It was his invention, always his, and now was finally likely, once again, to remain that way.

CHAPTER 22

[New York City, June, 1899 AD]

Charles was stretched out, ill and exhausted in the Millennium Club's infirmary. His last act, before he surrendered to the bed and instructions that he should rest, had been to get Bertram out of a back door, and home to his brownstone on West 73rd Street, where he could recover from his gun wound in private, away from police scrutiny.

It fell to Astor and Tesla, aided by Hastings the young doorman with the British accent, to tell and sell the police that no one in the club was responsible for Woodruff's death, or knew anything about it.

Astor and Hastings walked quickly from the infirmary to the front door of the club, where Tesla was explaining to the two policemen what had happened, in a thicker accent than usual, talking loudly and gesticulating.

"He was a strange looking man," Tesla was saying. "Hard to figure his age – definitely middle-age or older, clean-shaven, with slightly foreign eyes, if you know what I mean. I would say about 5'9" inches, 180 or so pounds. I have a good head for details – I'm a scientist!"

Astor instantly recognized the description, and now thought Tesla was a genius not only in invention but in brilliant prevarication.

The police recognized Astor. "You're John Jacob Astor the IV," one of them said, pleased to be in his presence. "My sister got married at your hotel last year – to a rich dentist from Baltimore!"

"Congratulations," Astor said. "It sounds like she did very well."

"We were talking about what happened here," the other officer said, not quite as enamored with Astor. He pointed to Woodruff's body, now covered with a sheet, with a half a dozen blood stains. "What can you tell us about this?"

"Well, I was unfortunate enough – or fortunate, in terms of giving you information – to walk up to the club just as the maniac was leaving," Astor said. "He looked just as Mr. Tesla described," he added, thinking the most fortunate thing about all of this now was his approaching this conversation just as Tesla was giving his description, so Astor could hear it. "Medium build, medium height, salt-gray hair—"

"Yes!" Tesla agreed.

"And he was talking to himself as he walked right past me, out into the street," Astor said. "He was saying something like, 'both Flannery and his partner got what they deserved, for what they did to my sister'."

"What did you say?" both officers asked Astor.

"The second part wasn't as clear as the first," Astor said, "I can't be sure about the sister. But I heard 'Flannery' as clear as a bell."

The cops looked at each other. They clearly knew that Flannery had been missing, and that nothing had been announced to the public. This made Astor's account extremely convincing, just as he intended.

"That's *very* helpful, Mr. Astor," the cop with the sister who got married said. "Thank you!"

"It was frightening!" Hastings spoke up. "Thank goodness he didn't stay here and take any other lives!"

The cop nodded. Two other policemen, non-uniformed, entered. "Please don't leave this facility," the cop with the sister told Astor, Tesla, and Hastings. "The detectives will likely have more questions after we give them our assessment."

"Of course," all three said.

The cops went off to brief the new arrivals, clearly superior, definitely detectives, Astor thought.

"I'll go check on Mr. Charles," Hastings said.

"Good idea," Astor replied. "Mr. Tesla and I will repair to the bar upstairs for a drink. My mouth is a little dry after all of that talking."

"Mine as well," Tesla said.

The two walked slowly up the stairs. "Impressive, bringing in Flannery," Tesla complimented Astor, who had told him about the Flannery ferry incident when they had first met in the Millennium, earlier in this remarkable day. "That should send the police off in the wrong direction for quite some time."

"Thank you," Astor replied. "But you win the prize for telling the police that the homicidal maniac looked just like Heron."

Tesla chuckled slightly. "I got a good enough view of him when he was standing transfixed at the bottom of that staircase with Porter and Woodruff. And he is in a sense responsible for Woodruff's death – who likely wouldn't have been here with his guns in the first place, had it not been for Heron."

[New York City, 2096 AD]

Heron took an automated car from Moynihan Station up to the

Millennium. He sat back in the seat and enjoyed the ride. The more he thought about what had happened in Massachusetts, the more he felt confident that the last copy of the *Chronica* had indeed been on that hairpin stick – why else would the android have fought so hard to keep it out of his hands?

Fortunately there was no one at the front door that he knew. And three Chairs were upstairs in the room, just as he had expected. One had been his, the other two had been taken here by Sierra Waters and Maxwell Marcus. With any luck, the two were dead on the floor now, three stories below in the Foster Square Facility. But he'd had his fair share of luck today, and it didn't really matter anymore whether those two were dead or alive. With all copies of the *Chronica* gone, and with it her ability to build time machines and interfere with his own, there would be little Sierra Waters could do other than observe him keep the world the way it was supposed to be.

[New York City, June, 1899 AD]

Heron got out of his Chair. He saw two other Chairs in the room. Could Waters and Marcus have survived and gotten back to the room in 2096, and fine-tuned the trip so precisely that they managed to arrive before Heron, but after he had left to go to 2096, when there had been only one Chair in the room, the one he had taken? Not likely, especially since Heron had been doing his best lately to make the Chairs less exact in their arrivals, as a way of slowing down some of Sierra Waters' plans. So who had used these Chairs here? It didn't matter, as long as they didn't get in his way now.

But it was a good idea to leave the club as quickly as possible. Heron moved as fast as he could down the spiral stairs, then down to the main library floor, and on to the top of the wide staircase that led to the vestibule and the front door. But he stopped as soon as he arrived at the top of the wide staircase. There were at least four police at the door.

Their presence here could be no help to him now, and could do some unexpected damage. There was another exit from the club – the door the servants used – no, not servants, workers in this time and place – but that door was his best option now. He turned quickly around and half-ran to the far side of the room with the bar and the dining hall—

"Sir?" a voice called out. "There's been an unfortunate incident in the club, and the police may want to talk—""

Heron pretended he didn't hear and continued to the door that would lead to the workers' entrance. The voice would have identified itself as the police, if it had been so.

"*Sir*?" the voice was louder and more insistent.

Heron ignored it and went through the door.

***

Hastings walked quickly up to Astor, who was chatting amiably with the bartender. "Sir, may I have a word?"

"Of course," Astor replied, and gestured to Tesla, who was drinking at a table, to join them."

"I believe I may have just seen Heron, based on the description you gave the police, leave the club."

"How?" Astor said. "He just walked by the police, and they forgot the description? You wonder why they're my least favorite profession – I'd rather take a fireman to dinner any day!"

"No," Hastings said. "He went out through the other exit – the one we used for Mr. Bertram."

"Ah, servant's entrance," Tesla said.

"Yes," Hastings said.

Astor nodded.

"Should we tell the police?" Hastings asked, "before he gets too far away?"

Astor thought for a moment. "No," he said. "And for two reasons. First, we told the police that the maniac left the club right after slashing that detective. If Heron is to be the maniac, and he appeared in the club now, that would invalidate our story."

Hastings nodded. "I see. And the second reason?"

"Heron in fact did not stab Woodruff," Astor said. "He presumably has no blood on him, bears no signs of a struggle . . . so his body would negate our story even further."

"Very true, as well," Hastings said. "Very good, Sir! Thank you for your clear thinking!"

"Any time!" Astor clapped him on the back. "Join us for a drink? We're just getting started."

***

Heron walked at a moderate pace down Fifth Avenue, as fast as he could without attracting suspicion. He had not changed his clothing in 2096, so his garb was still appropriate for this time. He hoped Porter and Woodruff were at the seafood restaurant near Grand Central, with the good news that the paper copy of the *Chronica* had also been destroyed. Heron's instinct said that it was, but he knew full well that instincts could be wrong.

Porter was at a table by himself, a bottle of scotch and a shot glass filled to the brim in his hands, which were shaking.

Heron sat down. "You look like you lost your best friend. What happened? Did you burn the *Chronica*?"

"Not my best friend – Woodruff – but it was horrible!"

"Good material for one of your photo-plays, I'm sure," Heron said. "Tell me the whole story."

Porter gulped down his scotch, poured himself another, and complied with Heron's request.

"It was the worst thing I've ever seen," Porter concluded, "his body just bleeding there!"

"But you put the *Chronica* into the fireplace, and you're sure the fire consumed it all?"

"Yes, yes! You've asked me the same question, five times, and I've given you the same answer!" Porter slammed his hand on the table. The bottle teetered on the edge. Heron steadied it.

"I don't blame you in the slightest for being upset," Heron said, soothingly. "But it was better him than you."

"I know, of course it was, I don't want to die," Porter said. "But —"

"I meant that more than personally," Heron continued. "You have a contribution to make to history. You will be lauded as a great master of the photo-play, believe me. As for Woodruff, he was just a police detective." Heron made a dismissive face. "A dime a dozen."

Porter nodded, still unhappy. "What do you want me to do now?"

"You do nothing," Heron said. "Just live your life. Let it play out. You can even see that whore of an actress, if you like."

Porter frowned. He wasn't going to tolerate Heron talking about his private life like that. "And what do I say if the police want to talk to me?"

"Just tell them you were indeed at the club, but you didn't happen to see Woodruff, and you left before the incident occurred," Heron replied.

"People saw me—" Porter began.

"They no doubt did, but you are still a nonentity at this point in your life," Heron said. "Nobody notices you. And if someone does speak up, it's your word against his. You and Woodruff arrived separately – the time that you were together with him after I left was very brief, right?"

Porter nodded.

Heron stood. He was feeling altogether good about the way events had transpired today. He put his hand on Porter's shoulder. "But you will be noticed soon. Stay with Edison – he's good at many things, when he's not poking his nose into other people's business. You will be something of a celebrity. Enjoy it."

Heron walked out into the June 1899 New York sunshine. He didn't want to stay in this year any longer. He wanted to savor the dissolution of all Sierra Waters had created from a safer vantage point, either in the past or the future. But he couldn't go back to the Millennium now. He walked instead to the train terminal. He picked up a newspaper.

Heron was a time traveler, but he could not see into the future, unless he already had been there. In two hours from now, there would be special editions, and newsboys hawking them, with a headline about the killing at the Millennium. They would carry a description of a suspect who looked like Heron. But the description would be vague, and could fit a thousand men.

Heron didn't know any of this, when he bought a ticket to Philadelphia, the city of brotherly love. He had had enough

CHRONICA

of Massachusetts, in any age. He would book a passage on the first ocean liner he could find in Philadelphia, to England, where he could travel to the past or the future, whichever he chose, at the Parthenon Club.

He took a horse-drawn carriage to the Hudson, presented his train ticket at the ferry, and enjoyed the short voyage across the river. The breeze off the water felt good. The sea was the first means of long-distance transport, and he'd always had a special love for it.

He boarded a train to the south, and enjoyed that slow clacking ride, too. For the first time in a long time, he felt at ease. He smiled at a boy bouncing a ball on the Trenton station. It seemed after all of these harrowing years that life and history were finally bouncing his way.

CHAPTER 23

[Foster Square Facility, Brewster, Massachusetts, 2096 AD]

She located Appleton in the lavatory, alive, "but not well," she told Sierra and Max, "because he was very weak already, and does not have much longer to naturally live."

Sierra went to get him.

"I thought the lavatory would be a good place to keep away from Heron, if he passed by here, again," Appleton said. "I would very much like to go home now, my dear, if that is still possible."

"Of course it is," Sierra replied. But she wasn't sure that it was. But she also was thinking, maybe it made sense, if they could bring him back, to bring him back to October, 1899, so he could die in peace at the time history had intended.

She walked with him, half holding him, very slowly, to the room with the android and Max and the two dead bodies. She knew better than to plead with Appleton to let her get him medical attention here, in the future. He wanted to be with his Mary.

"No sign of Heron?" Max asked, but he knew the answer.

Sierra shook her head no.

The android spoke. "Most of my surveillance equipment is badly damaged. But I'm getting a blurry reading of him approaching the Brewster fast-rail."

"Should we stop him?" Max asked, reflexively touching the hilt of his knife again.

"No need," the android said.

"Because Heron destroyed the last copy of the *Chronica* in the hairpin stick, and there's nothing we can do about that now?" Sierra asked.

Appleton smiled weakly and looked at the android. "We had a plan, and it seems that it worked," he said, softly.

"The *Chronica* wasn't in the hairpin?" Max asked, hopeful. "But, you said–"

"It was," the android replied. "That's what we needed Heron to think, so we needed to actually have a copy in there. That was mostly Mr. Appleton's idea – the hairpin was more convincing, more authoritative as the ultimate copy, than another paper manuscript. Just as it was Mr. Appleton's idea to distract Heron by giving a copy of the *Chronica* to Thomas Edison – that was convincing, too, and pursuing that copy took up a lot of Heron's time. I used that time to perfect the plan." She turned to Appleton and smiled. "You were just masterful."

He smiled again and took in the praise. "Publishing has always been a cut-throat business. I picked up some tricks along the way." He looked tenderly at Sierra. "I wanted to tell you. I tried. But there were too many dangerous people around. And then the rain got in the way."

Sierra squeezed his hand. "You were probably right not to tell me. But – wait, are you saying there's another copy!" Sierra said.

"There are more than one," the android said.

"But . . . of course! You have the copy in your brain! I should have realized that!" Sierra exclaimed.

"True," the android said. "But, as you know, digital media, including data banks, do not survive transfers across time in the Chairs. So, if that is all we had of the *Chronica*, it would be of limited use to you – less useful, ironically, than a paper manuscript or a scroll."

"I still don't understand," Sierra said.

The android smiled again. "It was your idea, in the future. Not to have my kind store the *Chronica*, but have us *be* the *Chronica* – that's how we're able to track changes in events across time, and initiate and implement events throughout history. We are not the words of the *Chronica*, we are its implementation. Not the Chairs described in the words, but what the Chairs with people in them do."

"You *are* the *Chronica*," Sierra said, finally beginning to understand. "I'll leave aside the paradox, for now, of how my future self got this marvelous idea in the first place – where it came from, if my future self built you on the basis of it, told it to you, and now you're telling me. But how long will Heron go without realizing it?"

"He has already gone a long time," the android said. "He had no idea what he was destroying when he set that Nitrian mob on my sister in Alexandria, and they tore her to shreds."

"You got some of your revenge today," Max said. "As someone once said, it's best eaten cold."

Appleton started coughing. Sierra helped him to a seat. "We need to get you home," she said.

Max agreed. "What about Astor? He helped us enormously – do we just let him go down on the Titanic?"

"Please be careful with any big changes you make in history," the android said. "It's not my place to stop you, but you know the risks."

Max took that in. "By the way, do you have a name? It gets a little confusing, not knowing what to call you."

"We don't like using names," she replied, "because in our basic appearance we all look the same. Androids who all look the same having either different names or the same name could be confusing. Also, having no name to begin with makes it a little easier for us when we adopt someone else's name, as my sister did with Hypatia."

"Ok, but surely you can tell us," Max said. "Just us. We won't get any more confused than we already are. We promise not to tell anyone."

The android smiled. "Chronica," she said. "Our name is Chronica."

Appleton managed another smile. "Your story will be told in manifest places."

APPENDIX

The following real people either appear or are significantly referred to in *Chronica* (along with characters for whom there is no historical record). The details provided below are what we know of them, as of the time of this writing (September 2014).

Alcibiades, 450-404 BC. Reputed to be handsome, amorous, wealthy, brilliant, brave, unpredictable, egotistical, and Socrates' favorite student. The two saved each other's lives as soldiers near the beginning of the Second Peloponnesian War between Athens and Sparta. Alcibiades later became an Athenian general, with mixed results. He fell in and out of favor with various oligarchic and democratic governments in Athens. While taking temporary refuge in Phrygia, on the east side of the Aegean, he was murdered by a band of Spartans (either loyal to Sparta, or hired by Alcibiades' political opponents in Athens). According to I. F. Stone in *The Trial of Socrates* (1988) and his sources, Alcibiades was surprised while in bed with a woman, and fought "naked, outnumbered, but brave with sword in hand" until the end.

Anderson, Mary, 1859-1940 AD. American and British stage actress, performed in *Pygmalion, Galatea, Romeo and Juliet,* and *The Winter's Tale.* Author of memoirs *A Few Memories* (1896) and *A Few More Memories* (1936).   May have played the role of Hypatia in the 1900 play of the same name. The credit is listed as Mary Aynderson, but there is no actress in any other historical record from that time with that spelling.

Appleton, William Henry, 1814-1899 AD. Became head of the publishing company, D. Appleton & Co – later referred to as "Appleton's" – when his father Daniel retired in 1844. Published Lewis Carroll, Charles Darwin, Thomas Huxley, John Stuart Mill, Herbert Spencer, and leading nineteenth-century scientists and philosophers in America. Offices in Manhattan. Owned the Wave Hill house in Riverdale, New York, overlooking the Hudson River and the Palisades, 1866-1899. Huxley was among his guests at the house. Theodore Roosevelt's family rented Wave Hill (when he was a boy in the summers of 1870 and 1871), as did Mark Twain (1901-1903) (see below for Twain).

Aristotle, 384-322 BC. Plato's student, Alexander the Great's teacher, one of the two titans (along with Plato) of Western philosophy. He emphasized the importance of observation and empirical evidence (in contrast to Plato's focus on ideas), and is therein one of the founders of the scientific method. Influential essays attributed to Aristotle span dozens of seminal topics including politics, biology, logic, education, poetry, and ethics in as many as 140 works, some or all of which are thought be lecture notes compiled by his students. Only a third to a half of these survive. We know about the lost works because they are mentioned in other sources. His view that the observations of the naked eye are more reliable than those made via instruments was used by the Church in its opposition to Galileo's telescopic observations (see below for Galileo).

Astor, John Jacob, IV, "Jack", 1864-1912 AD. Businessman, investor, author, scion of one of the wealthiest families in America. Wrote the science fiction novel, *A Journey in Other Worlds* (1894). Built the Astoria Hotel on 5th Avenue and 33rd Street in New York City in 1897, adjacent to the Waldorf Hotel constructed by his cousin in 1893. The two were connected by a corridor, and became known as the Waldorf-Astoria, which was torn down at the end of the 1920s and re-situated in its current location on Park Avenue. The Empire State Building was constructed on the hotel's original site in 1931. Astor left his first wife in 1909 and married an 18-year old woman, 29 years his junior. The press was unkind to him well before this, and referred to him as "Jack Ass". Astor and his wife were aboard the Titanic on its maiden voyage to America in 1912; Astor's wife, pregnant, was saved; Astor went down. His bravery and dignity in those moments have been noted and dramatized in books and movies about the Titanic. Chelsea Clinton got married at Ferncliff, originally Astor's estate, in Rhinebeck, NY in 2010.

Augustine of Hippo (St. Augustine), 354-430 AD. Arguably the greatest Christian thinker and philosopher, responsible for much of the Church's fundamental theology, which he presented at a time – the decline of the Roman empire – crucial for the Church's survival and growth into the future. Married ancient pagan philosophy with Christian teaching, in particular Plato's realm of ideal forms – the ultimate source of truth and beauty, never fully perceivable by humans – with the holy "City of God".

Barberini, Maffeo, 1568-1644 AD. Cardinal and Papal Legate, 1606-1623; Pope Urban VIII, 1623-1644. A patron of the arts and science – including, at first, Galileo's work (see below for Galileo) – Pope Urban VIII nonetheless called Galileo to Rome in 1633 to stand before the Inquisitor, where Galileo and his Copernican, heliocentric model of the solar system, supported by Galileo's telescopic observations, were put on trial. The resulting sentence found Galileo "suspect of heresy," subject to formal imprisonment (changed the next day to house arrest, where Galileo was confined for the rest of his life), and prohibited his publications. His books already published and in many influential hands – due to the printing press – nonetheless continued to disseminate his ideas, and the Scientific Revolution ensued. In 1992, Pope John Paul II admitted that the Church had committed errors in its treatment of Galileo.

Bellarmine, Robert, 1542-1621 AD. Cardinal, 1599; canonized 1930. As Cardinal Inquisitor, Bellarmine was one of the judges who sentenced Giordano Bruno (see below for Bruno) to be burned at the stake in 1600 for his "heresy" that the sun was just one of many stars with planets. In 1616, Bellarmine pressured Galileo to cease his support of the Copernican view of the solar system, which held, contrary to Ptolemaic and Church doctrine, that the Earth moved around a stationary sun (see below for Galileo). In 1623, Galileo resumed his development and presentation of Copernican theory.

Biden, Joseph Robinette, Jr., "Joe", 1942 AD -. 46th President of the United States of America (2021-2025), a strong supporter of railroad travel. Nicknamed "Amtrak Joe" for the 7,000+ train trips he made between Wilmington Station and Washington, DC while U. S. Senator from Delaware. Wilmington Station was renamed the Joseph R. Biden, Jr., Railroad Station in his honor in 2011.

Bruno, Giordano, 1548-1600 AD. Franciscan friar, whose views that the sun was a star – along with other stars in the universe which likely had planets – and divinity resided not in an anthropomorphic deity but the Universe itself as a whole (pantheism), led to him being burned at the stake by the Roman Catholic Inquisition.

Dickson, William Kennedy, 1860-1935 AD. Inventor and pioneering filmmaker. Built the kinetoscope motion picture player for Thomas Edison (see below for Edison), publicly displayed for the first time in 1893, on the basis of Edison's 1888 and 1889 preliminary patents. Also invented the kinetograph motion picture camera and perfected celluloid as a medium of film. Produced *Fred Ott's Sneeze* (5 seconds), the first motion picture copyrighted in the United States, for the Edison Manufacturing Company in 1894. Later, in England, Dickson produced the *What the Butler Saw* series, an early example of soft-core pornography.

Dvořák, Antonin Leopold, 1841-1904 AD. Czech composer, best known today for his Symphony No.9 in E Minor, *From the New World* – aka the *New World Symphony* – commissioned by the New York Philharmonic in 1893 and written while Dvořák lived at 327 East 17th Street in New York City. The symphony was immediately popular and frequently performed at The National Conservatory of Music of America in New York City. The song "Goin' Home" was adapted from the symphony with lyrics added by Dvořák's student William Arms Fisher in 1922, and was recorded numerous times in the 20th century, most famously by Paul Robeson. Neil Armstrong brought a copy of the symphony along with him on the first human visit to the Moon in 1969.

Edison, Thomas Alva, 1847-1931 AD. One of the most prolific inventors in all of human history and certainly the most prolific American inventor, not only in the number of inventions (1,093 US patents), but in inventions which transformed human life. These include the phonograph, a motion picture camera, and a long-lasting, easy-to-use electric light bulb. Edison was also an intrepid businessman, and pioneered ways of commercializing and mass distributing his inventions in corporate America. You could say he was the Bill Gates and Steve Jobs of his day, combined into one. Nonetheless, Edison initially missed the ultimate uses of some of his inventions, at first thinking of the phonograph as a recorder of telephone conversation (not a recorder of music) and motion pictures as providing visual images for sound recordings (rather than, in effect, bringing short stories and novels to the screen).

Ford, Henry, 1863-1947 AD. Revolutionized life and society by manufacturing, mass producing, and distributing the first affordable automobile in 1908. The Model T sold for $825 – equivalent to a little more than $20,000 today – and its price fell every year. He didn't invent but pioneered and perfected the assembly line manufacturing technique. Ford made his first automobiles – the very first was the Ford Quadricycle in 1896 – while in the employ of the Edison Illuminating Company as Chief Engineer (see above for Edison). Ford left Edison's company in August 1899 to go out on his own, but the two remained steadfast friends for life.

Galileo, Galilei, 1564-1642 AD. Astronomer and philosopher of science, his telescopic observations and treatises in support of the Copernican heliocentric model of the solar system were one of the watersheds and indeed the establishing event of the Scientific Revolution. Galileo pulled back under pressure from Cardinal Bellarmine (see above for Bellarmine) and the Inquisition in 1615. But he published his *Dialogue Concerning the Two Chief World Systems* and its stinging critique of Ptolemaic astronomy in 1632, for which he was put on trial in Rome, under the auspices of Pope Urban VIII (see above for Barberini). Galileo recanted under the implied threat of torture and worse. But the Church could not call back the mass-produced printed copies of his book already in many learned places in Europe, and his theory and championing of scientific method ultimately won the day.

Heron (or Hero) of Alexandria, 150 BC??-250 AD?? The years of his birth and death are debatable – Heron pops up throughout a 400-year span of ancient history. He was a prolific inventor of devices that embodied principles and techniques that were 2,000 years ahead of their mass application in the Industrial Age. These included a toy that ran on steam power (the aeolipile) and an automated theater that utilized "phantom mirror" and persistence-of-vision effects that are the basis of our motion pictures. Many of his treatises on other inventions, and mathematics, exist just in fragments, or are known only via reference to them by later Greek, Roman, and Arabic writers. His *Metrica*, considered his most important mathematic work, was discovered in Istanbul in 1896.

Hypatia, 355/370?-415 AD. Daughter of Theon, who was an astronomer, mathematician, and one of the last members of the Museum in Alexandria. Hypatia likely assisted her father in his new edition of Euclid's *Elements* and his commentaries on Ptolemy's *Almagest*, but she was considered a brilliant philosopher and mathematician in her own right, and led the Neoplatonist school in Alexandria. Renowned not only for her intellect, but her beauty and eloquence, Hypatia attracted many students and admirers. Hypatia was pagan, however, and her charm and accomplishments infuriated certain Christian fanatics, who brutally murdered and mutilated her. The death is thought to mark the end of Alexandria as an intellectual center of the ancient world; it was followed by an exodus of scholars. Charles Kingsley's 1853 novel *Hypatia* made her a heroine of the Victorian era, and she is today regarded as the first woman to have made a significant contribution in mathematics. (Kingsley is today better known for his 1863 urban fantasy, *The Water-Babies*.)

Jowett, Benjamin, 1817-1893 AD. Translator of *The Dialogues of Plato*, in four volumes, with extensive analyses and introductions, first edition, 1871 – still the standard English translation – as well as translations of Aristotle's *Politics*. Declining health prevented him from completing a series of essays about the *Politics*. He was for 28 years a tutor, and then for 23 years Master, at Balliol College, Oxford.

Morgan, John Pierpont, "J. P.", 1837-1913 AD. Leading financier in the first decade of the 20th century in America, the "Progressive Era". Arranged for the creation of General Electric, merging Edison General Electric (see above for Edison) and the Thomson-Houston Electric Company.

Bankrolled Nikola Tesla's attempt to develop radio at Wardenclyffe Tower in 1900 (see below for Tesla), but withdrew support in 1903 due to the success of Marconi with less expensive equipment.

Porter, Edwin Stanton, 1870-1941 AD. The most important filmmaker in the United States in the first decade of the 20th century. Joined Edison's Manufacturing Company (see above for Edison) in 1899, soon became its head movie director, and produced nearly 300 films between then and 1915, including *The Great Train Robbery* (1903), which was pathbreaking in its splicing together of simultaneously occurring action shots from different places and use of close-ups. *The Great Train Robbery* was highly popular and established motion pictures as viable commercial entertainment.

Ptolemy, Claudius, 90-168 AD. His *Almagest* and related astronomical studies provided an intricate and mathematically detailed, geocentric (Earth at the center of universe) mapping of the "epicycles" of the Sun, the Moon, and the five known planets at the time (Mercury, Venus, Mars, Jupiter, Saturn - Earth was not considered a planet). Ptolemy's model held sway until the Copernican heliocentric (Sun at the center) model developed by Copernicus (1473-1543 AD) and supported by Galileo (see above for Galileo) and his telescopic observations. The Church strongly opposed this model and continued its opposition until the 20th century. The accuracy of Ptolemy's lunar equations, notwithstanding its incorrect geocentric premise, has been noted, though flaws in his lunar model were corrected by Copernicus.

Régnaul, Jean-Baptiste, 1754-1829 AD. French allegorical and historical painter, best known for his *L'Éducation d'Achille* (1782), *Déscente de Croix* (1789), and *Socrate arrachant Alcibiade des bras de la Volupté* (1791). The title of the last is frequently rendered in English as *Socrates dragging Alcibiades from the Embrace of Sin*, or *Socrates dragging*

Alcibiades from the Embrace of S., and currently hangs in the Louvre.

Socrates, 470?-399 BC.   No texts written by Socrates have survived or are alluded to by ancient authors; all that we know of him are from the writings of his students, mainly Plato, and a few contemporaries. Socrates taught that the pursuit of knowledge was the highest virtue, and knowledge was best obtained through continuing questioning and dialog. He was no fan of democracy – in the *Phaedrus* (where Socrates also condemns the written word as conveying only the "pretense of wisdom"), Socrates asks why, if we would not trust a man ignorant of horses to give us advice about horses, should we have confidence in a government composed of everyday people with no philosophic training in understanding good and evil – yet Socrates, condemned by the Athenian democracy on charges of corrupting the youth of the city with his ideas, accepted its death sentence. Indeed, waiting in prison for thirty days for the return of the priest of Apollo from Delos (no death sentences could be carried out in his absence), Socrates refused an offer of escape and refuge made by his old friend Crito. Socrates explains in the Platonic dialogue of that name that to evade the death sentence would be to put himself above the state, which as a critic of the state he had no desire to do. I. F. Stone in *The Trial of Socrates* (1988) argues that Socrates may also have wanted his death penalty carried out as a way of publicly shaming the democracy he hated. In any case, that was certainly the result, and more than Socrates could ever have envisioned: his death by prescribed hemlock in 399 BC redounds as one of the worst cases in history of a dissident destroyed by government, all the worse because that government was the world's first-known democracy.

Synesius of Cyrene, 370-414 AD. Student of Hypatia (see above for Hypatia) and her devoted disciple. Christian Bishop of Ptolemais, 410-414. Synesius was earlier in Athens and

Constantinople. His letters to Hypatia show a deep interest in science and invention, and a profound affection for Hypatia. One of his last letters to Hypatia, written in 413, reproaches her for not writing to him, and avers that, if she had, he would be "rejoicing at your happiness". Whether or not his feelings for Hypatia were carnal, and whether or not they were consummated, is unknown.

Tesla, Nikola, 1856-1943 AD. A prolific and experimental inventor of devices (some 300 patents worldwide) using electricity, radio waves, remote control, and X-rays, most of which never attained widespread commercial success. Born in Serbia, Tesla came to New York City to work for Thomas Edison in 1884 (see above for Edison). The two soon fell out over a dispute about Edison's amount of payment for Tesla's improvement of Edison's motors and generators. Tesla resigned and the two became bitter rivals for most of Edison's and the rest of Tesla's life, to the point that Tesla wrote a scathing obituary when Edison died in 1931, criticizing Edison's "utter disregard of the most elementary rules of hygiene" and claiming his method of invention "was inefficient in the extreme." Tesla was on the cover of *Time* magazine the same year. He did much of his later work at the Waldorf-Astoria hotel (see above for Astor), where he lived. Tesla achieved pop-cult status by the end of the 20th century, mostly because of his "peace ray" or death-ray weapon, which he described but never built, operating as a high-energy particle gun. In the 21st century, conspiracy theories about "weather weapons" – use of tornados, for example, as weapons – have called upon Tesla's work for support. The all-electric and ergonomically sophisticated "Telsa" automobile was named after him in 2006.

Twain, Mark (pen name of Samuel Langhorne Clemens), 1835-1910 AD. Celebrated American author, best known for *The Adventures of Tom Sawyer* (1876), *Adventures of Huckleberry*

Finn (1884), and *A Connecticut Yankee in King Arthur's Court* (1889), a time-travel fantasy novel. He was known in the last decade of his life – the first decade of the 20th century – for strolling down Fifth Avenue in New York City, resplendent in his all-white suit.

Wells, Herbert George, "H. G." 1866-1946 AD. One of the deans or "fathers" of science fiction, along with Jules Verne. Wells' *The Time Machine* (1895) – his first novel, based on his short story "The Chronic Argonauts" (1888) – established time travel as a major genre of science fiction that continues and thrives to this day, as well as the appelation "time machine" as the standard way of describing a device that transports its passenger to the past or the future.

###

ABOUT THE AUTHOR

Paul Levinson

Paul Levinson, PhD, is Professor at Fordham University. His science fiction novels include The Silk Code (winner of the Locus Award for Best First Science Fiction Novel of 1999), The Consciousness Plague, The Pixel Eye, Borrowed Tides, The Plot to Save Socrates, Unburning Alexandria, Chronica, and It's Real Life: An Alternate History of The Beatles. His novelette "The Chronology Protection Case" was made into a short film and is on Amazon Prime Video. His alternate history short story about The Beatles, "It's Real Life," was made into a radio play, was a finalist for the Sidewise Award for Alternate History, and was expanded into a novel. His novelette, "Robinson Calculator," was published in the Robots Through the Ages anthology in July 2023. He was President of the Science Fiction Writers of America (SFWA) 1998-2001. His nonfiction books, including The Soft Edge, Digital McLuhan, Realspace, Cellphone, and New New Media, have been translated into 15 languages. He has appeared on CBS, CNN, MSNBC, the History Channel, and NPR. His 1972 album, Twice Upon A Rhyme, was re-issued in Japan and Korea in 2008, and in the U. K. in 2010. His first new album since 1972, Welcome Up: Songs of Space and Time, was released by Old Bear Records and Light in the Attic Records in 2020.

PRAISE FOR AUTHOR

The Plot to Save Socrates is "challenging fun"

- ENTERTAINMENT WEEKLY

In The Plot to Save Socrates, "Levinson spins a fascinating tale ... An intriguing premise with believable characters and attention to period detail make this an outstanding choice... Highly recommended."

- LIBRARY JOURNAL

Levinson "is one of my 'read on sight' authors . . . The Plot to Save Socrates is a tapestry of times and characters and philosophies, with an excellent look at history."

- BEWILDERING STORIES

The Plot to Save Socrates "resonates with the current political climate . . . . heroine Sierra Waters is sexy as hell . . . . there's a bite to Levinson's wit."

- CURLED UP WITH A GOOD BOOK

The Silk Code is "as twisted as a double helix."

- WIRED

The Chronology Protection Case is "a notable neo-noir addition to the intersection of time paradox and detective work."

- TIME ON TV

The Consciousness Plague is "a satisfying blend of murder mystery, police procedure, and science fiction."

- ORLANDO SENTINEL

In It's Real Life: An Alternate History of The Beatles, "one of my favourite moments treats us to a Beatles concert in Central Park"

- CORE DUMP BLOG

It's Real Life: An Alternate History of The Beatles is "a brilliantly written and fun sci-fi tale that is perfect for fans of the genre and music nerds"

- NTERESTING PEOPLE BLOG, SUBSTACK

"Paul is original -- his books and music are different than the norm -- they are clever!"

- BILLY J. KRAMER

BOOKS IN THIS SERIES

Sierra Waters

Sierra Waters, a graduate student in 2042, goes back in time to save Socrates and stop the burning of the ancient Alexandria Library. She encounters a time-traveling mastermind opponent, and her struggle to stop him takes her from 1890s New York to a future America in the middle of the 21st century, in which Joe Biden was elected President in 2008.

The Plot To Save Socrates

In the year 2042, Sierra, a young graduate student in Classics, is shown a new dialog of Socrates, recently discovered, in which a time traveler tries to argue that Socrates might escape death by travel to the future! Thomas, the elderly scholar who has shown her the document, disappears, and Sierra immediately begins to track down the provenance of the manuscript with the help of her classical scholar boyfriend, Max.

The trail leads her to time machines in gentlemen's clubs in London and in New York, and into the past -- and to a time traveler from the future, posing as Heron of Alexandria in 150 AD. Complications, mysteries, travels, and time loops proliferate as Sierra tries to discern who is planning to save the greatest philosopher in human history. Fascinating historical characters from Alcibiades to William Henry Appleton, the great nineteenth- century American publisher, to Hypatia and Socrates himself appear.

Unburning Alexandria

Mid-twenty-first century time traveler Sierra Waters, fresh from her mission to save Socrates from the hemlock, is determined to alter history yet again, by saving the ancient Library of Alexandria -- where as many as 750,000 one-of-a-kind texts were lost, an event described by many as "one of the greatest intellectual catastrophes in history."

Along the way she will encounter old friends such as William Henry Appleton the great 19th century American publisher and enemies like the enigmatic time travelling inventor Heron of Alexandria. And her quest will involve such other real historic personages as Hypatia, Cleopatra's sister Arsinoe, Ptolemy the astronomer, and St. Augustine -- again placing her friends, her loved-ones, and herself in deadly jeopardy.

Chronica

Sierra arrives in 2062, and find the world has somewhat changed. Joe Biden was President from 2009-2017, and train travel is much more prominent. Was this due to the scrolls that she rescued from the Library of Alexandria? Heron's Chronica, which describes how to build a time travel device and was one of the texts Sierra saved from burning, has not yet been published, and Sierra soon realizes that Heron is doing everything in his lethal power to prevent that from happening. Her attempt to safeguard the Chronica, which she left in William Henry Appleton's keeping, takes her to the end of the 1890s, where she dines, plots, and otherwise interacts with John Jacob Astor IV, Nikola Tesla, Thomas Edison, J. P. Morgan, film pioneers William Dickson and Edwin Porter, and other denizens of The Gilded Age.

BOOKS BY THIS AUTHOR

The Chronology Protection Case

When NYPD forensic detective Phil D'Amato takes a call from a lady physicist about her missing husband, he has no idea that her life, his life, and every other scientist working on a top-secret time travel project will soon be in dire jeopardy. As the number of dead begins to mount, D'Amato starts to realize that the suspect is not any one person or group but something much more sinister and dangerous.

"The Chronology Protection Case" was a finalist for the Nebula Award for Best Science Fiction Novelette of 1995. The story was adapted into a low-budget movie by Jay Kensinger, and an Edgar-nominated radio play by Mark Shanahan.

The Copyright Notice Case

Can a code embedded in our DNA millennia ago kill people who violate the warning in the code? NYPD forensic detective Dr. Phil D'Amato investigates. His main source of information: a researcher with two X chromosomes and green-violet eyes.

The Silk Code

Phil D'Amato, an NYC forensic detective (also featured in several of Levinson's popular short stories and two subsequent novels), is caught in an ongoing struggle that dates all the way back to the dawn of humanity on Earth--and one of his best friends is a recent casualty. Unless Phil can unravel the genetic puzzle of the Silk Code, he'll soon be just as dead.

Winner Locus Award for Best First Science Fiction novel of 1999.

The Consciousness Plague

Dr. Phil D' Amato returns from The Silk Code, winner of the Locus Award for Best First Science Fiction Novel of 1999, with another blend of biological science fiction and hard-boiled police-procedural mystery.Memory itself is the suspect in The Consciousness Plague -- more particularly, loss of memory, in slivers of time deducted from a growing number of individuals, which plays havoc with everything from the investigation of serial stranglings to candlelight dinners. D'Amato, NYPD forensic detective, investigates a spate of unusual cases and finds evidence of a bacteria-like organism that has lived in our brains since our origin as a species and may be responsible for our very consciousness. A new antibiotic crosses the blood-brain barrier and inadvertently kills this essential bug. Phil himself falls victim to this memory hole, and must struggle to get the proper authorities to pay attention before everyone loses so much memory that they forget that they forgot in the first place.

The Pixel Eye

Squirrels are spying on us in the park. Mice may have organic bombs set to go off in their brains. Holograms are taking the place of real people. Phil D'Amato investigates a case that pits civil liberties versus national security as he seeks to ward off a major terrorist attack on near-future New York City.

The Loose Ends Saga

Jeff Harris goes back in time to prevent the explosion of the space shuttle Challenger, but gets pulled into November 1963, and has 23 years to plan his intervention with the Challenger. He discovers that his actions in the past may result in the Soviet Union continuing in the 21st century. He strives with Laura and Karina to prevent this, and also the murder of John Lennon and the September 11 attacks, but the resilience and interconnections of history make it unlikely that they'll be able to stop all of those calamities, and the personal survival of at least one of them may be incompatible with their goals. The Saga contains "Loose Ends" - the novella nominated for Hugo, Nebula, and Sturgeon Awards - and its sequels "Little Differences,""Late Lessons, "and "Last Calls".

Ian's Ions And Eons

Ian's Ions and Eons is the name of a time-travel agency in the Riverdale neighborhood of the Bronx. This anthology contains the three "Ian" novelettes published thus far: "Ian's Ions and Eons" (2011) "Ian, Isaac, and John" (2011) and "Ian, George, and George" (2013). The time travel stories involve Presidential elections, rock music, television

and movies. Real historical personages who appear include Al Gore, George W. Bush, William Rehnquist, David Bowie, John Lennon, Dick Cavett, and Orson Welles.

Marilyn And Monet

It all started in the hot summer of 1960, when Marilyn Monroe walked off the set of The Misfits and began to hear a haunting song in her head, "Goodbye Norma Jean" ...

Robinson Calculator

The Calculators -- a secretive group of androids -- have been living off the radar for centuries or longer. Why are they now burying their dead in plain view?

The Other Car

James Oleson is beginning to see everything in perfect duplicate -- two identical models of cars which are the same down to scuff marks and license plate, two old philosophy books with the same torn pages and inscription in old ink, and twin mail men. Is he losing his mind, or experiencing the birth of a new alternate reality via binary fission?

Borrowed Tides

August 2016 brought news -- real news, in our reality -- that an Earth-like planet was discovered circling Proxima Centauri, the third star in the Alpha Centauri system, just over four light years travel from Earth. This is exactly what happens in Borrowed Tides, first published in hardcover in 2001, re-issued in Kindle in April, 2016. It tells the story of the first starship to the Alpha Centauri system in 2029, employing a new technology which can move it through deep space at almost half the speed of light. But it requires an enormous amount of fuel, and can only carry enough for a one-way trip. A philosopher of science and his childhood friend, an anthropologist with a specialty in Native American culture, have a daringly bizarre plan, and talk the government into putting them in charge of the Light Through starship voyage.

Slipping Time

Tripping in the rain can be very helpful ...

The Last Train To Margaretville

A painter desperate for money finds a way to collect what's owed him from his deadbeat clients -- via teleportation, the tunnels under Fordham University, and the train to Margaretville.

Peter Brown Called

This collection combines science fiction and fantasy stories that have music as a theme, as well as original song lyrics that deal with far-off suns, robots, and time travel.

Urban Corridors

A collection of urban fantasy and science fiction stories, ranging from alternate realities to time travel to ghosts and androids and other strange things in the city.

Extra Credit

Unexplained charges on Jon's credit card are due to something far more profound than identity theft.

In The Dybbuk's Pocket

Beware whom you take presents from ...

The Orchard

In the 22nd century, humans have discovered numerous planets teeming with life, but none with human-level intelligence. Teams of exo-biologists have been dispatched to the most promising places. The fifth planet of the Beta Hydri system has patches of trees that bear delicious fruit. Will it kill the exo-biologists before they can prove the planet has deliberately planted orchards - a sure sign of intelligent life -- and get the news back to Earth?

The Orchard was a finalist for the 1998 Sturgeon Award for Best Short Science Fiction.

The Suspended Fourth

Have birds on the second planet of Delta Pavonis been bred to sing songs that warn the inhabitants of deadly danger?

It's Real Life: An Alternate History Of The Beatles

It's 1996, and in this alternate history novel about the Beatles, WFUV disc jockey Pete Fornatale walks in the tunnels under Fordham University, then travels downtown to Grand Central Terminal and finds the world of music that he inhabits is very different. As he struggles to understand how to get in and out of alternate realities, and make sure John Lennon is not killed in any of them, Fornatale will actually dine with John Lennon and David Bowie, consult with Leonard Cohen, attend a Beatles concert with Diana Ross in Central Park in 1996, and work with a variety of real life characters you may or may not have heard of. The short story this novel is based upon won the Mary Shelley Award for Outstanding Fiction in 2023, and was a Finalist for the Sidewise Award (short form) for Alternate History 2022.